I MEANT TO TELL YOU

a novel by

Fran Hawthorne

STEPHEN F. AUSTIN STATE UNIVERSITY PRESS

For more information:
Stephen F. Austin State University Press
P.O. Box 13007 SFA Station
Nacogdoches, Texas 75962
sfapress@sfasu.edu
www.sfasu.edu/sfapress

Managing Editor: Kimberly Verhines
Cover and Book Design: Meredith Janning and Kimberly Verhines
Distributed by Texas A&M Consortium
www.tamupress.com

ISBN: 978-1-62288-934-1

FIRST PRINTING

To Barbara, for the Write Sisters

PROLOGUE

IN HER YELLOW CAR SEAT BEHIND MIRANDA, Tali danced her soft stuffed fox on its two rear legs and sang loudly in a mix of Hebrew and English: "Here comes the sun. Here comes *ha-shemesh*."

Ronit, in the passenger seat up front, screwed and unscrewed the cap of her water bottle. Shut. Open.

Miranda lifted her hand off the steering wheel to wave backwards at Tali, and the car swerved briefly. "Hey, over there," Miranda called.

"Hey, up there." Tali giggled.

Turning partly around, Ronit also waved. Then she checked her watch.

The highway guardrails glided by like ribbons unfurling. Rain slapped the windshield in front of Miranda as the sky darkened and they crossed the Potomac River from Maryland into Virginia.

Glancing toward Ronit, Miranda mouthed: *Are you okay?*

Ronit leaned forward and fiddled with the radio, until Celine Dion's clear soprano abruptly drowned out any other sound. *"For every dream you made come true/For all the love I found—"* Before the line was finished, Ronit stabbed the button for a different station. Very softly, her mouth barely an inch from Miranda's ear, she whispered, "It will be fine after we land in Tel Aviv. I'll call Tim from my parents' apartment."

"He's going to be furious."

A minivan was slicing into their lane directly in front of them. Raggedly, Miranda moved leftward; the car just behind her in that lane immediately honked. "Sorry. Sorry," she mumbled.

"I have spent six years—" Ronit's voice rose; Miranda quickly put a finger on her own lips, nodding toward Tali. "I have spent six years," Ronit repeated more quietly, "doing what Tim wants so he won't be furious."

"I know."

"I made the coffee too strong. I made it too weak. I put Tali to bed too early. I put her to bed too late."

"I know."

"He cut up my driver's license, Miranda! He canceled my credit cards! He said he makes all the money, so he'll decide how I spend it."

"He's crazy."

"If I don't go now, before he figures out somehow to block Tali's passport…" Ronit crossed her arms on the dashboard. "Last week …"

"What happened last week?"

"He just—He told me he would get custody of Tali, because my English isn't good enough."

"What? That can't be true."

"I don't know. He makes me so upset, I forget all my English."

"He hasn't—done anything again—in front of Tali?"

"Not since my wrist."

"Tali doesn't talk about it?"

"No, thank God."

"That's good. I guess." Miranda tapped the steering wheel, keeping her hands more or less at nine and three. Raindrops were plopping more heavily now. Brenda had said that the dashboard lights on the Toyota sometimes blinked for no reason, but she hadn't mentioned that the windshield wipers squeaked and missed big patches when they swept the glass. "You're sure he doesn't know about this trip?"

"How could he know? Who would tell him?"

"I don't know."

"You didn't tell Brenda why you wanted her car?"

"Of course not. And you did everything on the list? You prepaid your rent for next month? You forwarded the mail to me?"

"*Betach.* Yes, yes." Ronit unscrewed the water bottle cap again. "It will all be okay, as soon as we're in Israel."

"I just worry… I could see Tim spying on you. Following us." The rearview mirror showed only the lights from the angry car that Miranda had cut off, but it was definitely possible to imagine Tim, his fingers gripping the wheel of the old black BMW, his brown hair falling over his eyes, tearing down the interstate after them at seventy-five, eighty, eighty-five. Even in the rain. Coming right up against Brenda's trunk. Did he have any idea what kind of car Brenda owned?

"I'm sorry I'm bringing you into all my problems." Ronit began hitting her lap with her water bottle while she spoke.

"It's okay. That's what friends are for."

"I just need my family, for a while. I need my mother."

Tali had fallen asleep, her head resting against the side of her car seat, her dark curls squished underneath her cheek.

"Tim always has some reason why Tali and I can't go to Israel, not even to visit for three days. Every year. Even before we started this divorce."

Washington Dulles International Airport, five miles, a sign said.

Brenda's faded air freshener, swinging from the rearview mirror, reeked of sickly-sweet pine. The radio announced a spring sale at Sears.

"When are you going to tell your lawyer?" Miranda asked.

Ronit turned the radio louder. "Maybe tomorrow. The lawyers can finish the divorce without me. They're almost done anyway."

"I still think you should've…."

Tali stirred; her fox dropped to the floor.

The windshield wipers smeared water.

The car behind them honked.

Ronit checked her watch.

"I'll get you to the airport in plenty of time, don't worry."

Rain.

White lines.

Guardrails.

Exit sign.

The asphalt underneath Brenda's red Toyota rolled away at seventy miles an hour, onward to Ronit and Tali's waiting El Al airplane.

Two miles.

THEY HAD TO WAKE TALI WHEN THEY PARKED in the short-term lot at Dulles. Lifting the girl out of the car seat, Miranda rested her, full-length, against her own body, her arms wrapped in an X across the small back in its thick jacket. She nestled her cheek against the curls matted around

Tali's warm neck. Tali murmured and wriggled closer. "*Eema*? Aunt Randa?"

"You can carry her?" Ronit asked. "She's heavy, I think." She kissed the top of Tali's head.

"She smells so sweet. Like apple juice."

Tali wobbled a little as Miranda lowered her to the ground, and Miranda kept an arm around her shoulders. Ronit picked up Tali's little yellow suitcase and the fox in her left hand, pulling her own wheeled bag behind her with her right. They walked slowly to the terminal.

The El Al counter was mobbed, the check-in line snaking around two turns. "Saturday night," Ronit whispered to Miranda. "There are no flights on Shabbat, so now, after sundown, now everyone wants to go to Israel." At least five ultra-Orthodox families were spread through the line and the nearby rows of plastic chairs, the women with smart black caps atop their wigs and solid-colored skirts falling below their knees, the men in identical wide-brimmed black fedoras and long black overcoats over black suits and white shirts. A flurry of boys darted in and around the chairs, their side curls flying. There was also a pair of hikers with tall, metal-framed backpacks and a tour group in matching blue T-shirts whose leader held up a vivid royal-blue-and-white sign: "Arlington JCC." Tinny-voiced announcements echoed through the glaringly bright concourse. *"Keep your personal belongings in your sight at all times." "Smoking is permitted in designated areas of the airport only."*

"I'll stay with you as long as I can," Miranda offered. "I guess, until you get to the security machines."

"I think we leave the suitcase at these counters first. Then the people from El Al will ask us a lot of questions. They're so stupid. 'Where are you staying in Israel? Why are you staying there? What Jewish holidays do you celebrate? What do you do on Friday nights?' " Ronit took Tali's hand.

Tali grabbed the fox. "Where're we going, *Eema*?"

"For an adventure. You'll see."

"I'm going to miss both of you." Gently, Miranda twirled a silky cluster of Tali's hair, until Tali shook free.

"We'll miss you, too. So many years we've been friends. You've been like I have a third sister."

"Your mother's cauliflower-pomegranate salad."

"The silly statue with the fish."

"Here." Miranda slid the bigger suitcase away from Ronit. "Let me do something to help." They inched a step forward in the queue. "How long do you think you're going to stay there?"

Instead of replying, Ronit craned her head toward the front of the line, and Tali tugged at the hem of Miranda's windbreaker. "Aunt Randa, guess what? *Eema* got a squirting thing that makes roses for icings, so we're going to make cupcakes with yellow roses."

"That sounds delicious."

"And beautiful," Tali added.

It was their turn at the counter. Miranda hoisted Ronit's bag onto the scale, as Ronit gave her and Tali's tickets and passports to the agent.

"Ah, I hope the suitcase isn't too heavy for the weight limit," Ronit murmured.

Someone was pushing behind them; impatient travelers trying to jump the line? The ticket agent was starting to ask Ronit something.

"Don't move! Police!"

A powerful light was flashing in Miranda's face. Tali's fox was yanked away. Tali was screaming, Ronit was screaming, there were shouts behind her, in front of her, loud voices, deep voices, angry voices, two strong hands had grabbed Miranda's hand, both hands, thrust them behind her back, there was hard heavy metal around her wrists, something hit her shin—It was Tali's little suitcase, cracking open; a snowfall of papers and clothes flipped against her. Then a rough hand was pulling Miranda backwards away from the counter, from Tali, from the suitcase, cinching tight around her upper arm, like a vise, and something scratched, something stung sharply; "Ronit!" she yelled, "Ronit, what's happening?" and Ronit was crying, and Miranda's shoulder bag was sliding down her arm, banging her hip, while two hands now dragged her, and her feet jerked hard, again and again across the ice-slippery tiled floor, big tiles of green and grey and white, and the steel slapped against her wrists each time her feet hit the tile. More lights were flashing. More voices shouted, called, demanded; in English, in Yiddish, in Hebrew. *What the hell? What did those women do? That poor little girl.* "Tali!" Ronit screamed. "Daddy!" Tali shouted.

"You are under arrest," a man declared sternly, somewhere near Miranda's ears, "for violation of federal statute 18-1204 and Maryland code 9-305.

Attempting to remove a child from the United States with intent to obstruct the lawful exercise of parental rights, and acting as an accessory to abduct a child to a place that is outside of the United States."

"Come on, Tali," Tim's calm voice said. "Let's go home."

CHAPTER ONE

"YOU'D BETTER WARN YOUR MOM." Reaching his fork over Miranda's shoulder, Russ speared the last two pieces of rigatoni from the bowl that Miranda was lowering into the kitchen sink. "The FBI might want to ask her about those protests at Columbia where she met your dad."

"Why would the FBI care what my parents did thirty-five years ago? Everybody was protesting the Vietnam War back then."

Standing so close, nearly a head taller than her and wide-shouldered, his messy blond hair pale in the weak overhead light, Russ had a dab of butter on his bottom lip and smelled faintly of oil-and-vinegar salad dressing. Miranda tapped the smooth skin just above his jawline. "You need to wash your face," she added.

"For the security vetting for my job. It's not just me they care about; now they also want to investigate you, as my fiancée, and your family." With a kiss on Miranda's forehead, Russ walked back to the table and picked up the last of their dinner dishes. "You know, ever since 9/11, the federal government's gone nuts about security and terrorism."

The water in the bottom of the sink was sharply hot.

"What do they want to know about my parents and me?"

Russ opened the refrigerator and pulled out a box of Entenmann's chocolate doughnuts. "Oh, the usual: Do you take drugs? Do you have a criminal record? Are there any alerts on your credit history?" He grinned.

Miranda rinsed the grey-blue rigatoni bowl a third time, then carefully placed it in the plastic dish drainer.

Russ's grin became a laugh. "Did *Law & Order* ever base an episode on anything you did? Was your face ever on a Wanted poster? And don't get me started on those glitter pens you shoplifted in fifth grade."

Actually, Russ, seven years ago, when I was helping a friend who was going through a horrible divorce, we were arrested for kidnapping her daughter.

Miranda turned toward Russ.

"Did you ever kill anyone? Or kidnap anyone? Did you ever commit armed robbery?" He kissed her forehead again. "You know, the big felonies. Don't worry, sweetheart, it's nothing you would do. Just bureaucracy."

It wasn't really kidnapping. Not the way the FBI would define it. She was my friend's own daughter. Anyway, it's not kidnapping anymore, legally. because the court reduced it to a misdemeanor.

"Why—?" She coughed. "Why does your office care about my history?"

"I'm not sure. I think they worry that I could be blackmailed if you had a serious felony on your record—murder, kidnapping, major drug dealing, like I said—and they might not want to have an attorney on their staff who was a blackmail risk."

"I thought your security investigation was supposed to be finished ages ago."

"Yeah, now they say it'll be a few more weeks. Right after the new year." He glanced away from her toward the clock on the microwave. "Hey, speaking of *Law & Order*, it's almost time. I'll dry the dishes later. I really will."

The ideal job. That was what he'd told her last August, while they rested on the sprawling steps of the Capitol, sharing stiff chunks of a lukewarm pretzel and gazing down the Mall to the Washington Monument, the marble of the steps hard under their butts. It was the kind of job he'd wanted ever since he'd volunteered on the river-pollution lawsuit against G.E. when he was at Yale. He would be prosecuting sleazy companies and corrupt government officials as an assistant U.S. attorney in the fraud and public corruption section of the Office of the U.S. Attorney for the District of Columbia. He spoke the long title carefully, word by word, as if he was savoring each syllable like the salt on each piece of his pretzel. The office handled cases like the banker who was sentenced to six months in prison for stealing a quarter of a million dollars from customers' accounts and the business owner who defrauded Medicaid of $600,000. "I'll be helping real people, Miranda— families and customers and employees and taxpayers who've been screwed by those CEOs and bankers that my father loves to hobnob with. I'll be able to get them restitution for the money they've lost, and maybe even put some of those bastards in prison." Of course, the job was only provisional, pending an FBI background investigation including drug tests, fingerprinting, credit check, tax-filing record, references, addresses, criminal record... But that investigation would be a cakewalk for Russ.

As he'd talked, he'd slid his heavy sapphire class ring off of his own finger and down hers, jiggling it at the bottom where it hung loosely. "You have skeleton fingers," he joked. His warm, rough thumb and first two fingertips massaged her skin as he gradually eased the ring back up toward her nail, millimeter by millimeter, breath by breath, and her flesh vibrated like a thousand harp strings.

And then, a month later, it turned out that he'd actually been measuring her finger for an engagement ring, a small diamond on a thin band that fit her narrow finger precisely.

In the warm kitchen, Russ wrapped one big arm around Miranda's shoulders to guide them both toward the living room, carrying the box of doughnuts in his free hand.

"Are my father's arrests really going to be a problem for you?"

"Nah. I think getting arrested for protesting the Vietnam War is a badge of honor by now. I just don't want your mother to be surprised."

"If the FBI is that picky, what about my speeding tickets?"

"Tickets? Plural? You had more than one?" Abruptly, Russ stopped walking. He frowned.

"Only two. And the first one was before I knew you."

"Crap, Miranda, I know everyone speeds sometimes, but twice?" They fell onto the black leather couch at the same time, and Miranda snuggled against his arm and side, as comfortable as a bed of firm pillows. Breaking a doughnut in half, he put a piece in her lap. She shifted her thigh, and from underneath she pulled out the dirty T-shirt he'd left on the cushion again.

They looked perfectly matched yet also mismatched in the photo on the bookshelf next to the TV. It was right after the Georgetown alumni cleanup of Rock Creek Park last May, the two of them in their dirt-splattered jeans, laughing, Miranda's wavy brown hair sprawling out of her rubber band, Russ holding up a rake like the farmer in the Grant Wood painting and towering over her.

"How about, oh, a misdemeanor?" she asked. "Something small. Like disorderly conduct?"

He chewed. "Misdemeanors are a crime, too, of course, though I don't think the FBI'd care much. It's hardly in the same category as felonies like murder or kidnapping. But what the hell, Miranda, where are you coming up with all this? Why are you asking about misdemeanors?"

"That's what people often got charged with, when the police broke up protest marches, according to my mother."

Russ laughed, and maybe the laugh wasn't actually extra hearty, but it sounded that way. "So that's what it's about. Sweetheart, if the U.S. Attorney's office fires me because of your parents' political activism, believe me, I wouldn't want to work there."

On the TV screen, an ambulance was screeching down a wide Manhattan avenue. Two teenagers were shouting at each other. One waved a gun.

Now one of the TV teenagers was on the sidewalk, writhing and bleeding.

"Don't say anything without your lawyer," Russ murmured to the teenagers.

Miranda put a small piece of the doughnut in her dry mouth and tried to chew it. Her teeth finally ground it into a million splinters tiny enough to swallow, as she cuddled against Russ's shoulder.

CHAPTER TWO

BRENDA STRODE DOWN FOURTEENTH STREET alongside Miranda, her shoulders thrust back and her hands dug into the pockets of her cherry-red wool coat. "Why the fuck didn't you ever tell him?"

"Tell him what? 'By the way, I was arrested for kidnapping my friend's daughter seven years ago'?"

A faint smell of roasting chestnuts drifted toward them from somewhere on the long stretch of the Mall off to their right. To their left, a single red falafel truck weirdly played the wordless tune for "She'll Be Coming 'Round the Mountain," to an empty sidewalk. A few tourists stood on the withered December grass at the base of the Washington Monument, taking pictures.

The one time Ronit and Miranda had brought Tali to the Monument, Tali had moped at first because they weren't allowed to climb the stairs. But she'd agreed to ride the elevator to the observation deck, and once they were there she'd run from window to window pointing to every Lego-size building she could see on the ground. She'd counted them up to twenty, in English and then in Hebrew, which was as far as she knew her numbers.

"Come on, Miranda. You could've figured out a way to tell Russ." Halting, Brenda leaned over, pulled off a black mitten, and retrieved something from the sidewalk. "A quarter! That's big money for the beer collection."

"Why should I? By the time I met Russ, it was already five years after Dulles. I'd moved on with my life. I kind of forgot about it."

"You forgot that you'd been arrested?"

Miranda tried to tug her wool cap lower down over her ears, but it really was too small to fit over her mass of hair. "How much did you and I talk about it, after the first year? I finished probation. You got your car back. Ronit and Tali weren't in my life anymore, though I wish they were. When

Russ and I started dating, I was a totally different person from the Miranda who was arrested; it had nothing to do with my life or who I was by then. Why should I tell my boyfriend about something that was irrelevant?"

"Because it's a big deal. Being arrested."

"Would you tell a new boyfriend that you broke your leg on a biking trip four years ago? It was a big deal for you at the time."

"But now that Russ asked outright?"

A family was dashing across Fourteenth Street from the Washington Monument, holding hands, two parents, two kids. On the Mall side, the father lifted the thick black chain of the waist-high fence, and the kids ducked under.

Seven years ago, Russ, I was …

You're a kidnapper?

It was impossible.

"That's not actually what he asked, Brenda. He asked about major felonies, and the kidnapping was plea-bargained to disorderly conduct, which is only a misdemeanor. Like being drunk and throwing up in the middle of Constitution Avenue, that's all a misdemeanor is. A nothing. Russ said the FBI wouldn't care about misdemeanors. So why should I create unnecessary problems by telling him about a kidnapping that legally never happened? My lawyer said it's completely erased from my records. Even a new employer wouldn't see it, if he did a background check. Like, when I finally pull myself together to leave Mort and the Center and look for another job. Which I will do. Soon."

Brenda was walking more slowly, rubbing an index finger across one dark eyebrow. Her black suede boots made soft, rhythmic thuds on the pavement. "I don't know."

"Russ wouldn't understand. You know how goody-goody he can be. He doesn't even jaywalk. I mean, I love that about him, but not exactly now."

"I'd cross the street without him and let him catch up."

"Did I ever tell you about the Chips Ahoy! cookies?" Miranda stopped walking to ask Brenda, face to face.

"What? I thought he likes Entenmann's doughnuts."

"They were my sister Lily's cookies. Last summer, she found a bug in a package she'd bought at Safeway, and she told Russ when we went to my mom's house for dinner one night. So he got all fired up; he said she should write to the manager of the local Safeway, and the CEO of Safeway's parent company, and the CEO of Nabisco, and I don't know who else—he said it was corporate malfeasance and endangering the public health. He and Lily sat down and wrote a bunch of letters together. Well, you know Lily. She forgot about it two days later. But Russ kept calling that Safeway to talk to the manager, and he also called the PR department at Nabisco. And guess what? Safeway sent Lily an apology with a gift certificate for a hundred dollars."

"No shit."

"Lily made Mom give her a hundred dollars cash before she'd hand over the gift certificate."

Brenda grinned momentarily. Then she resumed walking, moving faster now. "I guess…" she mumbled in her throaty voice. "If you haven't told Russ about the kidnapping in all this time, and you didn't tell him two days ago when he asked you about your arrest history, you can't suddenly change your tune. So don't say anything to him. But whatever you do," and her voice picked up volume and speed, "I need food and a beer, and we've already used up ten minutes of my official lunch break, and even if weird Mort doesn't care how long you take for lunch, the U.S. Department of Agriculture is very strict about its employees' hours. Let's not waste a lot of time walking to a restaurant, yeah?"

"In other words, I still don't get to try the new Afghan place I want to review for District Foodie?"

"You don't mind?"

At the corner of Fourteenth and Constitution, cars were speeding through the final seconds of a yellow light. Brenda kicked the heel of one of her boots against the sidewalk, then the other, then the first again, while they waited. "It's not just the way they clock our lunch breaks that's driving me friggin' nuts at work," she began, as cars started rushing in the other direction, and more and more pedestrians collected around them. "Last week, for example, I tried to point out to my boss that it would make a lot more sense if I handled the data analysis on chickens, as long as I'm doing egg production anyway, instead of Joe down the hall doing chickens and fruit. Why would you put chickens and fruit together? Is he making dinner? And my boss tells me to go fill out a form for the suggestion box. Do you want to guess the last time anyone ever looked inside that box? Probably 1832."

"Could you talk to—what's the guy's name—the one who does chickens now?"

"He probably likes chickens." Brenda shrugged.

The 'walk' signal finally flashed. "I was thinking," Miranda said carefully. "I could try to contact Ronit."

The other people on the crosswalk and the sidewalk were hurrying in both directions, pushing past Ronit and Miranda.

"Why?" Brenda asked.

"Just to, you know, talk. Get her advice. No one else can really understand what happened that night." Her hat had ridden back up on her head, and Miranda tugged it down again, over her raw, cold ears.

"Didn't you already try writing to her ten times, and you never heard back?"

"Only twice."

"And the birthday presents you sent for Tali? She never thanked you."

"Oh, I don't know if they ever got any of the presents or letters. I might have the wrong address for Ronit's parents."

"You sent Tali's presents all the way the fuck to Israel?" Brenda demanded.

"Where else am I supposed to send them? Ronit's lawyer didn't know where she'd moved. I figure Ronit's parents could ship them to her."

"That's the dumbest thing I've ever heard."

"Some eight-year-old in Tel Aviv is probably playing with the make-your-own-necklace kit I sent to Tali four years ago."

"So if Tali isn't even getting the stuff, what's the point?"

"I have to do something to keep the lines open with Ronit. It's only once a year."

"And you still don't swear, do you? Because you promised Tali."

"Well, so what?"

For a moment, Brenda was silent. Then she said quietly, "Leave them alone, Miranda, like Ronit asked you to."

"And abandon Tali, too?"

"That's what Ronit wants."

They turned left onto Twelfth Street.

But Brenda hadn't known Ronit as well as Miranda had, back in their days together.

Stumbling on the path during their run in Rock Creek Park, when Miranda was sure she'd twisted her ankle, and they must have been at least a mile from any inhabited streets. Ronit immediately crouched and told Miranda to climb onto her back, and she insisted even when Miranda said it wouldn't work. She would carry Miranda piggyback back to civilization. Of course she could barely go four paces; she was taller than Miranda but just as scrawny. In the end they walked the whole mile or whatever, Miranda leaning against Ronit, baby step by baby step in the twilight. It took them over an hour to reach a little deli. Ronit wrapped an arm around her like a mom protecting a child.

Ronit, six months pregnant, arriving in Miranda's dorm room with a stack of her normal-size blazers, blouses, slacks, and skirts folded carefully in her big canvas shoulder bag. She put them together in various combinations—navy blazer with orange blouse and flared khaki skirt; black blazer with grey linen slacks—and studied Miranda modeling every single set. (Yes, she ordered; Miranda had to try all of them.) So that Miranda could have something classier than her denim skirt from high school, to wear to the interview with Mort Davis for a possible internship at the Center for Liberal Alternatives.

Because that was what friends did for each other.

When Miranda had asked Brenda if she could borrow Brenda's car for a few hours on Saturday night, Brenda had said yes, no hesitation, no questions asked. And when Miranda called on Sunday morning, Brenda again said yes and took an expensive taxi ride to the police station to bail out Miranda.

Tim took my wallet! I don't know what to do.

He cut up my driver's license, Miranda!

Can you drive Tali and me to the airport?

That was also what friends did for each other.

Wouldn't Ronit remember any of that?

CHAPTER THREE

MORT'S COMPUTER MONITOR SAT ON THE parquet floor of his office, next to his crowded steel desk and dangerously close to a brimming mug of coffee. A light bulb had burned out in the six-armed brass chandelier that hung down from the high ceiling.

"Say, would you care for a croissant?" At his desk, Mort waved a grease-spotted, white paper bag toward Miranda. "I'm afraid that it's from yesterday, but I find that the plain croissants seem to stay tolerably fresh for a second day, much better than the almond or chocolate variety. Do you agree? I don't have any napkins, I apologize, but I think there are some paper towels in the kitchen."

From the small marble table near the office door, Miranda picked up the two envelopes that were her mail. This was her chance to grab Mort's attention, while he was still thinking cheerfully about croissants and before he brought up the stupid drug-price data for the Senate health committee.

"How are you coming along on the drug prices?" Mort added, kicking his swivel chair fully around to face her. "How many years' worth were you going to analyze? Was it ten years?"

"Fifteen."

"Really? Fifteen?"

"Yes. To provide a broader context, remember?"

"Fifteen?"

"You know, Mort—" She strolled casually toward the desk "—as long as the committee has only started writing the legislation, I could contribute a lot more than statistics."

Mort frowned.

"For instance, I'm sure you know that there's talk in Congress about giving the federal government the authority to negotiate drug prices. That was a big section in my report on prescription drugs last winter. Why don't I write up a couple of pages about that to go with the statistics?"

Still frowning, Mort stared into the bag of croissants. He tugged at his skinny dark-blue tie, which he'd once told her was a high school graduation present in 1970. "I don't know. I don't think we want to get caught up in any political fights… "

"We wouldn't have to!" Miranda's elbow hit a pile of folders on top of Mort's desk, and she grabbed a few as they started to slide. "We can easily avoid the politics. I'll stick to the facts. I've already done detailed cost comparisons between the U.S. and Canada, which regulates drug prices. And how about this: I could include some of my interviews from the times I rode on the bus with the seniors going to Canada to save money on their prescriptions. Politicians love real-life stories."

A year ago, she'd written that report, and now that drugs and health care were a hot topic in Congress and the White House, her report was still moldering somewhere on Mort's desk while he obsessed about his stupid statistics. Her parents hadn't sat around looking up statistics about Vietnam. Grandpa Seymour hadn't spent his life doing research on factory injuries while someone else led the strikes. Russ didn't merely write reports about companies that cheated their workers and customers; he prosecuted them! She should be advocating for her ideas, adding her thoughts to a Senate bill, offering her unique contribution built from months of investigations, that would, even in the smallest way, make life better for people.

"The committee only asked us for the pricing data," Mort mumbled.

"We'd give them the data, I'm not saying we'd ignore that part. But with the Center's resources, we can do so much more to shape the legislation, to help write a good law that will lower medical costs for patients."

"That's true."

"And isn't that really our ultimate goal? To help people get better health coverage?"

After a pause, Mort shook his head. "Let's just stay with what the committee asked for. They'll decide how to use it."

"But what—?"

Mort was shaking his head again.

The kitchen was two rooms away from Mort's office. Jean was already at the counter, mixing fruit and ice cubes in the blender for her energy drink —bananas and strawberries, judging by the smells. Miranda took her mug and her box of green jasmine tea bags from their spot on the shelf over the sink.

Of all the rooms in the first floor of the townhouse the Center occupied, the kitchen looked most like what it must have been back in 1981, when the rich family who owned the building was still living there, and they let Mort use the parlor rent-free for his new think tank. There was a chunky, 1960s-vintage yellow stove and matching refrigerator, blue-and-yellow flowered curtains at the window, and a square, wooden dining table with four chairs neatly tucked in. A full set of china had been left in one of the glass-doored cabinets, although nobody from the Center used any of it.

Jean poured her concoction into a cup. "What did Mort do now?"

"What?"

"You're dipping your teabag up and down in your mug, but you don't have any water in it. So I figured something's bothering you, and the odds are, it's Mort."

Miranda promptly turned on the burner under the tea kettle. It might not be a bad idea to ask Jean's advice. Jean had been the first person Mort hired, a year after he started the Center; she'd gone to his wedding, and she'd even predicted the marriage wouldn't last. She probably knew him better than anyone except his cat. But how to frame her own complaint diplomatically? If Jean was that tight with Mort, she might not be open to too much criticism of him. "You're right," Miranda began. "I'm trying to figure out... I've been doing a historical price analysis for the Senate's Medicare bill, and I wanted to include some recommendations and information from the report I wrote last winter on prescription drugs. It would fit in perfectly, and Mort refuses to consider it."

"Did you ask him directly?"

"Yes. Just now."

"Hmm." Jean sipped from her cup, then stirred the contents.

"What good does that report do anybody, sitting on my shelf? This is the perfect chance for our work to have a real impact!"

"You have to remember the Center is his baby," Jean said calmly. She smiled a little. "He created it when he was only thirty-four, straight from

Missouri, because he was horrified by Reagan's election. He was going to pick up the fallen banner of liberal values. Mort Quixote. He doesn't put its imprimatur on anything lightly." She took another drink, grimacing. "But your idea sounds reasonable. Why don't you refine it and try him again in a couple of days?"

"Would it make a difference?"

"You know how he changes his mind all the time."

"I've never really pushed him. Well, not repeatedly."

"Let me tell you a story. When my oldest, Paul, was born, I asked Mort if I could bring him into work with me for a couple of days because I was still figuring out child care. Mort said sure. Well, for the next seven years I basically turned my office into a full-time day care center for both of my kids, from maternity leave until kindergarten. I had toys all over the floor, I was nursing, and Mort never said a word. I don't think he even noticed."

"Oh come on!" As the tea kettle whistled, Miranda switched off the burner. "He's not that oblivious."

"Look, he's amazing when he focuses on something. His ability to uncover connections and trends, to pinpoint issues. That's why the Center has lasted this long and is pretty damn well respected. But he sees only what he sees, if you get my point."

"So the question is, what will he see, if I push?"

"He might see that you've worn the same slacks every day this week," Jean continued. "Or he might not even see you at all."

What? Was she really wearing the same slacks? The grey wool ones? But they were perfectly appropriate for working on a report in an office, weren't they?

"People also say he's a fairly good golfer. For whatever that's worth." Opening the freezer of the sturdy old refrigerator, Jean plopped two ice cubes into her cup. "Try him again in two days with your idea."

Miranda walked slowly to her office, cupping her mug between her palms. Mort swinging a golf club. Mort clinking Champagne glasses at his wedding. Wow. Of course there were plenty of sides to Mort she didn't know and vice versa. What would Mort think if she told him that she wrote restaurant reviews for the District Foodie blog and had over four hundred followers? Or that seven years ago she'd been arrested for kidnapping? He wouldn't believe it, of course. He'd known her for more than a decade, and he knew she wasn't a criminal.

At its turtle pace, her computer warmed up. In the rich-family days, her office most likely had been the maid's room, with its unadorned fireplace, tiny sink, and flowered wallpaper faded to hints of yellow above the wainscoting.

Just for the heck of it, she started typing… Maybe Ronit's parents had a new address. It couldn't hurt to look. *Search Tel Aviv, Israel, within 30 miles…*

"Why are you reading about Tel Aviv?" Mort asked, peering over her shoulder.

Mort?

Quickly, Miranda erased the last three words in the Search bar and typed new ones. *Ministry of Health* "Israel's got great national health insurance, just like Europe. I want to see what's happening with drug prices there. I figured I could add some statistics from foreign countries, in addition to our data. For comparison." What was Mort doing, spying on her? She hadn't typed anything too revealing. Searching Tel Aviv. She wasn't sending her report to the Senate committee behind his back. Yet.

Mort tugged at his high-school tie again as he edged away from her shoulder. "Yes, that's true, and certainly Europe, the Scandinavian countries, are the gold standard…"

"Shall I include them with our U.S. data?"

"Do you think it would add anything?"

"Context. Broader global context."

"I don't… No, I don't think so. Anyway, I came in to tell you that Scott from the Senate committee said they hope to start marking up the bill right after the new year…"

When she switched back to her original Google search, all that showed up was the same address in Tel Aviv where she'd always sent Tali's gifts.

CHAPTER FOUR

RUSS STOOD OUTSIDE THEIR TALL APARTMENT building, one shoulder propped slightly against the beige-brick wall, hatless in the January evening cold. A weak beam from the front-door light flickered over his face and his dark-grey wool coat, where his big arms were firmly crossed.

"Why didn't you tell me you were arrested for kidnapping in 1996?"

His voice was a shard of ice, quietly slicing the night. His pale lips barely moved. Miranda halted, close enough that she could almost have kissed him.

How did he find out?

"Did you actually think the FBI wouldn't discover that you were arrested?"

But the plea bargain? Disorderly conduct.

"It's standard procedure," Russ continued. "The FBI always asks the local prosecutor for the full case file when there's an arrest record."

Of course she would explain. *It was for my friend Ronit. I was helping her. Wouldn't you help your friend if she was in trouble?* Why wouldn't her mouth move? She was too cold, standing on the sidewalk in front of their building, where their neighbors could walk by at any minute. "Can we talk about this inside? Do you want to get some Indian food?"

"This is not a dinner date."

He wasn't letting up. Staring at her, in the flickering light, as if she were a real criminal.

"Could we at least go in the lobby?"

Russ just kept speaking, spitting out his words in brittle clusters. He moved away from the wall to stand up straight, arms still firmly crossed. "Lou, the section chief in the office, came over to me today. He asked what this kidnapping arrest for Miranda Isaacs was all about, and why I'd lied on my security questionnaire."

"Lied?"

"I didn't include your arrest."

"That's not a lie. It's—it's an omission."

"Don't be cute."

"But it's something I did—me, not you—seven years ago. How much can that matter for you?"

"'Any false statements or inaccurate information during the employment application process may result in revocation of the position, as well as collateral consequences.'"

"Is that what your boss said?"

"That's what the rules say. I could lose my job."

Her breath was locked somewhere in her throat. Her arms were shivering, and she wrapped them around herself, gripping tightly just above her elbows.

I'm sorry. She had to say that.

A snake of frigid air began to slither up her spine.

Russ could lose his job. His ideal job. Because of her. Because she hadn't told him about the night at Dulles, but that was ridiculous. He'd gotten a glowing year-end review and an important new assignment. "They won't fire you. They gave you that big Veterans Affairs bribery case."

"So what? They'll give it to someone else."

"Just explain to them that I never told you about the arrest. It's my fault, not yours."

"It's not that simple."

"Why not?"

Across the street, in front of a shorter, red-brick house, a woman was yelling something. A man shouted back. A husband and wife, fighting?

"Why didn't you ever tell me, Miranda?" Abruptly, Russ kicked a foot against the brick wall. "I don't understand. We've been together for two years, and I'm a goddamn prosecutor, and I even asked you to marry me, and it never fucking occurred to you?"

"Because I didn't see any reason to tell you about something from a long time ago that has nothing to do with us or the person I am now."

"Not when I point-blank asked if you had an arrest record? When you knew the FBI was investigating everything about you and your family, and my job was at stake? You somehow forgot to mention that you were arrested for a major felony?"

"I thought it wasn't a felony anymore. It was plea-bargained."

"Kidnapping is a felony."

"I never think about it that way, Russ. I was helping my friend."

"By kidnapping."

"I just told you, I don't see it as kidnapping."

"Sneaking a kid out of the country?"

"Helping my friend."

"What other crimes have you committed that I don't know about?"

"Stop bullying me!"

"How can I believe anything you say?"

"Haven't you ever had a friend who needed help?"

"Not anything illegal."

"You have no idea what Ronit was going through. Her husband was crazy, Russ! Literally crazy. He took her driver's license and her credit cards. He yelled at her for everything. He threatened to cut off the phone. He'd even hit her a couple of times. She needed my help. She and her daughter had to get away for their own safety."

The crowds at the El Al check-in line. The ultra-Orthodox women in their hats and wigs; the boys with the side curls. The men in their black fedoras. The backpackers. The Arlington JCC sign. *Keep your personal belongings in your sight at all times.* Tali, smelling of apple juice, in the bright lights overhead. Her little stuffed fox. Her yellow suitcase.

Where're we going, Eema?

I just need my family, for a while. I need my mother.

Can you drive Tali and me to the airport?

Miranda inched one foot forward, toward Russ. "What happens next? Do you have some kind of hearing?"

"The FBI expands its investigation. Now it has to investigate your arrest and also my lie." His tone was quieter; almost tired.

"So I'll go talk to your boss—what's his name? Lou?—I'll explain that you didn't know. I'll explain why I never told you."

Russ looked away, across the street. "It's not the first one," he muttered.

What?

But he didn't say anything more, even as a man in a dark winter coat walked past them and the corner streetlight changed, sending forth a stream of cars.

"Before I got offered the provisional job," he finally went on, turning back to her, "the U.S. attorney himself interviewed me. His name is Jack Mason. It's just a formality, usually. But in this case, the second thing he said to me, after a jovial 'hello!' was to ask whether Henry Steinmann was my father. He said they'd been friends since Harvard." Russ exhaled. "I said no."

"No?"

"I know I was an asshole for doing that, okay? I didn't think about the security vetting, or even about goddamn Google. I just didn't want to be connected with Henry Steinmann in any way, and I didn't want to be hired because of my relationship to him. So I said he wasn't my father. You want me to say it? I lied." He kicked against the sidewalk this time.

"I realized within five minutes that after one search on Google, they'd find out," Russ continued, his voice still edged with anger. "The next day, I went to Lou, who was going to be my supervisor, and I told him. He seemed fine about it, said he figured his kids would discover new ways to rebel against him, too. Legally, it doesn't count against me, because it was only an informal conversation. It wasn't on any paperwork. But don't think Lou isn't counting it. And now your lie makes two."

"I'm sorry, Russ."

"I thought I knew you."

What?

His light blue eyes were homing in on her now. Arms crossed, rock-faced, like a prosecutor interrogating a suspect. He looked even bigger than usual.

"The Miranda Isaacs I thought I knew for the past two years is a—a smart, caring, loving, funny woman who wants everyone to have good health care. Who wants to change the world the way her parents and her grandfather did. Who would never kidnap a little girl and would definitely never lie to me about it."

Her cheeks stung from the cold air. On her left hand, her woolen glove pressed her small engagement ring into her finger.

"I thought we were building a life together."

"What are you trying to say, Russ?" No! She didn't want to ask that. She didn't want to hear the answer. It was too late to take it back.

"I don't know who you are anymore."

"I'm still the same Miranda. Look at me: Did I suddenly grow straight blonde hair? Did I stop going running in the morning? Did I start liking asparagus?"

"Did you kidnap a little girl and lie to me?"

"One lousy lie!"

"How do I know it's the only one?"

"How many times do I have to keep proving myself to you? I'm sorry, I'm sorry, I'm a thousand times sorry."

His long nose with the three freckles. His round chin. His eyes, glaring at her. His chapped lips, pressed together like the sealed flap of an envelope. He wasn't going to hear a word she said.

They couldn't linger out here on the sidewalk forever talking past each other as the night grew colder and colder. But then what? To sit across the kitchen table, poking at their dinner plates in silence? To apologize again and again; to be called a liar again? And what about going to bed? Each of them curling up at the edge of their side of the mattress, as far away from the other person as possible?

Her legs were shaking like an earthquake, but there was nothing close enough to grab for support except for Russ.

"Maybe we should just—you know. Take some time apart. A couple of days. We're too upset to talk now." She pulled a clutch of hair, wrapping it around a couple of her fingers.

Behind Russ, the glass door to their building swung open and a man emerged. Luckily, he headed away from them.

"What?" Russ shifted his weight on his feet. "I guess. Okay."

Was it okay? No. Encouraging separation was a bad idea.

"I'll go stay with my parents," he mumbled.

"With your father?"

"I'll survive."

"That's stupid. You stay here. I'll go to my mom and Bill's house." What was she saying? She was going to show up in Silver Spring on a Wednesday evening with a backpack full of clothing, as though she was dropping by to use the washing machine? "I'll make up an excuse. I'll tell them the toilet in our apartment exploded."

Why didn't Russ push back? Why didn't he suggest going to a bar, so she could have the excuse that she'd had too much to drink and she didn't know what she was saying? Why didn't he say he wanted to work things out? Now she was stuck.

CHAPTER FIVE

IT WAS EIGHT O'CLOCK, BUT BILL WASN'T SITTING in his armchair in the living room, reading his Italian magazine. Nor was his fat Italian-English dictionary on the marble-topped table next to the chair.

"Hi, Mom? Anyone? It's me. Miranda." Behind her, Miranda closed the front door and dropped her bulging backpack on the rug.

Russ and I are having some problems, so can I stay here for a couple of days?

I never told Russ I was arrested seven years ago and now he might lose his job and he's mad at me.

There was a fire in the living room of Russ's and my apartment. An electrical fire. Can I stay here for a couple of days?

We got this really bad leak in the apartment all of a sudden, and the bathroom's flooded.

"Miranda?" Her mother strode toward Miranda through the living room, barefoot, wearing a silky pale-blue blouse along with baggy jeans, her eyeglasses hanging around her neck on a ragged red string. "What's up? Hi." She kissed Miranda lightly on the cheek, bringing a whiff of sweet tomato sauce with her.

"Mom, where's Bill? Is everything all right?"

"Sure." Her mother palmed the door, although it was already shut. "Do you want some tea? Lily's in her room, doing homework. I assume. Or listening to music. Or both. Did I tell you I got her hooked on my old Jefferson Airplane CDs?"

"Mom? What's going on?"

"Let's talk in the kitchen."

The swinging door from the living room to the kitchen flipped back and forth and back again, almost hitting a wall, as her mother pushed it too powerfully.

A pile of file folders, an opened notebook, and a thick book were spread out on the kitchen table, along with the empty Lucite napkin holder and a fork. Underneath the window, the old radiator hissed faintly.

"Bill," her mother began. "Bill. He and I have, uh, separated. Temporarily. To think about our lives."

"Yikes."

With a flickering smile, her mother took two unmatched mugs out of the cupboard next to the framed "Make Love Not War" poster and turned on the water. But she filled the mugs too high and they overflowed, so she spilled out some water before placing the mugs into the microwave. "I mean, that's how we explained it to Lily and Ted."

"So why did you and Bill really separate?"

"Well, how about, because he's moved in with his girlfriend?"

"What the—"

"You can say 'fuck,' " her mother finished, as she sat down.

"Bill?"

Miranda knelt next to her mother and wrapped her arms around her mother's silky blouse and bony back, and they rested their heads together, a mass of wavy shoulder-length light-brown hair and thicker, frizzy, grey-brown hair. "Mom. How—? Oh, Mom."

After a moment, her mother resettled in her chair, and Miranda took the one next to her. "Let's keep our voices down a little," her mother semi-whispered. "Not that Lily would hear from upstairs anyway, with her music and her earphones."

"Bill actually has a girlfriend?"

"Yes."

"Who is she? A desk calculator?"

"Miranda!"

"I'm sorry."

"She's a financial consultant that he interviewed for his magazine. I think, last summer."

"How long—?"

"Since he moved out? About a week. It was a couple of weeks after

New Year's. I'm not sure when it all—uh—started."

The microwave beeped. The radiator let out a loud spurt of steam.

Bill Higgins was cheating on his wife, Judith Isaacs Higgins. Bill was cheating on Miranda's mother. Bill had a girlfriend. Skinny Bill Higgins with his rimless eyeglasses and skimpy, faded-red mustache and stubby fingers covered with red-blonde hairs, the nails trimmed perfectly straight across; Bill who read two articles in *L'Espresso* every evening from exactly eight o'clock to eight-thirty, laboriously looking up most of the words in his Italian-English dictionary. Bill who ate egg-salad sandwiches on white toast for lunch every single day. Bill had a girlfriend.

In all their years of marriage, since Miranda was ten years old, had she ever seen Bill and her mother even hold hands?

The summer after her freshman year at Georgetown was the last time Miranda had lived in this house with her mother and Bill, while she worked at a refreshment stand near the Lincoln Memorial, and Ronit flew home to Israel to see her family. One afternoon she was sitting in the backyard, partly reading, partly getting a suntan, partly watching Lily, who must have been two years old, toddling around the grass. Bill was supposed to be playing catch with Ted; he was Teddy back then. First Bill kept throwing the ball too hard, and Teddy was angry because he couldn't catch it. Then Bill threw such namby-pamby tosses that the ball dropped hardly a foot away from him, and Teddy got angrier. "You can't even throw a ball!" he'd screamed, running inside the house to find their mother. Bill had turned to Miranda; she'd turned away, as though she was absorbed in watching Lily. Because his face had looked so forlorn and helpless. *Don't look at me for help!* she'd wanted to yell at him. *You're the father. Go help your four-year-old son.*

Of course she hadn't told her mother, that summer. What was there to tell? It would only be Miranda criticizing Bill again.

"How are you? Are you okay?" In the kitchen, Miranda inched her chair closer to her mother.

"I feel ridiculous. Pitiful and ridiculous; being dumped like a teenager. I'm fifty-two years old. I'm a wife and a mother and a social services supervisor for the federal government. What kind of damn cliché am I? How the hell—" She pushed the folders and notebook toward the center of the table, and the notebook kept going, flying onto the floor. Miranda picked it up. "I'm furious at him, but I'm furious at myself, too, Miranda. Why didn't I see it coming? What's wrong with me, that I married someone who wouldn't keep his most important promise?"

"It's not your fault. He's the one with the problem."

"But I'm still the dumpee."

"Don't call yourself that, Mom. Don't belittle yourself."

Her mother shrugged. There were bags under her eyes now, and thin lines at the sides of her mouth. Her hair was an overgrown tumble of grey-brown frizz, as if she'd missed her last three appointments for a trim. She wasn't wearing her wedding ring.

"Is the girlfriend a lot younger than you?"

"I don't know. Who cares?"

"I'm sorry. You're right. It stinks no matter what."

"She lives in Virginia, is all he said," her mother added, her voice calmer. "It can't be too far away, if he's still getting to his office every day."

The room was growing too warm. Miranda tugged off her fleece jacket. "How did he—you know? Tell you he was leaving?"

"Oh, another cliché. He left a note for me on the table. This table." Her mother waved vaguely over the crowded tabletop. "In a sealed envelope, while I was at work. And his clothes were gone. Well, only his winter clothes."

"Did he give any reason?"

"Reason? What kind of reason is there for cheating on your wife?"

"Yeah. No."

Bill had been cheating on her mother. Bill Higgins and a sexy financial consultant from Virginia, holding hands in a dark corner of a candle-lit restaurant. Eating egg-salad sandwiches on white toast. No. All the words, put one after another, still made no sense, no matter how many details her mother spelled out.

As Miranda carried the two mugs of green jasmine tea to the table, there was a muted thumping from Lily's bedroom overhead, maybe Lily dancing to one of their mother's old Jefferson Airplane CDs. Or throwing her books on the floor. Or perhaps she'd decided to take up kickboxing. A couple of branches from the maple tree in the backyard scratched against the window.

"He wasn't acting weird recently at all? Like, I don't know, impatient or angry all the time?" Bill, angry? That was a stupid question. Miranda sat back down.

Her mother shook her head.

"Midlife crisis? Suddenly buying a slew of tie-dyed T-shirts and jeans?"

Her mother didn't even crack a smile. "No."

"Just...bam?"

"Bam."

Steam from the tea danced around Miranda's chin.

"What do you want to do next?"

"I'm trying to figure that out. See if it blows over? Chuck the rest of his clothes out the window? Sometimes I want to hire a divorce lawyer immediately, and sometimes I want to strangle both of them. No, not strangle; throw boiling hot coffee at them. No, I don't want to do that, either, because I never want to look at his goddamn face again. And then of course I tell myself to calm down and let my emotions settle. Maybe I miss him, but I don't realize it because I'm too caught up in feeling angry and pitiful. We've been married twenty-two years, Miranda; you don't just drop twenty-two years in the garbage can. That's why I didn't say anything to you before now. Why should I get you upset, if he and I end up reconciling next week? And you and Russ are so busy planning your wedding, I wouldn't want my shit to mess up your happiness."

"How are Ted and Lily taking all this?" Miranda raked her hair back from her face.

Tea splashed over the sides of the mug as her mother nudged it away. "I think they're kind of sleepwalking through it, to be honest. Of course, Bill hasn't been gone all that long. And you know I didn't tell them the worst of it, about his girlfriend. Ted's pretty much out of things anyhow, now that he's away at Duke and focused at the moment on trying out for the baseball team. And Lily's sixteen; do you remember what that's like? The world revolves around her friends and their music and her newest hobby and maybe a few spare minutes for school and SAT prep—and now she's gotten interested in the big protest against war in Iraq next month."

"I guess so."

"Really, with teenagers, how much do most families do together?

Other than taking Ted to Duke, I think the last time we went on a family trip was Niagara Falls, back when Ted was in middle school."

"But I can't believe Lily didn't tell me anything." Lily had called her just two days ago, to get Miranda's opinion of the poem she'd written for the junior-senior talent show. The day before that, she'd wanted to know if Miranda and Russ were going to the anti-Iraq war protest.

"Hmm. I asked both of them not to tell other people about our so-called separation. I suppose Lily thought that 'other people' meant her own sister, too."

Miranda swallowed a quick gulp of lukewarm tea. "I'll go say hi to her and see how she's doing, and that way I can let her know casually that I know about Bill. I want to find out what happened with the guy from Starbucks anyway."

"Which one is that?"

"The guy with three earrings she went to the movies with last week. But then I'll come back down here, if you want to keep talking. Or just to give you a hug. Whatever you want."

At the bottom of the staircase, her father's photo stood on the oak credenza, as always. Black-and-white, eight-by-ten; heavy silver frame. He sat on his Harley, one long leg stretched to the ground to prop him in place, the other foot on a pedal, leaning slightly forward into the handlebars, grinning, wearing jeans with ragged cuffs and short boots and aviator sunglasses, his dark hair tossed around his shoulders. His second official date with Judith, not counting all the intense days they'd spent working on the protests at Columbia. Forever nineteen and a half. Thirteen years younger than his own daughter was now. Jerry Isaacs would have only two and a half more years, before dying in the stupid, stupid car accident, when Miranda was barely six months old.

Forever nineteen and a half. Itching to rev the engine and join the Revolution. Summer of 1968, so he would've been heading to Chicago, to the big demonstrations at the Democratic National Convention. His second arrest.

His second arrest?

That didn't make sense. Her father had been arrested three times at major protests; in fact, he'd been one of the main organizers behind those protests. Yet the FBI and Russ's boss hadn't investigated him? They only cared about Miranda's kidnapping arrest that had been plea-bargained to a trivial misdemeanor anyway?

Maybe they hadn't investigated because Jerry was her father, not Russ's. Or because his arrests were so long ago. Or maybe the FBI just hadn't gotten around to questioning her mother yet. She should've warned her mother, as Russ had advised. Yikes, that was the last thing her mother needed, a bunch of government agents hassling her.

Miranda returned to the kitchen. "Dad's photo reminded me. It's so stupid, but the FBI might contact you for Russ's security clearance."

Her mother was fitting their mugs into the dishwasher. "What?"

"Oh, they're—you know, they have to investigate every tiny thing. Dot every I, cross every T. Russ thought the FBI might ask you about the protests you and my father organized. I suppose, about him being arrested."

One of the mugs slipped. It knocked something, which rattled the glasses on the dishwasher rack.

"Has anyone from the FBI called you yet?"

Her mother shook her head.

"Well, be forewarned. I mean, I don't know if they will call. They can hardly investigate everyone who protested the Vietnam War."

"What do you think they'd ask me?"

"I don't know. Like I said, probably about your anti-war stuff."

Latching the dishwasher door, her mother smiled at Miranda. "Fuck knows, right? Oh, tell Russ not to worry. I didn't blow up any buildings. I won't say anything that will get him in trouble." She frowned. "By the way, why are you here on a weeknight? I doubt that you had some flash of ESP about Bill and me. Not that I mind seeing you."

The frown dug deeper pairs of lines around her mouth and above her nose. Even her thick eyebrows were turning grey.

We got this really bad leak in the apartment all of a sudden, and the bathroom's flooded, so can I stay here for a couple of days? I can sleep in Ted's room.

That would have to be the story. Only for a couple of days. Her mother had her own marital problem to deal with.

CHAPTER SIX

Shalom *Miranda,*

Thank you for your letter to us. We are well, and also Ronit is well. Yes, we remember you as Ronit's friend at university, and we hope that you are well. Ronit says you should email to us, and we will send it to her. Good luck in your new marriage.

Leah and Yossi

BRENDA RUBBED HER EYEBROW AS SHE READ the email on Miranda's laptop. "Weird."

"I suppose it's good news that Leah and Yossi replied, for once," Miranda suggested. "Maybe it's because I wrote to them personally, instead of only sending a gift for Tali." Sitting on Ted's narrow bed, next to the desk with the laptop, she pulled out the scrunchie that held her hair and then twisted it back on.

Brenda lifted her bottle of Coors Light to her mouth and swallowed.

"Or because I hinted that it was urgent."

"What'd you say?"

"Something like, 'Hate to bother you but there's an important problem regarding my fiancé's job and I could really use Ronit's help. Blah blah blah.' But Brenda, I specifically asked for Ronit's mailing address or email address or phone number. So that I could write to her or call her myself, you know? I didn't say, 'Please forward my message to Ronit and then forward her message back to me and then forward…'"

"So why didn't they give the address or phone number to you? Why're they doing this cloak-and-dagger bullshit?"

"Exactly! And on the other hand, if Ronit still doesn't want to hear from me, why would they tell me it's okay to send an email?"

"Good question."

"And why didn't anyone ever answer me until now, all those years when I sent Tali's presents?"

"Like I said, it's weird." Brenda rubbed her eyebrow again. She sat back on the black swivel desk chair, settling her elbows on the armrests. "Maybe they've been sick. Didn't her father have some medical reason why they couldn't come to the U.S. to see Tali?"

"Yeah, he had a heart attack. But that wouldn't prevent both of them from writing to me for seven years."

We are well, and also Ronit is well. The email didn't even say anything. Where was Ronit living while she was being well? What kind of job did she have? Had Leah and Yossi actually seen Ronit and Tali?

If Ronit lived within a few hours' drive of Miranda, in Maryland or Virginia or even as far as New York, if Miranda could show up at Ronit's door in person... Of course it would be awkward. Worse than awkward; Ronit could be truly angry. *What are you doing here? I told you to write to my parents, not me.* The door might well be slammed in her face. But if Ronit would only let Miranda speak for one minute—or even better, if she invited Miranda inside, and Miranda saw some sort of memento from the past that she could point out to Ronit—

"Over there on the bookshelf? Is that your old menorah, with the little Maccabee soldiers?"

Ronit might let out one of her whoops. "Yes, but now I bought my own candles."

"You mean Brenda didn't steal some for you?"

In the first weeks after their arrest, Ronit had made her decision sound so reasonable. Every step she took had to be prudent, cautious, and above the slightest suspicion, she explained, while her criminal defense lawyer negotiated a plea bargain with the prosecutors and her divorce lawyer negotiated custody and visitation with Tim's lawyer. It was awful enough that she was allowed to see Tali only for half an hour per week—and even that had to be in the stark, cold Child Protective Services office, where the two of them sat at a bare table, a social worker eying them the whole time from a few feet away. No phone calls between visits. No letters. No time alone with Tali. No excursions to the zoo and the Washington Monument. Ronit might be permitted to bring Tali an occasional book or toy, but only if the social worker inspected it first. She could not risk losing that precious contact with Tali, minuscule though it was. Everything she did, Ronit said, had to be geared toward the two paramount goals: getting more time with Tali and staying out of jail. If she and Miranda were to write or phone each other, the judge might think they were still conspiring. Thus, Miranda had to be discarded.

Fine; Miranda didn't want anything to do with Ronit anyway. Ronit had dragged her into the whole mess, and Miranda had her own plea-bargain negotiations to worry about. Of course she wanted to see Tali, but Ronit obviously wouldn't be any help with that. Could Miranda, on her own, send Tali an occasional note or gift? Absolutely not, her lawyer insisted.

As the negotiations went on, into the third month, her anger at Ronit began to weaken. Whatever Miranda was suffering, it had to be a million percent worse for Ronit. Three or four times, Miranda tried phoning. No one picked up. No one returned messages; then there was no answering machine at all. She even went to Ronit's apartment in Tacoma Park once, which probably violated every legal protocol her lawyer had warned her to obey. It was a wasted trip anyway. Ronit didn't answer the doorbell. With the window blinds tightly shut, Miranda couldn't tell if anyone was inside. She left a note in the mailbox.

Finally, Miranda's plea deal was signed, her kidnapping charge was erased—supposedly—and she called Ronit's lawyer. They had all moved away, Tim and Tali and Ronit, he said. To Houston or Atlanta, as Tim had once fantasized? The lawyer didn't know.

By then, Ronit's phone number in Tacoma Park was disconnected. The only email address Ronit had ever used was her account at the child care center where she'd worked, and it had been immediately deactivated. Over the years, whenever Miranda checked, no one named Ronit Harrison was ever listed in the Houston or Atlanta areas in Superpages. There were thirty-four Timothy Harrisons near Houston and twenty-three in Atlanta the last time Miranda had Googled. It would take hours to contact all of them, and why would Tim talk to Miranda anyway? For that matter, maybe Tim hadn't taken Tali to either of those cities. Or they could have moved there, and then moved again, and yet again. It was nearly seven years ago by now; Tim was so impatient, they could have changed cities half a dozen times. They could be in Peoria or Poughkeepsie or Paris. With his MBA, Tim could probably find a job anywhere, and with his personality, he'd keep getting fired. He would move on to yet another city, and another, always confident that in the next location he'd finally land a position prestigious enough for his talents where the bosses weren't idiots. And Ronit would follow, every address. The judge had ordered Tim to give her that much, her lawyer said.

If they did traipse from place to place, Tali would probably have viewed it as an adventure at first. After all, she'd loved hearing Ronit's stories about far-away Israel and practicing with the Hebrew flashcards Ronit had made using pictures cut from magazines, in preparation for someday visiting *Savta* and *Sabba* in Tel Aviv. They studied together, Tali and Miranda: *Ehtz*, for a tree to climb. *Shual* for fox. *Tzahove*, yellow. "Yellow for sun!" Tali exclaimed. *Shemesh*. "Yellow for Mommy's hair," Miranda suggested. Also scissors, another of Tali's favorite words, for some odd reason: *meesparayeem*. Tali cut out pictures for the flashcards with her blunt little yellow *meesparayeem*.

After a while, though—especially as she grew older and planted roots— wouldn't Tali come to hate changing homes again and again? She would have gotten used to her school, her friends, her favorite playground, her special ice cream parlor in each city. Maybe there was a local zoo with fennec foxes. Little girls vowed to be friends forever. Would Tim have listened to her and stayed put, after the third or fourth transfer?

On the computer, Brenda had logged onto Google and was typing *Bicycle Rentals Washington DC*. "I suppose you might as well go ahead and do what Ronit's parents offered. Send her an email via them. She can hardly complain, since it's their idea."

"I don't see that I have any other options." Miranda shifted her weight. How had her brother managed to sleep for eighteen years of his life on this mattress that was as thin and hard as a prison bed?

"Did you ever consider saying no," Brenda said slowly, "when Ronit asked you to drive her and Tali to the airport?"

I thought things would get better when he moved out, but he's worse. And Tali sees it all.

He cut up my driver's license, Miranda!

I can't do this anymore.

I just need my family, for a while.

Can you drive Tali and me to the airport?

"A person doesn't say no when a friend asks for help."

"To anything?"

"Oh, come on, Brenda, do you want to invent nonsense hypotheticals? What if Ronit had asked me to murder Tim? What if she asked me to shoot up Tali with heroin? This was just a ride to the airport."

Angling her empty Coors bottle against the desktop, Brenda began languidly twirling it, clockwise, then counterclockwise. "You've told me you regret doing it," she murmured.

"Sure. In hindsight. And I'm sure Ronit regrets asking me. Don't you regret lending me your car that night?"

"Fuck yeah."

"All right. I know that if that whole night had never happened, Ronit and I wouldn't have been arrested, and Ronit and Tali would probably still be living here, and Russ's job would be safe. So it's her fault, it's my fault, it's Tim's fault, too, for that matter. What's the point of hindsight? I can't change the past."

Brenda had stopped twirling the beer can.

"Anyway, if I hadn't driven her, she would've taken a taxi. You know Ronit."

"If, *schmiff*," Brenda agreed, swiveling around toward Miranda. "Speaking of Russ's job, have you heard from him?"

Miranda shoved Ted's pillow under her butt, but it was as flat as the mattress. "Just some emails about logistics. Do I need anything from the apartment? My copy of *Bon Appetit* magazine came in the mail. Stupid stuff like that." She untwisted and retwisted her hair scrunchie once more. "Yes, I know his job is in jeopardy because of my arrest, and he's angry that I never told him about it. I blindsided him, you could say. I get that. But he's behaving like a child now. It's been four days. He can pick up the phone and call me."

It would've been his fourth morning waking up without her; waking alone in the queen-size bed. Wearing, probably, a sweaty T-shirt and his boxers, the shirt's soft cotton clinging to his shoulders and belly. Had it felt empty to him, to stretch out a bare leg leftward and hit nothing? Had he called toward the bathroom that morning, while he pulled up his socks and laced his sneakers, as though she was there to answer: "Do you want to go running on the loop around the Lincoln Memorial and across the bridge?" And then thrown his T-shirt on the floor, expecting her to pick it up?

"What's your plan for Russ?" Brenda asked. "You always have a plan."

"Oh, I don't always…"

Brenda pointed the Coors bottle toward Miranda.

Miranda grimaced. "I know. I've been waiting for him to make the first move, because he's the injured party, more or less, and I didn't want to push him. But it's been long enough. I can perfectly well call him now and say 'Let's go get coffee and doughnuts.' And that's what I'm going to do."

"Okay."

"After I write to Ronit."

"Why—?"

"That'll be quick, and then I can focus on Russ."

"Oh?"

"Besides, maybe Ronit will have some advice on what to say to him."

"Hey!" Lily suddenly shoved open the half-ajar bedroom door, almost hitting the foot of the bed with it. "Miranda, do you have anything like a denim jacket I could borrow? My hoodie would look dumb with this, wouldn't it?" She had on a purple-and-yellow plaid wool shirt, red shorts, and tall, tight, leather boots that laced on the front, ending halfway up her thighs.

"Sure." Miranda walked two steps to Ted's tiny closet. Where was—? Oh, her denim jacket was probably still at the apartment. Russ's apartment. Their apartment. "How about fleece?" She slid her dark-green fleece jacket off one of the crowded hangers.

Lily frowned. "I dunno. I don't think the colors work together. What do you think? Miranda? Brenda?"

"It seems fine to me," Brenda replied. "But I only wear black, except for coats, so I'm the wrong person to ask." She was wearing a black turtleneck and black jeans at the moment, for instance.

"Are you colorblind?" Lily asked.

"Nah. I just like black."

Miranda spread out the arms of the fleece to form a T against Lily's torso. "I see your point. I guess it would be a lot of colors."

"Don't ask her advice, either, Lily. She hasn't bought clothes since

1992," Brenda said.

"That's not true!"

"I love Miranda's clothes. It's kind of a party tonight," Lily added, "and I want to be, like, unique, but not dumb."

"I don't think you'd look dumb. But if you don't think it works together..." From the top of Ted's dresser, Miranda pulled out her neon-yellow Lycra running vest. "Try this?"

"Cool. Thanks."

"You'll be the belle of the ball." Miranda squeezed Lily's shoulder.

"In the future," Brenda said casually, "let me know if you ever want something special. I can probably get it."

"Really?"

Miranda glared at Brenda. *Shoplifting again?* she mouthed.

Brenda shrugged.

"Lily," Miranda asked, "do you remember Tali? My Israeli friend Ronit's daughter? They've moved away, and she's going to be twelve next month. What do you think a twelve-year-old girl would like for her birthday?"

DEAR RONIT.

I know it's been a long time. What have you and Tali been doing for the last seven years?

I've been thinking about you.

Remember when I thought I'd twisted my ankle in Rock Creek Park?

Remember when we were arrested at Dulles Airport?

Dear Ronit,

I know you asked me never to contact you, but

Dear Ronit,

I'm writing because

Dear Ronit

I know it's two months early, but I'm sending Tali's birthday present

Dear Ronit

I apologize that I'm breaking the silence you requested. I wouldn't write if it wasn't important. To be brief: I'm engaged to a truly wonderful man named Russ Steinmann. He's a lawyer, and he's been hired for what's really his dream job, but because it's with a sensitive government agency, they asked about the criminal records of his family, including his fiancée. Me. And now Russ is angry that I never told him about my arrest at Dulles, and it could cost him his job.

So I guess I'd just like to talk with you about that night. Maybe that would somehow help me stabilize and clear my thoughts. You're the only person I can truly talk to about what happened.

Could you tell me your phone number? If you're living anywhere near the District or Maryland or Virginia, maybe we could have a cup of tea. (Or wine?)

No matter what, I want you to know that I think about you and Tali a lot, and I hope you're both well and happy.

Miranda.

Dear Ronit
I'm writing because I miss you.

SEVEN YEARS. RONIT COULD BE LIVING anywhere, working at almost any job. She could be riding the escalator at a subway station somewhere while Tali walked up and back next to her. She could be baking yellow-rose cupcakes with Tali. She and Tali could be running together through the tree-lined streets of whatever city they lived in, just like Miranda and Ronit used to do.

CHAPTER SEVEN

EVEN THOUGH THERE WAS A STURDY WOODEN chair right next to him, Scott remained standing behind the desk in his airless Senate committee office, jutting his head forward and slashing his right hand sideways into his left palm while he speed-talked. He had a booming deep voice and mousy brown hair that flopped over his black-framed eyeglasses, and he chomped urgently on his chewing gum as soon as he finished every sentence.

There was also a matching chair in front of the desk, but were visitors actually supposed to use it if Scott never sat down? Miranda didn't.

"Bottom-line, you're saying that U.S. spending on prescription drugs is up an average eighteen percent annually since the late 1990s—Correct? One hundred seventy billion last year?" Scott chomped.

"Yes. And also—"

"Did you break that down by categories in your report? What percentage of the increase is attributable to price hikes? What percentage is other factors? Did you provide charts, I hope?"

"Yes. And—" Almost every muscle in Miranda's body was aching from standing up for the past ten minutes—her back, her neck, the soles of both feet, both legs, both arms. She shifted the folder with the pricing data from her left arm to her right, as her briefcase began to slip from where it leaned against her calf. Her hair, at least, was staying decorously bound by its scrunchie. "We also—"

"Good. I'll give it a read." Scott reached out his hand, presumably to take the folder.

"I also have another study!" Miranda clutched the folder against her chest. She had to speak as fast as Scott did, before he took her folder and ended their meeting. "Last winter we actually looked into the question of federal authority to negotiate drug prices, and I've brought a copy of that report with me."

"Why?"

Why? "Because it's relevant. Because isn't that one of the topics the committee is considering for the bill?" Because Mort hadn't exactly given Miranda a Yes.

She'd mostly followed Jean's advice. A few days ago, when she'd emailed Mort to update him on the status of her data-collecting, she'd mentioned in the second-to-last paragraph that she might bring a summary of last winter's report to her meeting with the Senate committee's chief of staff. Mort hadn't replied. If he disapproved, he'd have to say something. Of course, his nonreply could simply mean that he hadn't noticed the couple of sentences, as Jean had predicted, and as soon as he paid attention, he might order her to back off and stick to the boring numbers Scott had asked for. However, if Scott himself wanted Miranda's report from last winter—if he wanted her to contribute to the broader debate about drug coverage—then how could Mort object?

"Thank you," Scott said, sounding bored. "We have a lot of research on the issue of price negotiation already, so I think I'll pass on your offer." He stretched his hand toward Miranda again. "I'll be in touch if I have any questions."

"But we did some unique research."

Scott took a step toward the door.

"We have examples of people who've been going to Canada to get their prescriptions filled because the prices there are typically seventy percent lower."

"We know that. They've been doing it for years."

"But these are people I actually met on the buses to Canada. Real people. I have their real stories."

The office was small and almost empty, the last in a series of small offices on the fourth floor of the Russell Senate Office Building. One wall held a poster of the Grand Canyon, its edges curling, and a fat cactus with a short arm was growing half-bent over in a black tub against another wall.

"Are they seniors?" Scott asked.

"A lot of them. They charter buses."

Scott abruptly grabbed the wooden chair near him and sat down. Without glancing at Miranda, he started writing on a notepad.

She fell into the seat of the matching chair. Now, of all stupid times, she needed to pee.

"Would they be willing to testify in person at a committee hearing?" Scott kept writing while he spoke.

"I can ask." Would they? The Laceys, in their matching jackets, holding hands the entire bus ride. Mrs. Patterson, who'd never been out of New York State before. The Lauterbachs, who took turns filling their prescriptions because they couldn't afford to pay for both sets of meds every month.

"I'll take a look at what your bus-riders have to say. Can you give me ten to fifteen examples?"

Fifteen? Ten? She ought to have ten. She'd find ten. She'd go back to Canada to get them. Yes!

It was just past five o'clock. Outside the blindingly white-marble Russell Building, aides and secretaries and lawyers and researchers from the nearby congressional offices were starting to trickle onto the twilight sidewalk, toward their constellation of Metro stops. Her mother worked in the HHS building straight across the Capitol; they could take the Metro to Silver Spring together and celebrate Miranda's small victory. No, it was too soon for her mother to be leaving work. At least Miranda wouldn't run into Bill on the train, since he presumably would be taking one of the lines that went to Virginia and his girlfriend.

From his office about fifteen minutes away from where Miranda was standing at that moment.

Which he always left at six o'clock.

So what?

So, if she wanted to talk to him, she knew where to find him, and she would have plenty of time to get there.

And why in the world would she ever want to talk to a creep like Bill Higgins who'd cheated on her mother?

For exactly that reason: Because someone had to make him confront what he'd done. Someone had to ask him why he'd walked out on his wife and his own kids, Ted and Lily, after more than twenty years. Her mother had said she didn't want to look at his face, which was her right, but that didn't mean Miranda couldn't.

If she could change Scott's mind, she certainly ought to be able to have a chat with Bill Higgins.

Straight downhill on Constitution Avenue. Past the Capitol and its leafless winter trees and rolling lawn, past the hulking Labor Department headquarters, a right turn onto Third Street, up that long block and left onto D Street, and—Oh great, now she was in Judiciary Square, the heart of Washington DC's criminal justice system, surrounded by the District of Columbia District Courthouse and the District of Columbia Court of Appeals and the U.S. Courthouse annex and the District municipal police and only a couple of blocks from the U.S. Attorney's office where Russ was still working unless they'd fired him because of Miranda but there was no point pondering the irony of Miranda Isaacs, ex-criminal, walking among these overpowering stone-and-columned headquarters of police and prosecutors and judges. Anyway, she was leaving the accusing square, onto ordinary Sixth Street, then a block and a half to a narrow, five-story, dull-brick building. The offices of *Your Finances* magazine, on the second floor.

Almost immediately, the door of that building opened. A figure in a dark, knee-length coat emerged.

Already?

No. Bill always wore a camel-hair coat.

A pale blue sedan emerged from the underground garage next to Bill's building and whizzed up the street, followed by a white car.

On second thought, trying to confront Bill directly was a stupid idea. He was more likely to evade and mumble for ten minutes, rather than answer her questions. And her mother might be annoyed if she found out. Maybe, instead, it would be more fruitful to be indirect. To follow Bill, secretly. With luck, Miranda might be able to track him all the way to the girlfriend's home and see what sort of place she lived in, perhaps even catch a glimpse of her. Maybe she lived in an apartment building with a friendly doorman who would be eager to gossip about the hot new romance on his watch.

Directly across the street from Bill's office was a much wider and newer beige-marble building, with revolving doors deeply inset from the sidewalk where Miranda could loiter, probably unseen.

Two women, chattering, sauntered out from Bill's building.

Someone crossed in front of them on the pavement.

A skinny, not-very-tall guy in a camel-colored coat and grey slacks, with dull-red hair and rimless glasses, pushed the door of Bill's building partway ajar. With another push, the guy was outside. He turned left and began walking.

It was too early.

He was walking too fast.

It wasn't Bill. And it was.

Miranda ran out of her hiding place.

She had to stay just enough behind him, like a detective in the movies, so that she could see him but he wouldn't see her. If he rounded a corner, she didn't dare lose him. If he caught her, what story would she tell him?

He turned at the next corner, and then another, a right turn onto brightly lit Seventh Street. Past McDonalds, an Indian restaurant, a cell phone store, a cupcake shop, a strong whiff of chocolate. His balding, dull-reddish head and camel-colored coat bobbed among people swerving in and out of doorways and around each other. Suddenly he was going into a small, signless store. A newsstand. Getting his regular bottle of lemon iced tea for the ride home? *The Wall Street Journal?* No, he would have read that at work, hours ago. She ducked behind a grey minivan. Really, this was too ridiculously like a movie.

He was back on the sidewalk, moving forward again among the crowds, toward the Gallery Place Metro station at H Street.

And he paused once more. Now it was a flower stall. He was buying— flowers? Bill? A bouquet of red roses.

A peace offering, for her mother? Of course not. He had never, since Miranda had known him, bought flowers for her mother.

Holding the flowers above his shoulder, he stepped onto the escalator to descend underground to the Metro.

Well, then: Onto the escalator for her, too.

If she lost sight of Bill, once he got to the turnstiles, it would be almost impossible to find him again. Three subway lines, six directions, two of them going into Virginia. He was five spots below her, as the escalator descended; he was locked in place. So far so good. One by one, like a line of automated toy soldiers, the riders glided onto the stone floor at the bottom. Man, man, woman, man, teen, teen, Bill, man… But Bill didn't immediately head leftward into the station's dimly lit tunnel like all the other passengers. After he reached the bottom, he pivoted a little to his right into a slight empty space next to the wall, just a couple of inches from the escalator, and fumbled in his coat pocket. The escalator continued to descend, inexorably, inches away from him. Woman, woman, man, woman. There was no way to stop it; there was no way to turn around and clamber back up. There was no way for Bill not to see her, unless he kept his eyes fixed on his pocket. Three more people moved off, and then it was Miranda.

Bill straightened up.

Miranda stood in front of him. She had nowhere else to go.

"Miranda?" he asked.

CHAPTER EIGHT

SIX LONG-STEMMED RED ROSES FELL NEXT to Bill's brown loafers, while three more dangled from his left hand. The person getting off the escalator behind Miranda elbowed past her.

"That's a nice bouquet."

Silently, Bill crouched down to retrieve the partly crushed flowers from a cluster of cigarette butts, his perfect fingernails scraping the stone floor. It took him four fumbling tries.

"Does she like roses?"

"Yes…"

Riders kept pressing against Miranda while the escalator descended, pushing her sideways, a step toward Bill. So much for interrogating the doorman and subtly spying on the girlfriend's apartment; so much for delicately catching Bill off-guard with just the right question. Well, they couldn't stand there forever, blocking other people. What would two colleagues do if they were having a disagreement? "Can we sit down somewhere and talk?"

Clutching the roses in both hands, Bill stared at her as if she was insane.

And she was. A sit-down chat? The two of them? Coffee? The cup two-thirds filled, skim milk, no sugar, for Bill. To sit across a table from this man who'd cheated on her mother, while he precisely stirred his precisely prepared coffee so that he didn't spill a drop. His hairy fingers. His stupid little mustache. She couldn't. She should never have followed him.

"Okay," he mumbled. "We can go to the Copper Tea Pot. Near my office."

Would it be the same coffee shop as twenty-three years ago, when her mother had taken Miranda to meet "her friend" for lunch? The restaurant then had smelled of French fries and had pink Formica tables and thick, glazed plates in bright colors: pink-orange for Miranda, royal blue for her mother, Kelly green for Bill. He'd ordered an egg-salad sandwich on white toast, and her mother got some sort of green salad. Bill had asked a few questions, leaning forward with his hands flat on the table and his nails trimmed evenly across, while Miranda ate French fries and a hot dog and built a tiny house with the sugar packets from a bowl that had come with Bill's and her mother's coffee. He asked what Miranda liked to do at recess, and if she had a best friend. Her mother mentioned Miranda's friends Marcia and Beth. Bill explained that he became a financial journalist because when he was approximately Miranda's age—which was nine years old, wasn't it?—his favorite uncle bought him five shares of Disney Company stock, which had pictures of Mickey Mouse and Donald Duck and Pinocchio and Bambi and Cinderella and Dumbo and Tinker Bell on the stock certificate, and the uncle showed him how to follow the price every day in the newspaper, and so Bill started saving up part of his birthday and Christmas money every year—which began at ten dollars for birthdays and five dollars for Christmas but then increased to fifteen dollars—in order to buy more shares of the Disney stock with Mickey Mouse's and Donald Duck's and Pinocchio's pictures, so that by the time he was in high school he owned sixty-seven shares, which fluctuated somewhat in value over that period but essentially maintained a steady upward rise, and by the time he was ready for college the price per share had more than doubled. On Bill's green plate, the white chunks and squished dark-yellow mass of his egg salad oozed out from the bread. No, Miranda had said, she didn't want dessert.

Now Bill and Miranda glided silently up the escalator, Miranda one step ahead. At the sidewalk, she waited without looking at him. "This way," he said, still swallowing his words.

However, he immediately raised a palm and turned his back to Miranda, clamping his phone to his ear.

Of course he would be calling the girlfriend, presumably to let her know he'd be late. Waylaid by his stepdaughter who'd never liked him. Miranda kept walking, not fast, not slow. Let Bill rush to catch up, or tell her she was going in the wrong direction.

Too quickly to have lingered over romantic telephone murmurings, he was almost next to her—too close!—his loafers scraping the pavement. Miranda jerked away. "It's two blocks from here," he said. "The other side of the street. If you don't mind a coffee shop?"

That didn't count as a question she needed to answer. Miranda walked, keeping a forearm's length from Bill, and she crossed the road where he gestured, just as the traffic light switched to the red palm signal for *Wait*. He pointed, unnecessarily, to a sign on a wide, lighted window that announced in brassy letters: The Copper Tea Pot. Shoving open the door, Miranda strode to a square table with two wooden-backed chairs near the front.

If it was the same restaurant as twenty-three years ago, it had acquired new dishes. The abandoned cups and plates at a nearby table were made of sturdy white china, edged in blue. The tables were still Formica, however.

"Why did you do it?" she demanded.

Bill finished sitting. "Miranda, it's not that simple…"

"Apparently it was, for you. You left my mother."

Bill set his bedraggled bouquet on the table.

A waitress in a white-and-blue apron suddenly arrived next to them, proffering a Pyrex coffee pot that was tilted dangerously near horizontal. "Coffee?"

"Yes," Bill replied. "Thank you. Just fill it two-thirds full, please. With skim milk on the side. No sugar. Thank you."

"Jasmine green tea, thanks," Miranda said.

Bill let in and out a long breath and moved his flowers onto his lap.

All right. She was here, about to drink a cup of tea with this jerk. She could have refused, and she hadn't. Well then, if she wanted to have any sort of conversation and hear what he had to say for himself, then she needed to lighten her tone of voice. Being too hostile wouldn't help. "What's her name? Your friend."

"What?"

"I mean, if we're going to talk about her, I guess I should know her name, shouldn't I? That would be nice." She managed a paltry smile.

"I'm not sure that we… have to. Talk about her."

"She's someone you interviewed for your magazine? That's how you met?"

"Yes. In a way."

"Is she a stockbroker?"

"Not really."

"Is she also studying Italian?"

"Italian? No, she—no."

"Do you have a picture of her?"

"What? No. That is, I do."

"Can I see it? I'd really like to see what she looks like."

"I—I don't know."

"Is she pretty?"

"I guess so. Yes. She's got long hair. Uh. Like Lily."

"Long hair? That's nice."

"Look—Can we talk about something else?"

All of a sudden, she was fiddling with her own hair. Just because Bill mentioned Lily's and the girlfriend's hair? Miranda dropped her hand. This conversation was going nowhere. The girlfriend had long hair and didn't speak Italian. How was that going to help her mother? "What would you like to talk about?"

"How, uh, how is your mother doing?"

"What?" Miranda snapped.

A sharp drop of water hit Miranda's forehead. Directly above her, the waitress was holding a quivering cup of steaming water in one hand, a saucer containing a Lipton's teabag in the other. As soon as she got the cup and saucer to the table, the waitress darted away.

"You're asking how Mom is doing, after what you did to her?"

"I mean... Does she need any financial help?"

Miranda plopped her teabag roughly into the cup. How could her mother have ever married this cheating, boring, clueless jerk? Even from the way they first met, she should've been forewarned. Rushing to pick up little Miranda at a new babysitter's house, she'd gotten off at the wrong Metro stop. She'd been disoriented for a moment, standing on an unfamiliar corner. Of course she'd been grateful when a man in a camel-colored coat stopped to ask if she needed help. But surely she should have thought it was weird that the man had memorized the map of the entire Washington DC metropolitan area Metro system? It was the only seriously stupid thing Judith Isaacs had ever done.

"I'll obviously keep on, uh, supporting…" Bill's nails, as he wrapped his palms around his coffee cup, were still trimmed perfectly, and his fingers were still covered in reddish-blond hair. "Ted and Lily…"

"We close in fifteen minutes," the waitress whispered, hurriedly dropping the check on the table between their cups.

Bill tugged his light-brown wallet out of his pocket. When he shifted his weight, some of his roses slipped onto the linoleum floor. "Ted and Lily," he repeated, clutching the wallet without opening it. "I'll be seeing Ted next week. I'm going to Duke, to interview an economics professor. So I'll take Ted out for dinner…"

"What did you tell Ted and Lily about all this? I suppose I should get the same prettied-up cover story they have."

"Just what Judy and I agreed."

Judy. Her name was Judith! Always.

"That we both need some time apart to, um. Think," Bill continued. With two fingertips, he inched the check slightly toward his coffee cup.

"And Ted and Lily didn't ask anything more?"

"Oh, kids. They don't pay attention to their parents."

"Yeah. That's true. That's what Mom said, too."

Bill nodded.

The waitress scuttled past them, to lock a bolt on the front door.

"Still, it might be hard for me to keep up that cover story." Miranda tapped the string from the teabag against her mug. "To say that Mom 'agreed' or 'needs time.' As though this was her choice."

"Well, maybe it was."

"What are you talking about? She didn't kick you out."

Suddenly, it was a different Bill Higgins facing Miranda, a man whose bushy red eyebrows hovered over his eyeglasses like two bear pelts, who wheezed sharp breaths out of his broad nose and glared at her and clenched his manicured nails into fists on the Formica. "Maybe there isn't room in one house for Judy and two husbands…" that man said, beginning with a gunshot of words but trailing into a mumble, like the old Bill.

"What's that supposed to mean?"

"Maybe I'm…" Bill looked down at the flowers in his lap. "Tired of living with the ghost of a martyr who saved the world."

"My father?"

"Not just the ghost, but his photo staring me in the face every time I come down my own stairs. His favorite poster in my kitchen."

"Too bad, if Mom likes it."

"My own house."

"And her house."

"A ghost that even my own daughter adores."

"I'm not—"

"Now Lily wants to go to that Iraq protest next month just like the sainted Jerry and Vietnam."

"Don't you dare!"

"And I'm expected to live with that hero-worship every day in my house?"

"That's right!"

"Grandpa Seymour the brave union organizer. Saint Jerry the—the saint." Bill slapped his napkin against the table. The rest of the roses dropped off his lap.

Miranda grabbed the check. "That's my father you're talking about, and my mother loved him. So you just shut your mouth. You're jealous, and you think that gives you permission to cheat on Mom?"

"Why don't you Google your Saint Jerry sometime?"

"Duh. I've Googled both of them a zillion times. There wasn't an Internet in 1968. And by the way, Mom hates being called Judy, in case you forgot."

The only possible thing to do after that, of course, was to dramatically pull a bill out of her pocketbook, without looking but hoping she'd grabbed at least a five and not just a single, shove the money under her teacup, and walk out the door. And also hope that Bill would double-check her payment and if she hadn't left enough, he'd add a couple dollars more. He owed her and her mother that much.

HER FATHER COULD HAVE BEEN QUOTED in a lot of newspaper articles back in 1968; after all, he was among the leaders of the big sit-in by students that shut down Columbia University that spring because of the Vietnam War, and he was arrested for taking over the university president's office. But so few of the news stories from those days had ever been uploaded onto the Internet.

There were too many protestors at the Democratic Convention in Chicago to pick out individual faces in the photos from that chaos.

All the reporting about the grape boycott in California focused on the farmworkers union leader Cesar Chavez and the horrible conditions in the fields. No one paid attention to the people behind the scenes like Jerry Isaacs.

He'd never graduated from Cooper Union, so he wasn't on any alumni lists.

The car accident that killed him in February 1971, when Miranda was just six months old, would have been too minor to merit a write-up in *The New York Times*.

After the funeral, his family dropped all contact with Judith; he'd been alienated from those conservative, Nixon-voting relatives for years.

The only Jerry Isaacs or Jerome Isaacs that Google ever found was Jerome Isaacs, PhD, who was six years old when Miranda was born and was currently an associate professor of business psychology in North Carolina.

Maybe, her mother had said, he was one of the three long-haired, twenty-something men in jeans standing near the microphone on the tiered staircase of Low Library at Columbia, in the *Times* photo of the 1968 sit-in that had once cropped up on the Internet. He could have been the guy speaking at the mic, or the one slouched against the bottom of a large bronze sculpture of a seated woman, or the one with his arms crossed; in the small, fuzzy picture, they all looked like him. Judith and her friends Kim and Marilyn might even be the girls in half-profile, off to the side of the photo, clutching schoolbooks to their chests. Or not.

What could Bill possibly know? Nothing! He was inventing suspicions out of spite and jealousy, as if trashing Jerry would justify his cheating on Judith. He was the second-choice husband who would never be as sexy or young or idealistic as Jerry Isaacs had been.

If Jerry had truly done something scandalous—shot a policeman? bombed a draft board office?—his name would have appeared in at least one Google search.

And if there was anything so horribly violent or headline-making in his past, the FBI would have flagged that long before they found Miranda's little misdemeanor, no matter how many decades ago it was or how distant Jerry's relationship was to Russ. *We didn't blow up any buildings,* her mother had said. *I won't say anything that will get him in trouble.*

No, there was likely no scandal, but also no public glory. Jerry Isaacs would apparently never get the credit he deserved for his efforts in those idealistic, crazy days. He'd been one of the people who truly lived by their beliefs, protesting a wrongful war, racism, police brutality, inhumane treatment of farmworkers, all sorts of evils, in order to make the world a little bit better for Miranda and all future generations. But he didn't need many physical artifacts:

A long, wrinkled piece torn vertically from a flyer calling for students to support a sit-in at Columbia, its typewritten paragraphs smudged in random spots, with a blurred phone number scribbled on the blank side.

A fuzzy newspaper image of three twenty-something guys on the staircase of Low Library.

A picture postcard from Big Sur, California—a sky of swirling purple, gold and red; a turquoise ocean that crashed into jagged black cliffs—postmarked September 25, 1968, addressed to Judith at Grandma Bessie and Grandpa Seymour's apartment in Brooklyn, and signed, in perfect classroom script, "Peace and love, Jerry."

Miranda's birth certificate from Brooklyn Jewish Hospital, September 19, 1970. Father: Jerome Isaacs. Mother: Judith Isaacs.

A black-and-white photo of a guy with windblown hair and sunglasses, sitting on a Harley.

CHAPTER NINE

THE BILLS ARRIVED IN MIRANDA'S EMAIL, CC'd to Russ:

Owed to the photographer by February 18: A deposit of eight hundred dollars for four hours of photography for a wedding on Sunday afternoon May 18, including a maximum of 160 proofs plus a video.

Owed to the caterer by March 18: A second installment of a thousand dollars for a buffet dinner Sunday afternoon May 18 for an estimated fifty people, including five vegetable/dairy hors d'oeuvres, choice of salmon or pasta entrée, house salad, two hot side dishes, dinner rolls, fruit salad, assorted pastries, wine with dinner, soft drinks, tea, coffee. (Wedding cake and Champagne to be provided by the customer.)

The Indian caterer in Alexandria would have been more fun. The delicate, flaky *goan* salmon curry; the tangy-sweet chicken *tikka masala* in creamy tomato sauce; the four types of *naan* bread; the fried crescents of sweet-and-sour eggplant... "But we don't have the chutzpah to do an exotic wedding dinner, do we?" Miranda had said at their tasting in November, and Russ, his mouth full of chicken, a dab of tomato cream sauce at the edge of his lips, nodded unhappily. And therefore, they'd also rejected the Vietnamese restaurant near DuPont Circle that she'd given four stars in her review for District Foodie. (Too weird for Bill and Lily.) And no Chinese food. (All the pork, lobster, and shrimp would drive Russ's father berserk.) Maybe the upscale Italian restaurant that Miranda had also rated four stars, where Russ's friend Greg had his wedding reception? But it was beyond their budget.

"We could spend more on food, and cut back on something else," she'd suggested.

"Like what?"

"Eliminate the music?"

"What? How will you walk down the aisle?"

"You can hum."

"Or use my iPod?"

"A group singalong?"

"Ask Lily to play guitar?"

"Russ, you know Lily. Guitar was three months ago."

"Okay, I'll play."

"Guitar? Since when do you play guitar?"

Russ broke off a piece of the airy *naan* bread. "I don't now." Fleetingly, he smiled. "I had a band with a couple of friends when I was fifteen, sixteen. Like every sixteen-year-old, I was sure I was the next Dylan. We even got a few gigs. At schools. Contests. But then I became more involved in the debate club and the environmental club in high school, and music pretty much disappeared. Although…"

"Although what?"

"Well…" He broke the *naan* bread in two uneven pieces, and then again, and again. "My mother went to all of my gigs. Which was embarrassing, okay. When you're sixteen?" He put one of the middle-size pieces in his mouth. "I also liked having her there, I guess. That she was proud of me."

"Was she interested in music?"

"She'd studied piano pretty seriously at Juilliard. That's all I know." He chewed the bread.

"Really? Did she ever have a career in music? Was she in an orchestra?"

"Not that I know of. I can't remember even seeing a piano in the house. So don't count on me for the wedding entertainment, sorry."

Pizza. McDonald's. Entenmann's doughnuts. The White House chef. Martinis and steak with the lobbyists at The Monocle. A picnic by the Tidal Basin under the cherry blossoms—Oops, no, it would be too late in the season for the cherry blossoms. So they would move their wedding a month earlier! On the steps of the Lincoln Memorial, where Miranda used to pretend to be Martin Luther King Jr. giving his "I Have a Dream" speech when she was a little girl! They got giddier and giddier over the weeks, not only from planning the ceremony, but also from Miranda's moving into Russ's apartment, and getting her own set of keys, and buying bath towels together, and making dinner together every night, and watching *Law & Order* cuddled on the black leather couch after dinner. Their couch. Their TV. Their future. *I thought we were building a life together.*

"THIS IS EXACTLY WHAT YOUR GREAT-grandfather Jacob would have seen, on the steamship from Russia!" Russ exclaimed, pointing straight ahead as he and Miranda leaned side by side against the grillwork railing of the ferry *Miss New York*. Ellis Island loomed in the distance beyond his finger, the overpowering brick-and-limestone fortress with its green-spiked towers and huge windows trimmed in a lacy white design, like the icing on a giant's birthday cake. "Do you think he was picturing streets paved with gold and all that crap?"

"Or maybe he was just angry. After all, Sarah's family pretty much exiled him to America to keep him away from her."

"Which didn't work. Luckily for you and me."

There was no point trying to place Russ's family on any ship to Ellis Island. His father had already traced the tree of Steinmanns back to Josef Steinmann the peddler who came to America from Kissingen in Bavaria in 1841, long before the riffraff were landing at Ellis Island, and established the little shop in Philadelphia that became a classy, nationwide department store chain. As his father made sure that Russ and his brother knew.

Inside the fortress, they stood in the vast, two-story-high Registry Room as Russ swept his arm from the red-tiled floor, to the tall windows that lined the walls, to the three chandeliers hanging from the vaulted ceiling. "This would've been jam-packed with people waiting in lines, for hours, probably."

"All those old folks, standing for so long. And the little kids. How did the parents keep their kids from running around and getting lost?"

Russ pulled Miranda over to the display of passports in one glass-walled nook on the far side of the floor. "Maybe we'll find your great-grandfather's passport!" There were travelers from Italy, Russia, the Irish Free State, the French mandate in Syria and Lebanon…

They took turns reading aloud the first few columns of names on one of the ship manifests, mounted on another wall.

They grabbed a kiss in a corner of the small, wood-floored Medical Room when no one else was around.

They climbed to the third-floor balcony and surveyed the Registry Room below them.

"Can't you see Jacob there in the lines, carrying his carpetbag?" Russ asked. "And then Sarah, when she came years later?"

"In her long black skirt and shawl."

"The U.S. government didn't like it when single women were by themselves, even if they were going to be joining their fiancé. When Sarah showed up, they might have demanded that Jacob marry her on the spot."

"I suppose that's what Jacob and Sarah wanted, anyway." Miranda giggled.

That was when Russ got down on one knee and took a ring box from his pocket.

Just before the French teenagers barged past them.

NOW THE WEDDING WAS LESS THAN FOUR months away. The thousand-dollar deposit they'd already paid the caterer was nonrefundable. The six hundred-dollar deposit for the keyboardist and singer was sixty percent refundable. All the vendors had different terms, musicians and photographer and printer and caterer, and some could be delayed. The rabbi, who was a friend of Miranda's mother, wasn't charging a fee but had asked them to make a donation to his temple, which they hadn't done yet. The invitations hadn't yet been mailed. The vows had not been spoken. Everything could be canceled.

They weren't canceling anything! They just needed to talk.

Except that Russ refused.

One email from him, finally, after Miranda's email and two phone messages. After a week of solid silence: *I'm sorry, but I'm not ready to talk. Maybe soon.*

Ten words, on a screen. From the man she was supposed to marry.

He wouldn't even talk to her to explain why he wouldn't talk. He hid behind an email. It couldn't be just that he was still deeply hurt and shocked because of her arrest, not after so much time. This was pure punishment, and she didn't deserve it. Yes, she hadn't told him about Dulles—call it a lie if he wanted; fine, she'd lied—but she'd admitted it as soon as he confronted her. She'd been willing to listen to his accusations and try to explain. She'd even been willing to explain to his boss. He owed it to her to answer her questions, at the very least.

Unless he'd actually been fired. Because of her. And therefore he was too furious to talk.

Turning in his ID badge. Clearing out his desk. Packing up the photo of her at Ellis Island, along with the copy of Upton Sinclair's *The Jungle* she'd given him when he'd started the job. "To remind you of how muckraking reformers can change the world," she'd explained, as she kissed him.

If he was going through that… What could she possibly say now? *I'm sorry. I'm sorry.*

Now she was getting carried away. Before she started imagining all the worst-case scenarios, she ought to find out, as best as she could, what was really going on. Obviously, she couldn't ask Russ. He might have confided in Greg. Their friendship went back more than a decade, to when Russ was in law school and they'd both volunteered on the river-pollution lawsuit against GE. What was his phone number? His last name? He worked for a small consumer nonprofit, but which one?

Or she could give Russ more time.

Or email him again in a couple of days.

"THE ONE YOU REALLY SHOULD BE…" Brenda's throaty voice disappeared from Miranda's cell phone for a few seconds

"What?"

"…trying to talk to is Russ's boss."

"Are you nuts?"

Bright rectangles of white light flashed past the window in Miranda's Metro car. The automated announcement intoned: *The next stop is Metro Center. Transfer is available to the Orange and Blue lines on the lower level.* Metro Center, where Miranda used to meet Ronit and Tali, coming from the opposite direction on the train, and Tali ran endlessly up and down the steep escalator to F Street, and they couldn't pull her away until finally Ronit suggested *gleeda.* Ice cream.

"The big problem is making sure Russ keeps his job, isn't it?" Brenda was saying.

"Unless he's already been fired."

"But if he hasn't been, then you want to prevent that, yeah? That's the key. If Russ keeps his job, none of the rest of this bullshit will really matter. It won't matter that you were arrested at the airport, and it won't matter that you never told him, and it won't matter that he didn't include your arrest on his questionnaire, because the main reason those matter is if they cause him to lose the job."

"I don't think it's that simple. He still thinks I'm a criminal and a liar."

"Forget about that! Once the worry about saving his job is out of the way, he'll relax, and you two can kiss and make up and you can tell him all about Ronit."

Doors opening. Step back to allow customers to exit. A cluster of commuters squeezed in at the same moment that only a few shoved their way out. They grunted, coughed, jostled Miranda against the pole she was clutching, wriggled their feet around other feet. Someone smelled of bacon. Someone else had thick, oily hair. "Watch out!" a woman snapped, when Miranda's heavy shoulder bag rammed her thigh. The train doors slid shut.

"And that's why you have to talk to his boss, to save his job. If Russ won't talk to you, then you have to go to his boss and explain exactly what you'd tell Russ if you could: You were only helping a friend. It was a long time ago, so you never think about it anymore. Whatever. The point is to humanize this thing, to show Russ's boss that you're a real person—"

Brenda's voice was suddenly cut off again, maybe because of a Metro tunnel on Miranda's end.

Miranda waited a half-minute. "You're forgetting a key point." Her elbow was crunched against her ribcage as she tried to hold her phone to her ear. "I already offered to talk to his boss." Someone grabbed the pole directly in front of her chin.

"And?"

"Russ didn't exactly jump at my offer."

"But he didn't say no."

"Brenda—No! I am not going behind his back. Our relationship is in enough trouble, without me sneaking around."

All the strangers within inches of her voice were probably wondering what kind of scandal Miranda was talking about: *Unless he's already been fired. He still thinks I'm a criminal and a liar. Our relationship is in enough trouble.*

"I can't really talk, Brenda. I'm on the Metro."

"Is there someone else who could do it?"

"Drop it, Brenda."

"How about Russ's father?"

"What? I thought I was the one with the crazy plans, not you."

"That's even better than talking to Russ's boss. Go to the top: The U.S. attorney himself. You told me Russ's father knows him. They went to Harvard together."

At the next station, more people pressed past Miranda. She pulled herself right up against the pole, twisting away from someone's hard-edged briefcase. "So what if he does?"

"I'll bet they still keep in touch. Season tickets near each other at the Kennedy Center. Their wives were probably best friends at Bryn Mawr."

"No, Russ's mom was a piano prodigy at Juilliard."

"But they grew up on the Main Line together. Or the Upper West Side of Manhattan."

"I don't know if that's true. You're creating a stereotype."

"Just ask Russ's father to drop a little hint to his buddy the U.S. attorney. You know how those kinds of connections work in this town."

"And you know that Russ and his father hate each other. They've barely spoken since Russ's bar mitzvah. Not to mention that his father doesn't think much of me, either, in case you've forgotten the disastrous history seminar I took with him senior year."

Russ had refused to use his father's connections for references when he applied to law school, and he'd refused to join his father's old fraternity when he ended up at Yale, and he refused to shop at the department store chain that Josef Steinmann's son had founded a hundred and forty years ago. He'd even lied to the U.S. attorney about not being Henry Steinmann's son, which could have cost him the job before he'd started, because he wanted nothing to do with his father. The engagement dinner at Russ's parents' townhouse last October was supposed to be the great reconciliation; they didn't make it past the broccoli-almond soup. That was the point when Russ's father claimed that Enron was just one bad apple, and the government should keep its claws out of the free market.

"Bad apple?" Russ had demanded. "Twenty-four thousand innocent people lost a billion dollars of their retirement money. Thousands more lost their jobs. Not to mention the investors who were defrauded out of another tens of billions. That's a pretty fucking big apple."

"We don't need that language," his mother interrupted quietly.

"That is still only one apple, no matter how large," Professor Steinmann repeated. "One company, out of nearly three thousand listed on the New York Stock Exchange. Yes, that makes it an apple, not an orchard."

"It's only the first one to get caught! That's why we need stronger government regulation and prosecution, not less."

"Why? To depress investment and reasonable risk-taking?"

" 'Reasonable risk-taking'? With whose money?"

"That's right. Reasonable risk-taking is the engine that fuels economic growth, and if government bureaucrats who understand nothing about markets try to inject their fairy-tale theories—"

"So you'd leave the wolves to police the chicken coop?"

"Now you're claiming that all businessmen are wolves? You sound like you've taken lessons from Miranda's Communist grandfather."

Jumping up, Russ had dramatically kicked his carved mahogany chair backwards to the floor and shouted, "Miranda and I are proud of her grandfather who helped working people get decent wages, unlike my own grandfather who exploited his employees!"

Doors opening. "Brenda? It's DuPont Circle; it's my station. I have to get off. I'll think about what you said."

No she wouldn't. There was nothing to think about. It wasn't like Brenda to have such a crazy idea—at least, not at nine in the morning without drinking a few beers.

Besides, Russ might be ready to come out of his sulk in another day or two. The next bill for the wedding wasn't due for almost three more weeks. Miranda could sleep a while longer on Ted's hard mattress.

Then she was in the middle of the rushing crowd on the red-tiled platform, trying to edge around slowpokes and dodging briefcases toward the Q Street exit.

CHAPTER TEN

"YOU'VE BEEN WONDERFUL, MOM. LETTING ME camp here for so long." Miranda pulled out the chair on the far side of the kitchen table from her mother, who was typing at her laptop. "Actually, I might need to stay, um, longer than I thought."

There was nothing on the table to fiddle with. A short stack of printed papers at her mother's left side, two or three books at her right. The Lucite napkin holder, empty of course. The pottery bowl Lily had made in sixth grade, with a pile of M&Ms inside. A porcelain bowl crusted with a rim of brown.

"You don't mind?" Miranda added. "I'm not in your way?"

"Stay as long as you need to, sweetie. This is your home." Her mother took a scoop of M&Ms.

Since when did Judith Isaacs Higgins eat candy?

The bags under her eyes were bigger now, and there was a lot more grey in the underside of her hair where it was held back by a faded macramé headband. Deeper lines tugged downward at the corners of her mouth.

Miranda reached into the M&Ms bowl, too. "How are you doing? Have you heard from Bill at all?"

"A note that he'd paid the mortgage. He calls Lily every few days. I don't want to hear more than that from him, believe me."

Just as the microwave sent out a long beep, the kitchen door swung powerfully open, and Lily in green sweatpants, a pink-flowered pajama top, and multicolored socks ran straight toward the beeping. The toes on the socks were separated, like the fingers on a pair of gloves.

"Hey Miranda." Lily dropped into the empty seat between her mother and sister, carrying a greasy paper towel with two slices of pizza. "Are you and Russ still going to the big protest about the war in Iraq?"

"We were … I don't know if Russ can do it." Miranda forced a laugh. "You know, it could jeopardize his job with the U.S. Attorney's office if he's protesting government policy."

"That's bullshit, Miranda. Free speech."

"It's a joke, Lily."

"So can me and my friends come with you? We've been talking about it a lot at school."

"Really?" Miranda mumbled.

"Mom," Lily went on, while she bit into one of the slices, "do you think it could be as big as some of the Vietnam protests you and Miranda's dad organized? What did you guys do to protect yourself from tear gas?"

"Oh shit. We soaked bandanas in vinegar and water, I think. Some people wore swimming goggles. And you should always have extra water—But I'm not sure any of that worked," their mother added quickly. "The stuff really stings. You don't want to be near it, I promise."

"And they said we shouldn't bring any ID. That way, they can't arrest us."

"What?" their mother demanded.

"Who said?" Miranda asked at the same time.

"Like, you know. I read it on a website."

"I don't think it's true, about IDs."

"So what works for tear gas?" Lily repeated.

"You run. And you stay out of trouble and don't get arrested." The laptop monitor had reverted to its screensaver, the out-of-focus Rosh Hashanah photo Bill had taken maybe nine years ago, with Miranda, Ted, and Lily on the plaid couch, all wearing different shades of blue. Lily was in the middle, giggling as she turned toward Miranda. Ted was sticking his tongue out. Miranda had stretched one arm along the top of the couch, behind Lily's back, and made the old Sixties peace sign with the other hand.

"I might be," Lily persisted. "Miranda's dad got arrested a lot of times, and Grandpa Seymour bailed him out, you said."

"Well, yes. And Grandma Bessie was not happy."

"But Miranda's dad was trying to stop the war in Vietnam! Grandma didn't support the war, did she?"

"No. It was more like…" Their mother's fingers fluttered above her keyboard. The wind had gotten stronger outside, dancing with the topmost branches of the maple tree so that they almost scratched the kitchen window. "When Jerry—Miranda's dad—came to our apartment for dinner, after he got out of jail one time," she added, suddenly cheerful, "do you know what he and Grandpa Seymour talked about?"

"What?" the two sisters asked together.

Their mother grinned. "The Mets."

"My father was a baseball fan?"

"The Mets were in the World Series, and I think everyone expected them to lose but they won because of some incredible catch. Or something. And Grandpa and Jerry were laughing and waving their fists in the air. I was pretty amazed, like you are now. There's Jerry, fresh out of the Tombs, sitting at our kitchen table with Grandpa and the challah and the Shabbos candles, laughing about the World Series."

"Dumb," Lily muttered.

"It was because the Mets are always the underdogs compared to the Yankees."

"My union-organizer grandfather and Sixties-radical father were baseball fans. Why didn't you ever tell me, Mom?" Miranda broke off an edge of Lily's pizza.

"You never heard about any of that?" Lily asked Miranda. "All those years when you and Mom lived in New York City with Grandma and Grandpa? They didn't talk about baseball?"

"I don't remember Grandpa ever watching baseball or reading the sports pages or anything like that. But we moved out of their apartment when I was six, to come here to Washington, so maybe I was too little to notice. I mainly remember Grandma doing crossword puzzles, and Grandpa taking me for walks to get ice cream. And reciting Martin Luther King's 'I Have a Dream' speech as we walked."

"Shit, yes," their mother agreed. "When I was a little girl, almost every Sunday Grandpa would do the same thing with me. He'd buy me ice cream, and then we'd go on excursions while he lectured me about history and politics and capitalism. We went to NYU to see the building that used to be the Triangle factory; have you heard of it? In the early Nineteen-Hundreds there was a horrible fire there that killed over a hundred people, because the workers were locked inside. And we went a lot to Inwood, which was Grandpa's favorite park because of the ancient Indian caves and the old glaciers—though he'd always complain that Robert Moses ruined the park when he cut through it to build the West Side Highway."

"And the civil rights marches you went to with him? The candlelight vigil?"

"Sure. After the church bombing in Birmingham, when the four little girls were killed."

"Did Grandma ever go to any of those marches?"

"No… She wasn't really interested in what she called politics."

"She thought civil rights was politics? That seems like an awfully narrow definition. What did she think of Grandpa's union work?"

"Don't get me wrong: I don't mean to make your grandmother into a right-wing harridan. I don't think she was against unions, but she was glad when Grandpa left the union and got his Civil Service job with the Parks Department, which she figured would be less likely to get him in trouble."

"I wish I'd met them both. Grandpa and Miranda's dad," Lily said, crumpling up her pizza wrappings.

"You know who would've hit it off with Grandpa?" their mother added. "Russ."

It was probably true: If Grandpa Seymour were still alive, he and Russ would be at the kitchen table eating poppy-seed bagels with whitefish salad and tomatoes, Grandpa with his thick white mustache and thick eyeglasses and plaid shirt buttoned up to his Adam's apple, and Russ with his broad shoulders and old tan sweater and the freckles on his long nose. Grandpa might challenge Russ on some points: Did the Steinmann department store employees belong to the Retail Clerks union? Did Steinmann buy from unionized manufacturers? Russ wouldn't defend his family's department stores, but he'd want to argue that unions can't solve everything; he'd stretch further and further across the table toward Grandpa and get more and more excited, pointing to the kind of enforcement work he hoped to do at the U.S. Attorney's office, prosecuting corporate bribery and cheating and corruption and the government officials that enabled it, as another way of making businesses honest. And Grandpa would shake his head. He wouldn't be angry, because he would actually like Russ. He'd just shake his head and say that those sorts of investigations were very nice but they don't get to the basic problem. Even unions can't solve the basic problem, because they can never have enough power. The real answer, Grandpa would insist, is to throw out the capitalist system altogether, because when workers are exploited, so are consumers, and the only fair system is where everyone has an equal share. That would definitely be a step too far for Russ, although he would listen to Grandpa's arguments.

And then they'd go out for ice cream. Grandpa would get one scoop of chocolate; Russ would get two scoops of flavors he'd never tasted before.

What if Russ could have met Jerry Isaacs? They would also sit around the table, while Russ soaked up Jerry's stories, his mouth slightly agape, maybe breathing a little fast, demanding more and more details. Was Jerry nervous when he spoke in front of large crowds? How did he and the other leaders determine that it was the right moment to call for a demonstration? Did he think the kind of mass movement that had forced the U.S. government to leave Vietnam could ever again be summoned for another cause—for instance, preventing war in Iraq? Or was there something unique about the Sixties? However, Russ the law-abiding, never-jaywalking attorney would no doubt be less enthusiastic about the things Jerry had done that had gotten him arrested. Three times. Taking over the president's office at Columbia. Fighting with police at the Democratic National Convention in Chicago. Organizing a huge antiwar rally in New York that got out of control. Taking over a university office was a bit beyond King and Gandhi, Russ might have suggested—patiently, not angrily.

"Was Grandpa ever arrested during his union's strikes?" Lily was asking, holding a large bottle of lemon-lime seltzer by the neck, the refrigerator door still open.

"Lily, why do you keep talking about being arrested?"

"Because that's why you guys won! Because you were willing to, like, risk your lives. Get arrested. Get tear-gassed. You got the U.S. out of Vietnam because of the public pressure and the TV news stories from all your marches and arrests."

Their mother stood up and slowly shut the refrigerator door behind Lily. "Sweetie, don't romanticize what Miranda's dad and I were doing, or the things that happened back then."

"I'm not romanticizing. I just want to stop this war, like you did with Vietnam. It's the same thing you protested, millions of people dying because a president starts a war all the way across the planet for no reason." Carrying the seltzer bottle, Lily moved toward the kitchen exit. "So Miranda, can me and my friends come with you to the Iraq march? I told them we'd all meet at the Metro—Hey." She halted. "Why are you still here, anyway? Isn't your bathroom fixed yet?"

They both looked at Miranda, then.

In fact, I meant to tell you, the bathroom's all finished and we're moving back tomorrow.

Maybe she could move back. If she and Russ could avoid each other for the indefinite future in a one-bedroom apartment. Or she could take a cheap hotel room in Virginia. If she could afford it; if Mort didn't fire her for pushing her ideas on drug prices and her interviews with the old folks on Scott at the Senate committee. If she didn't have to pay wedding bills.

"Yeah. Uh. Russ found another problem in our apartment. With the, um, kitchen sink. So I have to stay here for a while longer."

"But how can Russ live there, with all those plumbing problems? Is the bathroom usable at all?" her mother asked, frowning.

"Well, actually, he moved in with his parents. Temporarily."

Abruptly, her mother laughed; maybe it was her first big, real laugh since Bill had left. "Poor Russ. Now I see why you didn't go with him. Breakfast with the Steinmanns. A toasted bagel and no chitchat." The laugh became a trail of giggles. "But sweetie, he can stay here, if you want. I'm sure you miss him."

"No. It's fine. I mean, it's only for a few days. Think of it as if he were away on a business trip."

"Still, it must be hard on you."

"I'm okay. Besides, can you picture Russ in Ted's skinny bed?"

"Hah. At least you should invite him here for dinner. I'm sorry I didn't suggest it before now."

"You should sue the landlord." Chugging straight from the seltzer bottle, Lily left the kitchen.

Their mother picked up the crumpled paper towel and pizza crust that Lily had abandoned on the table, mushed them into a ball, tossed the mess toward the garbage pail under the sink, missed, retrieved the mushed paper and pizza from the black-tiled floor, and threw it in properly. "I don't know, Miranda. Lily will do something wild if she goes to that march about Iraq. But if I forbid her to go, she'll lie to me and go anyway. To her mind, anyone who doesn't go is endorsing Bush and war."

"It's hard to argue with her logic. You were leading protests when you were only a little older than she is, and those were a lot more dangerous than this one will be."

"No. They weren't really."

"It sure sounds like they were. You just told us about the tear gas. My father was arrested three times."

"But that wasn't—What if you said to Lily that you and Russ aren't going to the march, that you think it's a waste of time or, I don't know, some reason? That might give her pause. She really admires you."

"I don't know about that. She'd probably just think I'm a wimp."

Opening a cabinet door, Miranda's mother took out two cans, then put one back. "Did I tell you she got sent to the vice-principal's office last week for mouthing off to her history teacher?"

"Really? What did she say to the teacher?"

"It was about the last presidential election and why it's inaccurate to say Bush was 'elected.' But—"

"Lily's right."

"That's not the point."

"And you're probably the one she learned it from."

"Never mind that. The point is that we can't count on her to be responsible at some kind of mass event where there will be police and maybe worse. Do you truly think she'd listen if a cop told her to stay off a fence, for instance?" Miranda's mother returned the first can to the cabinet and retrieved the second.

"True."

"Of course, she could easily forget all about the march by next weekend. But if she goes, do you think you and Russ could keep an eye on her?"

Miranda covered her nose and mouth with her hands, her breath whistling out through her fingers.

"If you went with Lily, I'd feel a lot more reassured," her mother continued. "Don't worry, I don't expect you to babysit her. Just… be nearby. Keep watch. They're predicting a huge crowd."

"I don't know if Russ actually wants to go…" Miranda selected three M&Ms for herself: orange, green, and yellow. "Don't get me addicted to these things, please."

CHAPTER ELEVEN

THE SHUTTERS ON THE RED BRICK ROW house spread straight out from each of the eight windows like perfect rectangular wings, their white paint gleaming. At the edge of the sidewalk, three demurely trimmed shrubs bordered the cozy front yard's waist-high iron fence.

According to the class schedule posted on the Georgetown University website, Professor Steinmann would be safely out of the way, teaching, for another three hours (Europe between the World Wars; Three Empires and Their Legacies). Abigail Steinmann, however, should be home, if her routine hadn't changed since the fall: The Great Composers class she audited at George Washington University was on Tuesdays, the library board met on Wednesday nights, and she volunteered at the library on Thursdays. At any rate, two o'clock on a Monday afternoon was a reasonable time to take a late lunch break, put on the nice black blazer that even Brenda approved of, and plan on finding Abigail alone in the house. As soon as Miranda pressed the button to the right of the polished wooden door, three bells chimed inside.

The last chime tailed off. A moment later, the heavy door swung inward.

Poised at the marble stoop, one veined hand resting on the edge of the door, Abigail was wearing a soft-looking white sweater with matching wool slacks and a string of pearls that looped just below the neckline in a perfect C. Her seal-sleek black hair was fastened in its usual bun at the nape of her neck, exposing earrings that were large gold ovals. Her lipstick was a subtle shade of coral.

"Miranda." Abigail's tone was marginally surprised, as though Miranda were a UPS package that had arrived a day early.

"I apologize for not calling first. May I come in?"

"Of course." With one step sideways, Abigail held the door open wider, then pecked Miranda on each cheek.

Through the entryway, past the yellow tulips in the Waterford crystal vase, underneath the small brass chandelier, and into the parlor, with its larger chandelier and floor-length white curtains and walls flawlessly painted in muted slate above the molding, beige below. Abigail waved Miranda to a gold-brocade armchair and seated herself on the paired sofa perpendicular to it, one leg draped over the other knee. An enormous off-white conch shell rested on the far end of the glass-topped coffee table in front of Abigail, while the little table on Miranda's left side held a lumpy, pink-and-grey clay figure that looked vaguely like a mushroom and—so Russ had told her—had been made by his five-year-old nephew. If Miranda and Russ ever talked to each other again and got married and had kids, would Abigail display their little artwork, too?

Abigail settled against the back of the sofa and rested her hands in her lap before turning toward Miranda. "How are the wedding plans coming along?"

Wedding plans. Miranda crossed her own left leg over her right, mirroring Abigail. "Yes. We're getting to the final details. Do you have any suggestions for hors d'oeuvres?"

With a brief smile, Abigail lifted her hands, clasped together, maybe two inches off her lap, then dropped them. "It should be whatever Russell and you prefer, shouldn't it?"

"Sure. Yes. But we want our guests to enjoy themselves."

"Of course. And the biggest pleasure for everyone will be seeing Russell and you standing under the *chuppah.*"

"Of course. So, I was thinking of avocado cups with pomegranate salsa, and miniature pizza bianca slices, for starters." Miranda also clasped her hands in her lap.

"That sounds delicious."

"I apologize that we probably won't be using a kosher caterer, but I promise it will be kosher-style. No shellfish. Nothing *treyf.*"

Abigail merely flickered another half-smile.

"We've also been discussing the music."

"That will be very nice."

"I'd love to hear your opinion."

"You must have your favorite pieces."

"But you know much more than I do about music, from your studies—" Abigail's shoulders twitched slightly.

Stupid! Whether or not it was supposed to be a secret, Abigail's abandoned musical career was not discussed in the Steinmann household. There had never been a piano in sight, as Russ had told Miranda, nor any photos of Abigail at a keyboard. This was not the way Miranda was supposed to be starting this delicate conversation.

Thank goodness for Abigail's training from hosting endless dinners and cocktail parties; she knew how to glide out of awkward moments. "I think choosing music for one's wedding is such a personal decision, I certainly wouldn't want to give you any advice," she said calmly. "Would you like some tea?"

"Yes, tea. Thank you."

"Jasmine green." Abigail unhooked her legs, pressed her palms onto the sofa cushion, and rose straight up. "Without sugar, milk, or honey."

Of course it was nuts, trying to carry out Brenda's convoluted plan for Russ's father to lobby his boss. There were too many risky moving parts. It probably wouldn't succeed. Russ would be furious if he knew Miranda was asking his parents for help, on top of already being furious about her arrest. Not only all that, but this visit was going to last far too long to be a lunch break, and what if Mort actually noticed? Miranda should have outright taken the afternoon off from work.

Still, it might not be so nuts if Miranda spoke with Abigail instead of Russ's father, the way Brenda had originally urged. Miranda had never taken a history class from Abigail at Georgetown; Miranda had never had to plead with Abigail to raise her grade from a D to a C. The two of them had even sat together and talked a few times—about Miranda's job, for instance. Abigail had posed questions about health insurance and prescription drug prices as though she was genuinely interested. And maybe Russ didn't hate his mother as much as his father? After all, Abigail had gone to all of Russ's band's performances when he was a teenager. Now, with a wedding coming up so soon, wasn't it perfectly normal for a young woman to pay a visit to her future mother-in-law? Miranda was merely going to ask Abigail to ask her husband to drop a word to an old friend. A hint: *My son tells me how thrilled he is to be working in your office. I hear that my son is working for you in a provisional position; or is it permanent yet?* A little tap, to help give Russ every possible edge in the cutthroat business of job-hunting in Washington DC. A carefully prepared script. The kind of thing that happened every day in every city. The Steinmanns ought to want to assist their own son, no matter if they were barely on speaking terms with him and they thought his fiancée was a mediocre student who came from a family of Communist agitators. It was the longest of shots but Brenda was right about one thing: Saving Russ's job could make all the difference. And what was the worst that could happen? A chillier "How are you?" from Abigail next time?

When Abigail reappeared in the parlor, she was carrying a silver tray with one teacup nestled in a saucer; it was the everyday china, the design with a thin silver stripe around the edge. Resting the tray on the glass-topped table, Abigail handed the cup and saucer to Miranda. The steam from the cup rose politely away from Miranda's face.

"And what brings you here this afternoon?"

Miranda took a sip before replacing the cup and saucer on the tray. "It's about Russ's job, you know, with the U.S. Attorney's office in the District." There wasn't any obvious reaction on Abigail's face. "I know you and Russ's father and I, we all share the same desire for Russ to finally be permanently settled there. It's so perfect for him, chasing after corrupt government officials and corporate crooks and those sorts of, uh... misdeeds."

"It certainly seems so."

"In fact, isn't Russ's father a friend of the U.S. attorney? Didn't they go to Harvard together?"

"Jack Mason? Yes." Abigail frowned.

"So—oh, I'm probably being presumptuous—but do you know if Russ's father has talked to Jack Mason about Russ?"

Abigail clutched her knee as she sat up straighter. "Miranda."

It was crucial for Miranda to keep her focus directly on Abigail. No guilty glances down at her lap. No fiddling with her hair. Force Abigail to fill in the silence now, and whatever she said would be the clue for what Miranda ought to say next.

"Miranda," Abigail repeated. "You're suggesting that his father use a personal friendship to influence Russell's career?"

"Oh, as I said, I realize it's a little presumptuous of me." A sheepish yet charming little grin would be exactly the right touch. "But you can't blame a woman for trying to help her fiancé, can you? Especially when it's my fault."

What? Did she actually say that last sentence?

From somewhere beyond the main doorway and simultaneously from upstairs, at least three telephones sounded, but Abigail didn't move to answer them. After four rings, they stopped. That was a bad sign, that Abigail would let a phone call go to voice mail so that she could stay in the parlor and grill Miranda: *What did you mean, it's your fault?*

"To be candid, Miranda, I do think it would be highly inappropriate for Russell's father to get involved. In any case, I think Russell and you have both said that he's been doing well in the provisional position, and you're confident he'll be appointed permanently." There was something about Abigail's words that was even more precise than usual.

"Uh, yes. Sure."

"Did Russell suggest this?"

"No. No, not at—"

"I cannot believe he is doing this again."

With her fingers pressed against the glass-topped table, Abigail abruptly pushed the silver tray an inch away from her. The teacup and saucer rattled.

Again?

Abigail panted sharply as her shoulders rose and fell. "We told him the last time, if he'd decided to drop out of Yale and devote himself to his—his other interests… well that was his responsibility, and just what did he expect. And now he's sent you as his emissary for this new demand."

"NO!"

"I know that he paints his father and me as the villains, thank you, but this is truly going too far. After everything." Abigail was actually quivering, her legs in their white wool slacks clamped tightly next to each other, feet together.

"What happened," Miranda whispered, "at Yale?"

"I'm sorry, Miranda, but I'll have to ask you to discontinue this topic."

"But what happened?"

Russ had asked his father for a favor? For his career? As recently as law school? Russ, who wouldn't even shop at a Steinmann department store?

Abigail sprang up from the couch. "Russell should have talked to us himself, instead of sending you, if he truly was so—"

"Russ didn't send me!"

"Send you where?"

There was a low mahogany console across from the sofa, with three Chagall lithographs from his Jerusalem window series mounted on the wall above it. There was a second brocade chair at the other side of the little table that held the lumpy clay sculpture. And in the doorway to the front hall, there was Professor Steinmann, tall and wide-shouldered like Russ, with his trim grey goatee, wearing a beige sweater vest, a white formal shirt, and a solid brown tie, dressed as though he was in front of a classroom, and carrying a wineglass.

"You're not in class," Miranda managed.

"No."

Europe between the World Wars? Three Empires and Their Legacies? "The schedule. On the website. Said."

"Well, that's incorrect. My classes have all been canceled." He moved to the sofa and sat down near Abigail, who also sat.

No. No. This wasn't—She wasn't in his senior history seminar anymore! She wasn't at his annual student dinner party. She was not going to make a fool of herself. He couldn't give her a D on her report card ever again, and he was not going to argue her into corners, as he'd done at that party when she refused every bottle of wine he offered:

"My goodness, Miranda. Nothing from my wine cellar appeals to you?"

"No, no. I'm sure they're all great."

"Please tell me what vineyards you usually prefer."

"No, it's just—I just try to avoid wine—alcohol—all kinds of alcohol, you know? Because I get stupid when I drink."

"Ah, that's a new excuse for writing a C paper. I'll have to keep that in mind."

"No, that's not what I—"

That wasn't going to happen now. She was a grown woman—an experienced health care analyst whose research on drug prices might influence new legislation in the Senate.

"Russell," Abigail began, "has sent Miranda to ask—"

"No he didn't!"

"Miranda!" Professor Steinmann snapped. "Please let Abigail finish speaking."

"But it's not the way it looks!"

"Abigail, what was Russell sending Miranda to ask just now?"

"RUSS DIDN'T SEND ME!"

"DON'T SHOUT IN THIS HOUSE!"

"He didn't send me here!"

"In other words, he doesn't know you came?" his father asked quietly.

No, that wasn't—Oh no. Oh no. But Russ's parents would never tell Russ. They didn't even talk to him.

"You came to ask us for something without informing him," his father added.

She shook her head.

"It's one or the other. Either he knew that you were planning to come and didn't object, or you came here secretly."

How did he keep doing it to her? Turning her into a nervous college student. Twisting her words.

"What was Miranda asking, Abigail?"

"She was asking if you would talk to Jack Mason, to put in a good word about Russell."

It didn't sound too bad, the way Abigail phrased it.

"So," Professor Steinmann said, "this is another secret you're keeping from Russell."

What?

"Although not as serious a secret as being arrested for kidnapping."

Her hands couldn't hold onto the armrests. Her throat couldn't swallow.

"I do find it difficult to believe that you could think you would be able to hide such a major aspect of your background." Professor Steinmann stared at her, with the same pale blue eyes as Russ, as though they were back in his seminar and he was waiting for her to stop fumbling with the answer to an obvious question.

Russ would never have told his father about her arrest record.

"How–?"

"Jack Mason," his father said, "was troubled that my son would have omitted this fact from his security questionnaire. He wanted my opinion."

Professor Steinmann's opinion. Of her? Oh no. "They're hiring Russ, not me. It doesn't matter if you think I really deserved that D in your seminar, and it doesn't matter if I was ever arrested for anything, all that matters is that Russ is brilliant and he cares and he'll work his tail off, and that's what you should've told them, even if Russ ends up on the other side of the courtroom from your friends and he wins—Which I guess you don't want, is that it? Is that why you won't help?" She needed breath. She needed to shut up.

Why had she ever listened to Brenda?

Abigail was still sitting next to her husband but arched forward, as though she was ready to escape to the kitchen to bring more tea. Her eyes seemed to be looking sometimes at Miranda, sometimes at her husband, sometimes at the Chagall lithographs.

"What did Russ ask you to do at Yale?" Miranda dug her fingers into her thighs.

Professor Steinmann's arm, lifting his wineglass to his mouth, shook for an instant. He quickly brought the glass down to the table, without drinking. "I told Jack Mason," he said, his voice still quiet, "that the reason Russell didn't include your arrest is probably that you'd hoped you could put it behind you, because it was so many years ago."

Oh. That was actually pretty close to the truth.

"Nevertheless, Russell was legally obligated to include the information on his questionnaire. Jack can't brush that aside, not on a security matter. Not these days. Whatever I might say."

IT WAS A LONG WALK, PAST ONE PERFECT RED-BRICK row house after another, past adorable restaurants and boutiques tucked under the stoops of other row houses, from the Steinmanns' home, over the parkway, to the closest Metro stop. More than enough time to listen over and over to Russ's message on her cell phone. His voice was warm, as though they'd never fought.

I've been an asshole, and I'm sorry. I miss you. Would you like to go out on a date with me tomorrow night?

CHAPTER TWELVE

A FEW FLECKS OF CORN CHIPS WERE SPRINKLED just below the neckline of Russ's striped sweater. He picked up another chip, cracking it in two pieces. "Which movies do you think'll be nominated for Best Picture?" he asked.

Far behind him, the plate-glass front door of the bar opened and shut several times in a row, shooting in blasts of cold air.

He had a short growth of blond stubble on his round chin, as if Miranda had taken all of their razors with her to her mother's house so now he couldn't shave. The small pedestal table that held his whiskey-and-water, Miranda's Merlot, the cup of taco sauce, and the bowl of corn chips was too low for their bulky canvas chairs, and Russ's spread-apart knees repeatedly knocked against it. A couple of times his knees almost touched Miranda's—or maybe they did brush, just a breath's worth, two thick bones, barely felt through the light wool of his trousers and her long skirt.

His lips would probably taste of corn and whiskey and spicy taco sauce, if they kissed.

"I suppose all the Tolkien fanatics have been lobbying for *Lord of the Rings*."

"But you're rooting for *Gangs of New York*, because it's about an anti-draft riot?" Russ grinned.

"Because it's Leonardo DiCaprio." She returned a smile, smaller than his grin.

It was impossible. It was too hard. How could they flirt and make small talk about the Academy Awards and pretend that there were no elephants in the middle of this bar?

"Russ," she began.

"I know I—"

"I have to ask—"

"I need to explain—"

What did you ask your father to do at Yale?

"—the shit that's going on at my office," Russ finished, as he gripped his whiskey glass.

The noise level in the dark room was growing louder and slightly chaotic, voice tones rising into jokes or arguments, chair legs scraping, the cash register beeping, an occasional glass clinking, the mounted TV blaring laughter. The walls were made of some kind of ribbed metal, and the customers at their black pedestal tables formed a circle facing the center island where the bartenders mixed their drinks, like a theater in the round.

"Lou listened to my explanation of what you told me about your arrest, and he claimed he believed me," Russ went on, his words emerging between deep breaths. "But it's obvious he doesn't. And it's also obvious that he remembers my first lie, about my father not being my father. You can see the suspicion whenever he passes my door, like a shadow walking next to him. Whenever I send him a memo, he sends it back full of trivial questions. Questions you'd ask a first-year law student. 'Did you check the case history…?' That kind of crap. Not that he talks to me about the security investigation. Hell, he doesn't talk to me at all. He doesn't stick his head in my doorway anymore to bullshit about the Bulldogs' newest game—Okay, that may sound juvenile—"

"No, it doesn't. It's an important kind of bonding."

"And my security clearance still hasn't come through."

His blue eyes were staring right at her, but they didn't look angry. His eyebrows were only a bit furrowed. There were deep creases alongside his long nose, and his chapped lips were slightly parted. It was a face of pain, not anger.

"I can't get hired without it," he added.

"What else can they want from you?"

"Who knows? The government can't be careful enough when it comes to catching terrorists, right?"

"Have they given you any hint as to when you'll find out?"

"Of course not. This is the FBI. Meanwhile, I end up taking five times as long as I should on every memo, every brief, even my emails, second-guessing myself on every word. Should I say 'advisable' or 'recommended' in the first sentence? Is 'advisable' too wishy-washy? Hell, is Lou going to fire me over an adverb?" He circled a chip around in the bowl of taco sauce. "Or is 'advisable' an adjective?"

"An adverb. I think."

"I can't even decide how to say hello in the morning. That's not who I am, Miranda. You know that."

No, that wasn't Russ. This FBI investigation was creating a slew of Russes she'd never seen before, and none of them was as good as the big, loving, energetic, brilliant original. There'd been the angry prosecutor who'd confronted her about her arrest two weeks ago. The silent, sulking Russ who didn't return her phone calls. Now this anxious, self-doubting Russ. Not to mention the Russ from law school who had maybe asked his father for a favor.

"I told myself," Russ was saying, "that I'd give it another week, and then I'd ask Lou what's going on. But I know that would be one of the dumbest things I could possibly do. Never paint yourself into a corner."

"How about the other people in your office? Are they…. ?" *Friendly? Keeping their distance?* What was the gentlest way to phrase the question?

Barely inches away from Miranda's hand, Russ had started tapping the tabletop, almost as if he was playing a trill on his mother's old piano: index middle ring pinkie ring middle index. There was a new red line, maybe from a paper cut, along the side of his left index finger. "I can't tell. They seem mostly normal. But when I was going into the building the other morning, I saw Dennis, who I might have mentioned to you; we worked on a couple of cases together…." Index middle ring pinkie. "He asked me—He obviously felt uncomfortable asking; 'Is Lou pissed about something?' "

"Maybe Lou's pissed about something else. Maybe his kid got in trouble at school."

"He gave my V.A. case to another attorney."

It was as if Russ's face had melted, with the corners of his eyes, his lips, and his cheeks all suddenly sagging downward. Even his fingers stopped, flat and still on the table.

"The V.A. bribery?" Of course it was the bribery; that was a stupid question. His biggest case ever.

Russ exhaled. "Yeah."

Was there anything she could say? *Maybe they'll give you another big case, after this is all over.* That would be just as stupid. *I'm sorry.*

"I don't want to sound like I'm whining. And I know all this is no excuse for ignoring your phone calls and emails." Russ picked up a corn chip and started to push it around inside the bowl of sauce. "Do you want to tell me," he asked quietly, "the whole story about your arrest, from your point of view?"

While Miranda talked, Russ sat absolutely still except to place the bare corn chip, uneaten, on his plate.

"We'd been friends for almost seven years by then, Russ. What's a friendship built on, after all that time? I'm not saying blind loyalty; of course if your friend is planning to go to a mall with a shotgun, you don't hand her the bullets. You do everything you can to stop her. On the other hand, if she tells you a secret, you don't share it around. So if she's going through a horrible, unbearable situation, and she's tried all the usual steps—moving out, counseling, whatever the situation is—and you know that she and her daughter cannot stay where they are. And she asks for your help. Yes, seven years counts for something. Ronit asked for my help because she knew she could trust me."

Russ picked up the chip from his plate and dipped it into the sauce bowl again.

She could add: *I would do the same for you. That's what it means to be married.*

"I know I overreacted," Russ said, looking into the bowl.

He was admitting—? He wasn't upset about the kidnapping anymore?

"I think I called you a felon, didn't I?" The edges of his mouth looked like they were ready to turn upward into an embarrassed grin. "I'm sorry."

If Miranda reached out, she could brush the corn-chip crumbs off his sweater, and the sweater would feel soft and fuzzy.

Then Russ let out another long breath. "I still don't understand how the two of you could have thought that what you were doing was in any way legal—But never mind. That was something dumb you did a long time ago, as you say. You were helping a friend. You didn't think about the implications."

"Okay."

"The kidnapping isn't really the issue."

"So what is the issue?"

He chewed the corn chip until it must have been nearly liquid.

"Is it your job?"

"You talked about trust," Russ continued. "Your friend trusted that you would help her."

"Yes."

"You're right. That's a key part of a friendship. But how about the trust between people who are getting married?"

There was trust in so many little things. Co-signing for their joint bank account. Giving her the keys to what had been his apartment. Confiding: *I can't even decide how to say hello in the morning.*

"That I should be able to trust that you won't lie to me," he added quietly.

Once. One lie.

"Why didn't you tell me, when I warned you about the FBI investigation? Why did you lie to me?"

"We've been through this, Russ."

"But why?"

"I told you. I didn't think it was a big deal."

"You were lying to me while I was being investigated by the FBI. How can that not be a big deal?"

"I mean that the kidnapping wasn't a big deal—which you yourself are admitting now."

"Yes, the kidnapping isn't a big deal, but the lying is the issue. That's what I can't get past."

"How many times do I have to repeat myself? I. Didn't. Think. The. Kidnapping. Was. A. Big. Deal. So I didn't really think it was a big lie, either."

"How can I trust that you won't lie to me again?"

"Because of one lie?"

"This is a lifetime commitment, Miranda. Sharing a home. Making plans for years and years out. Relying on each other. Total trust."

It was pointless. It would always be Miranda the kidnapper. Miranda the liar, no matter how much she explained or apologized. One lie and a million truths in their two years together, yet it was the one lie that Russ would remember, after he forgot all the truths and all the good times, all the shared hikes and chicken *tikka masala* and even the visit to Ellis Island. He would forget why he wanted to marry her before he forgot the lie. *Why didn't you tell me you were arrested for kidnapping? Why did you lie to me?* Just like his father, he would always see her as the lousy student who really deserved a D, long after she'd graduated.

Where was the loving, understanding, warm-hearted man she'd known for two years? The Russ she was supposed to marry would wrap his arms around her, enfolding her like a thick bearskin rug, and say, "What the fuck have you done but I love you anyway."

"I want our life back," Russ said. "I want to be able to have that trust with you again."

"Well, how do you think it makes me feel, to have you doubting me every minute?"

Just like you feel every day at work, Russ. Wouldn't he see the resemblance?

Instead, he apologized a second time. "I'm sorry if I'm saying this all wrong. I don't mean to attack you. Can you understand that right now it feels like everything is being pulled out from under me—my job, you? I don't have any anchors left."

"Yes, I get it. I really do. But I'm not pulling any—" All of a sudden, she was sliding down her canvas seat. She grabbed the edge of the steel table.

"Are you okay?" Russ reached out his hand toward her. Then stopped.

"A little woozy from the wine, I think. That's all."

Russ moved his outstretched hand to the bowl of chips. "You want a chip? To help sober up." He offered a few in his palm. "We're out of taco sauce, sorry. Do you want me to call the waitress to ask for more? You should review this place for District Foodie."

There was no way to pick up one of the chips without grazing his palm's warm, smooth skin.

He popped the remaining chips in his mouth, brushing the crumbs onto the floor. Just as much of a slob here as he was at home.

Then he leaned across the table's short diameter and planted a peck on her cheek.

What was that for? What about trust?

"So," he said, his words coming out in jerks, "do you want to go out on another date sometime?"

Of course, that was the reason he'd suggested this date, to see if they could rebuild trust, sip by sip. Kiss by kiss. It would be nice, to snuggle into his big arms again. To run with him alongside the Lincoln Memorial; to visit Gettysburg and Appomattox Courthouse together ... There was a moist spot on her cheek in the shape of his lips.

And then to have to prove herself at each date? How? What were the course requirements she had to fulfill?

The answer to his question had to be yes. But.

CHAPTER THIRTEEN

THE TALL BLONDE WOMAN WHO ENTERED the noisy coffee bar near Miranda's office couldn't be Ronit. For one thing, her hair was cut in a stylish shag, instead of bouncing against her shoulder blades like Ronit's long pony tail. And the color was wrong—it was sunshine streaked with moonlight—where Ronit's hair had always been a single shade of dark blonde. Ronit wore tailored slacks and orange, pink and yellow blouses when she dressed up, the kind she tried to get Miranda to wear, too; not a dark suit with a pencil skirt and a floor-length, hooded black coat, as this imposter did. Besides, Ronit would have waited for a second or two by the door, surveying the too-bright room jammed with round wooden tables, deep purple armchairs, and photos of old Washington DC on the red walls. This woman plunged straight into the crowd.

However, it was the correct address and the correct time, as specified in the terse email that Ronit had sent two days earlier.

The woman who wasn't Ronit strode in the general direction of Miranda's small table in a style that was far more businesslike than Ronit's. While the real Ronit also moved briskly, there was a bit of a swaying to it, a Marilyn Monroe wiggle—not on purpose, she'd always insisted. "I have hips," she would protest. "What should I do with them? Tie them up with ropes?"

The woman halted in front of Miranda.

"*Shalom*, Miranda."

Her voice was almost Ronit's. Medium-pitch, the "I" in Miranda pronounced with a long "ee" sound, the "R" caught at the back of her throat. But the tone was too flat to be Ronit.

"*Mazal tov.* You said in your letter that you are getting married." The voice pronounced it the Hebrew way, as Ronit would: *mah-zahl,* with the accent on the "zahl."

After seven years of silence.

As Ronit began unbuttoning her coat, she fumbled momentarily. Then she finished with the buttons and wrapped the coat carefully over the back of the chair opposite Miranda.

Close-up, she was a more elegant version of the old Ronit: her brown eyes, her long eyelashes, her wide mouth, although coated in pink lipstick now. A pair of fat, circular, gold earrings peeked through the two-tone hair. No wedding ring. That was too bad. It would've been nice if Ronit could have found a good man to love, a good stepfather for Tali. On the positive side, she certainly dressed as if she had more money and a more professional job now.

How have you been?

Where are you living?

How's Tali?

Did Tali get my presents?

What have you been doing for the past seven years?

Where did a person begin a conversation, after a seven-year absence?

It's good to see you again.

"Do you want to go get yourself some coffee? I already got my tea." Miranda pointed to the thick white mug in front of her. What had Ronit liked to drink seven years ago? When they took Tali to the zoo or the carousel, it was usually a Coke, wasn't it? How could a friend forget something like that?

Ronit returned from the counter carrying a mug with steamy, milky foam. She took a sip the moment she sat down.

"You said you're here in the District for a conference?" Miranda asked.

"Yes. Until tomorrow night."

"What sort of conference?"

"About internships and fellowships in governments. Not very interesting."

"Is that what you do? You work for a government agency?"

"No."

Ronit was speaking as though she was answering a questionnaire, staring at her coffee mug more than at Miranda. "I work with many governments, not for one government," she abruptly added. "And what about you? Do you still have your strange boss?"

"Mort? He's not so strange."

"You are still helping people to get medical care?"

"I guess you could say that. For now, I'm working with a Senate committee that's writing a bill about drug coverage. Trying to expand insurance coverage." *Working with* was an exaggeration; all she'd done so far was give Scott a list of twelve names.

"That's what you always wanted. To make the world better for people, *nachon*?" Even saying these friendly-seeming words, Ronit's voice had no emotion or energy.

"I guess. Thank you."

When Ronit lifted her mug again, her napkin began to slide from her lap. She grabbed for it but missed, and it fell to the floor.

This wasn't Ronit, this elegantly-hairstyled, crisply walking woman who picked her words so carefully, as though she was still worried that if she said the wrong thing, the family court judge wouldn't let her see Tali. Of course a person could change a lot in seven years. And after all that time, it would be ridiculous to expect Ronit to immediately wrap Miranda in a giant, smothering hug, especially since Ronit had always hated "American hugs." But something a little warmer than these clipped clichés—some hint of the old Ronit—wouldn't be unreasonable. Ronit was acting as if she and Miranda had never giggled at the First Ladies gowns in the American History museum or chased Tali up and down the Metro escalators; as if she'd never phoned Miranda, her voice choked: *He cut up my driver's license, Miranda! I can't do this anymore.*

"Tell me about the man you are marrying," Ronit said.

Big. Cuddly. Smart. Loves Indian food. Loves chocolate doughnuts. Loves visiting old historical sites. Gets out of breath too easily when he runs. Has three freckles on his nose and two spots of skin as soft as a baby, in front of his ears. Furious that his fiancée hadn't told him she was arrested for kidnapping. "He's a lawyer. He wants to go after corrupt companies... He's big. Tall. Physically ... It's hard to describe someone you know really well. I guess it's because you take it all for granted." Miranda gathered her hair into the kind of ponytail that Ronit no longer wore and pulled it around her neck.

"You have a photo of him?"

"Sure."

From her wallet, Miranda slid out the top picture, the close-up of Russ laughing after he and Greg had finished the 10K fund-raising race for Greg's nonprofit agency, his sweaty hair dark against his forehead. Then four more, fanned across the table: Russ and Miranda holding hands, dressed up for the Center's annual dinner; Russ in profile and shirtsleeves, his tie loosened, poring over his computer; Russ stroking Miranda's cheek; Russ resting against the railing on the boat returning from Ellis Island. One by one, Ronit picked them up. At the picture from the dinner, she paused.

In that photo, Miranda was wearing the green linen cocktail dress that Ronit had helped her pick out at Hecht's.

"He looks very nice. Very friendly." Ronit stacked the five photos, then tapped the stack all around, realigning it. "He enjoys the outdoors?"

"We go running most weekends. I've shown him some of the routes you and I used to take, around the Lincoln Memorial and across Arlington Bridge."

"And the picture with the boat? You go boating together?"

"That was—well, that was the day he proposed to me."

"How beautiful."

Yeah. "We were visiting Ellis Island and the Statue of Liberty. That's the kind of nerdy thing we both like to do."

"How did you meet him?"

"Do you remember the dinner I went to senior year, at my horrible history professor's fancy Georgetown house? Where I did everything wrong?"

"Oh my God." Ronit clamped a hand over her mouth. "Of course I remember. You telephoned me right after it ended. You were crying."

Finally! Even if it took Russ's awful father to spark the connection. "Everything I said at the party was a disaster. The professor thought I was insulting his wine collection. Then I drank too much. Then I started arguing with him about Vietnam. The only thing I didn't do, thank goodness, was spill my wine on the carpet."

"I was going to go to right to his office if he didn't give you a good grade and tell him some kind of story; maybe I would say your mother had cancer, so he should be nice to you."

Really? Would Ronit have done that?

"He was at that party, your fiancé?" Ronit asked. "You told me about him? I'm sorry, I forgot that."

"Yes, he was at the party but no, I didn't tell you, because I hardly paid any attention to him. The professor is his father, and I think the professor just wanted him to show up and fill a seat, to make the dinner seem more popular."

"Ah, your professor was making a *shidduch*. A wedding match." Ronit grinned.

"I wish he was! But I had to waste almost ten years before I met Russ for real, at a Millennium-Plus-One party on New Year's Eve of 2001. And when I learned who his father was, I almost ran away."

Ronit was definitely grinning now. Laughing. Her wide mouth was opening wider, and any minute she might even let out a genuine Ronit whoop—Well, probably not a whoop, not in the middle of a coffee bar. But the old Ronit was emerging at last, and they could have a real conversation.

Are you dating anyone special?

Do you have any recent photos of Tali?

Tell me more about your job.

Do you remember how Tali would only ride the yellow horse on the carousel?

Why didn't you give me your address directly? Why did I have to go through your parents?

Why did we ever think it was a good idea for you two to sneak off to Israel without checking with your lawyer?

Miranda's mug of tea had grown cold. She took a swallow nevertheless. In a few minutes, she'd search for more hot water and offer to get Ronit a refill of her coffee concoction, but first she needed to keep the momentum going, now that Ronit seemed to be relaxing a little. "It's too bad you're only here for another day. But maybe we can get together another time. Where are you living now?"

Silently, Ronit picked up her spoon and held it horizontally above the table, the bowl in her right hand and the end of the shaft in her left. She'd stopped looking at Miranda again.

Oh no, were they back to the awkward, forced conversation already? Because of one ordinary question?

Miranda's mug shook as a stocky man brushed against their table, and then two other customers squeezed past him, talking rapidly.

"I work for a small—what are the initials you use? NGO, *nachon?*" Ronit's voice had returned to its questionnaire-answering monotone. "Our main specialization is the environment, but we have some programs with local governments also, which is why they hired me. Because of my degree in political science. I work with mayors and administrators to select employees to have fellowships with our NGO, and then we train them how to analyze the environmental impact of their work, so that they will bring that knowledge back to their jobs. To bring a greater awareness of the environment to their colleagues. I am also working all the time on other projects with governments. So there are many ways this conference can be useful for me." She paused. "That's why I came all the way from Tel Aviv, to be here."

"When did you—?"

Tel Aviv?

Ronit was staring at the spoon.

"How can you be in Tel Aviv?" Miranda demanded. "What about Tim and the custody—Did he just give up? Is Tali living with you full-time now? That would be wonderful."

Ronit's hands were steady, though her fingers looked tighter on the spoon. "Six years ago," she said. "We lived in Pittsburgh, Pennsylvania. Tali lived with Tim, and I lived a few streets away. I had a small apartment. I worked at a toy store."

Miranda could stop Ronit, right then, before the monotone went any further. She could take her black shoulder bag and run away.

"Tali was in the playground," Ronit continued. "She was climbing the bars, and they were very wet from the rain. She fell. She hit her head on another bar. The doctors called it an intracranial hemorrhage."

Tali. Climbed. And fell.

"That's why I haven't answered your letters or thanked you for your gifts, all this time. I couldn't look at the gifts. I couldn't write the words.

I'm sorry."

"Okay, Eema?" *Tali called from the platform of the Metro station, and she laughed as she began to run up the Down escalator.*

In her yellow car seat, Tali sang, "Here comes the sun. Here comes ha-shemesh."

It wasn't true. Ronit wasn't crying, so it wasn't true.

She needed to hug Ronit. No, Ronit hated hugs. She needed to say— she needed to say—

"I'm sorry," Ronit repeated. She stood up from her chair and pulled out the hooded coat from behind her, so she was the one who left the coffee bar first.

CHAPTER FOURTEEN
RONIT
C. 1988-1996

THE NUMBER ABOVE THE DORM-ROOM DOOR WAS the same as the number on the paper that the Georgetown University Housing Office had given Ronit, but the labels on the door, in the shape and color of monarch butterflies, said "Brenda" and "Miranda."

A thin girl who was probably a good ten centimeters shorter than Ronit, with light-brown hair that flared out from her head in tangles, was walking slowly down the hallway from the elevator, dragging a big tan suitcase streaked with dirt and staring at every door. She halted next to Ronit.

"You're Brenda?" Ronit asked her. "Or Miranda?"

"Miranda."

"You know this other girl? Brenda?"

"No. This is my first day at Georgetown. I don't know anyone."

"Me, too." Ronit sighed. "This is also my first day, and I also don't know anyone. My family lives near Tel Aviv, but I've been at Hebrew University in Jerusalem for the past two years. And you? You're from far away?"

The girl named Miranda replied with a bigger, dramatic sigh. "No. I live in Silver Spring—that's a boring suburb in Maryland—and my asshole stepfather actually wanted me to live at home instead of the dorm, to save money. Can you believe it? It's a good thing he gives in easily."

"You don't want—?" But there was no point asking Miranda; Americans were so careless about their families. Ronit set her oversized canvas bag on the linoleum floor, between herself and Miranda.

"Is this your room, too?" Miranda asked. "Are there three of us in the room?"

To the right and left and across the hall, all the doors had just two monarch butterflies, never three.

So it was another wrong room. "My name is Ronit. First the people in the Housing Office put me on a floor with boys. I guess they never met anyone named Ronit, so they thought my name is Ronald. All of the boys just shut up and stared at me when I came out of the elevator, with my bags." She waved her piece of paper. "I went back to the Housing Office, and they said, okay, this one will be my room, the number here, but my name isn't on this door. Well, I'll knock, anyway."

Inside, when the door opened, dark jeans and black sweatshirts and candles and little ceramic figures and boots and sandals and small decorated boxes and glittering jewelry and a hotplate and a mirror and more black clothes were spilled over the twin bed, the plain wooden desk, and the bunched-up orange rug on one side of the room. The girl who opened the door had round glasses like John Lennon, big hoop earrings, a black T-shirt, and muscled arms, and she was holding a pair of dangling earrings and also a glass mug of something golden, which could have been tea or it could have been whiskey. "Are you both Miranda?" Her voice sounded like it was coming from deep within her throat. "Come on in, whoever you are. I'm Brenda. You want some warm beer?"

More girls were wandering through the hallway and knocking on doors, with parents, with huge trunks, with cartons, with typewriter cases and tall lamps. The room to Ronit's right overflowed with incense even through the wall. "This is home for the next year!" someone announced.

"But what about you?" Miranda asked Ronit.

The efficient Americans would have a bed for her somewhere. Ronit hitched her canvas bag on her shoulder and picked up her blue suitcase from her other side. "Okay, I'll go to the Housing Office again." She nodded at the walls. "And when I get my real room, I'll make curtains for the windows. Even if my roommate again is a boy. Yellow, purple, green! These rooms need colors."

ON HER SECOND TUESDAY MORNING AT Georgetown, Ronit was a block downhill from the dorm when she heard Miranda calling, too close to ignore like the day before. She slowed until Miranda caught up to her, panting heavily. "I saw you yesterday," Miranda said, "but you didn't hear me. When I called. Do you want to go running together?"

They ran on the route in Rock Creek Park that the university phys ed department recommended, until Miranda thought she'd twisted her ankle. They ran to the Washington Monument and along the pebbly dirt pathways of the strangely quiet Mall with other joggers, and around the Lincoln Memorial and across the Potomac River on the Arlington Memorial Bridge to the big military cemetery, and onto any street that suddenly appeared interesting. They went past darkened office buildings, adorable eateries just warming up their bagels, sleeping bodies curled around bulky garbage bags of their possessions, and all of a sudden there would be a colorful street, or a pocket park, or a statue with an inscription to read. If Ronit switched direction toward one of those objectives, Miranda would always follow. As a running partner, Miranda was slower than Tzipporah back home in Israel, but she was like a radio, easy to listen to while she talked about school and her family and American politics. "I want to do something with my life that makes a difference, the way my parents and my grandfather did," she said on one run, as though saying it would be enough to make it happen. "I could do something on workplace safety, which would be a way of carrying on the ideals of my grandfather, who was a union organizer. Or health care. My grandparents both died of heart attacks when I was a little girl, right after my mother and I moved here, and I worry that there's a genetic tendency of some sort that Mom and I could inherit. But if I'm not a doctor, I wonder how much I can do in health care."

"What do you miss most about your home?" Miranda asked Ronit on another route.

Her parents and her sisters, Tzipporah and Michal, of course. The three orange trees in the front of her parents' apartment building. The sand-colored houses climbing up the hills of Jerusalem; the *shawarma* vendors and the abrupt, narrow little streets and the thousand different languages of the people crowding through the Old City. The Mediterranean lapping the long curve of the beach in Tel Aviv. The lushness of the forests up north in the Galilee, with all their shades of green and the hidden, rocky creek where she, Tzipporah, and Michal had waded when they were little. The stark Negev Desert that Abraham had wandered, and the beach in Ashkelon where a person could pick up three-thousand-year-old bits of pottery just strolling on the sand. The sounds of people speaking Hebrew all around her, the sonorous long U's and E's and the deep R's. The wild way her heart thumped every time she stood in front of the *kotel* even though she didn't think she believed in God.

She wore her Teva sandals from Israel until it got toe-numbing cold in November.

"Since I'm in the States for now, I want to be a tourist!" she told Miranda. "I want you to show me the most famous sights, so I can tell my family. The White House, the Washington Monument, everything. And then you also have to show me the places that the tourists don't hear about, all the secrets you know from living here."

Miranda took her to the tall stone staircase near campus where parts of the movie *The Exorcist* were filmed and to the beautiful desk in the State Department building where Thomas Jefferson wrote the Declaration of Independence. Twice, Miranda's mother Judith made Shabbat dinner for them. The first time, Ronit brought a big bowl of roasted cauliflower sprinkled with tahini, pomegranate seeds, and date honey, the delicious way that her own mother cooked it, and Judith immediately wrote down the recipe. Miranda's stepfather Bill asked Ronit to help him pronounce the Hebrew "ch" which he couldn't get right even after a dozen tries, turning it into something like a heavy breath. But he was very proud of his effort. Before the Kiddush blessing, he give a speech about the similarities between the Pope's skullcap and Jewish *yarmulkes,* which he ended by announcing, "Let us welcome our special guest, from across the ocean, from five thousand, eight hundred, and sixty-four miles away."

"He's sweet," Ronit said to Miranda, after Bill drove them back to the dorm. "Why do you make him sound horrible?"

"You wouldn't think he's sweet if you had to justify every penny of your living costs to him."

"At least you have your family nearby. You don't even realize how lucky you are!"

"Do you really want to compare losses?"

It was the first time Miranda had ever gotten angry. They stayed up until three o'clock in the morning, talking in Ronit's dorm room while her roommate was away. They smoked the joint that Brenda had given to

Miranda, a towel stuffed under the door.

"You remember anything about your father?" Ronit asked Miranda.

"Shit, I wish I did. Even something vague, like a smell. I was only six months old when he died. Well, to be fair, I don't remember much about anything until I was maybe three. I remember my grandfather holding my hand and walking down the street with me while I tried to grab the ice cream that was sliding off my cone." Miranda had been lying on her back on the roommate's bed, but she rolled onto her side so that she faced Ronit. "Of course I've asked my mother to tell me everything about every minute she ever spent with my father."

"What does she say?"

"For starters, they met at Columbia University during a big protest against the Vietnam War. A bunch of students had taken over the administration building, to try to stop Columbia from doing weapons research for the Pentagon, and my father was spending all day in the president's office writing speeches, because he was going to be talking to the TV stations and the newspapers and all. My mom was only a go-fer, which she admits."

"A gopher? Your mother was a little animal?" Ronit started to laugh, and then it felt almost like she was gulping huge breaths of air with her laughter, and it wouldn't stop. It was more laughing than she'd done in the entire three months she'd been living in Washington DC.

Miranda laughed, too. "It's slang. It means, you know, my mom went out constantly to get sodas and coffee and stuff, for the protestors. So that's how she and my father met. She brought him a Coke."

"She was a waitress!"

"No! Well, I guess you're right; she kind-of was a waitress, at first. But then she became almost as involved in the whole anti-war movement as my father was. Like at the Democratic Convention in Chicago in 1968, they were both socked with tear gas and chased by the cops."

"They were very brave, your parents."

"Yeah."

When Miranda handed her the joint, Ronit stubbed it out carefully against the side of a bowl of pistachio shells.

"You want to know something a little embarrassing?" Miranda asked, leaning closer over the rug that separated the two beds.

"What?"

There was a pause, before Miranda whispered, "I figure getting pregnant with me was an accident, and my parents had to get married. Look at how young they were. But what difference does it make?"

"You asked your mother?"

"Hell no! Why would I do that? It would just get Mom upset. Especially if I'm wrong."

Loud female giggling passed in the hallway outside their door. "Do you think they can smell the weed?" Miranda was whispering again.

"They can't tell which room it's from."

"Yeah. They're probably smoking in their own rooms." Miranda fell back onto the bed. "How about your parents? Leah and Yossi, right? Tell me about them."

Leah, in brightly colored stretch pants, on the stepladder checking the orange trees for any ripe fruit. Yossi, with his tight grey curly hair, running and limping alongside Michal when she was learning to ride her bike.

"My father tries to do too much, and then he jokes about it. For example, he was shot in his leg in the Six-Day War, and he has trouble walking ever since. But one year he told my little sister Michal that he was joining the Israeli Olympics weight-lifting team. So when it got closer to summer, she kept reminding us, 'We have to watch Daddy in the Olympics on TV!'"

"What a cute story. I could see my sister Lily doing that, too."

"He still jokes that he wants to climb Masada with me, to see the sunrise. That's a famous fort on top of a mountain in Israel, near the Dead Sea, where nine hundred Jews killed themselves so they wouldn't be captured by the Romans." Yossi had claimed that he didn't mind when she went to Masada with Tomer and Moran two summers ago, but it was so obvious that he did. She shouldn't have gone without him. "I know that I'm luckier than you," Ronit added. "I know that I'll see my father again, even if he's far away now."

"Are you going to move back to Israel when you graduate?"

"*Betach!* Of course."

Miranda didn't say anything after that; she was lying on her back, maybe too stoned to talk.

"But you must come visit me! I'll take you everywhere, Jerusalem, Tel Aviv, Tzfat, Haifa, every place you want to see and also the ones the tourists never go to. Just like you did for me here in Washington. We'll go hiking in the Galilee and on the beach in Ashkelon. We'll have a great time."

"It's a deal!" Miranda reached her hand over the rug and shook Ronit's. "It'll be a walking tour through the stories I learned in Hebrew school."

Ronit wrapped the remaining bit of the joint in a tissue and gave it to Miranda. For next time.

By November, she'd met Tim on the second floor of the Air and Space Museum. She was stretching forward, maybe too far, over the low metal fence surrounding the Wright Brothers' Flyer.

"Be careful. You'll fall over," a man next to her said.

"I can't believe that this worked. It looks like a child's toy. A very big toy."

The Flyer was impossibly long and flimsy, with strips of heavy muslin stretched over a series of spindly wooden poles.

"I think about how brave the Wright Brothers must have been, to do what everyone said men can't do. Fly."

"Now we have airplanes that serve us dinner."

"Maybe Orville Wright took his lunch pail on board."

The man was laughing as she turned to look at him.

By December they were dating steadily.

He had dark brown hair that was thick and smooth when she ran her fingers through it, and hands that were muscled and warm when he pulled her against him.

He would be graduating in June, and then he hoped to go to one of the top business schools in the States. Wharton, in Philadelphia, or Stanford, out in California, or Chicago, he said.

He knew something about almost any topic she could bring up—the popular new vampire novel, the U.S. presidential election, the Jewish refuseniks in the Soviet Union.

He wasn't Jewish, but he was so much like Israeli men. He didn't ask ten different people for their opinions before he did something. He just did it.

"Maybe," she told Miranda, "if things get serious with us, I'll ask if he will move to Israel with me, after he finishes his business school."

RONIT HAD LEAH'S MENORAH, WITH TINY MACCABEE soldiers as the candle-holders, and Miranda brought a box of plain candles for the first night of Hannukah. But on the third night, Brenda appeared in Ronit's dorm room carrying a set of longer, more elegant candles, each made of different pairs of colors that blended into stripes like a rich candy cane. Even unlit, they let out a faint sugary fragrance.

"Wow. Where'd you get those?" Miranda asked.

"Do you honestly want to know?"

"I shouldn't light them." Carefully, Ronit placed an orange-and-coral candle into a Maccabee helmet. "Then the beautiful colors will melt."

"What's the big mystery about where you got them?"

"They remind me of the special candles they make in Tzfat, in Israel."

Brenda gave a turquoise-and-pale-blue candle to Miranda and one with black and orange swirls to Ronit. "Have you been to that new place that sells candles and body oils and things? Near H and Twelfth?"

"No."

"Well, they have all kinds of great stuff sitting on the counters. And only one sales clerk, who gets flustered when they're busy." Brenda rubbed an eyebrow, that strange habit of hers. "If you get the picture?"

"You bought these beautiful candles at the new store?" Ronit asked.

"No."

Ronit frowned. "I thought you just said you did."

Miranda pointed at Brenda. "You shoplifted?"

What was "shoplifting"? Picking up a store off the ground? That word made no sense.

"Brenda, I don't believe you!" Miranda exclaimed. She sounded almost excited. "When I was in fifth grade, one of my friends dared a bunch of us to take some glitter pens from the drugstore, and we almost got arrested."

"You were almost arrested?"

"They don't arrest kids." Brenda batted Ronit's words away.

"The store manager threatened to. It was the one time my asshole stepfather was any use. He picked me up at the store and promised the manager blah blah blah whatever he was supposed to say. And he agreed not to tell my mom."

"You were probably too young, that's why you were caught. You have to plan it. First of all, don't dress sloppy. Dress like you can afford to pay for anything. And then when you're in the store, you make a big deal of picking things off the rack, putting them—"

"Stop!" But Miranda was laughing.

Were Americans really so casual about breaking the laws? Americans were supposed to be the ones who always liked to make rules, who always paid the price on the price tag. Well, maybe they weren't so strict.

ST. WILLIAM CHAPEL HAD A BEIGE CEILING crossed by wooden beams, coronet-shaped chandeliers, and tall stained-glass windows that were set into niches every few feet along the walls. On the right side of the aisle, Miranda, her boyfriend Seth, Brenda, Tzipporah, and Michal clustered in one pew, while Tim's parents, his grandmother, his sister, his brother, his sister-in-law, his aunt and uncle who lived in Virginia, a cousin, her husband, their three children, and two friends who were also going to business school with him spread across four rows of the left side. The *chuppah*, with Yossi's prayer shawl spread over the top, was planted under an archway at the front, where Tim waited.

He was the only person in a tux: a crisp black jacket and bowtie, a white shirt, and a white handkerchief folded in two sharp peaks in his breast pocket. His dark brown hair was slicked and parted on the side, a few sexy strands falling over his forehead.

And then Ronit was next to him.

She circled Tim seven times beneath the *chuppah*, while their parents watched from both sides.

"Timothy. Ronit," the rabbi intoned. "Today, we bring together not just two people, but also two cultures and two countries. And it is the beauty of the marriage ideal that the two of you will create one partnership, one Jewish home."

Ronit nudged Tim.

He raised his eyebrows at her.

He squatted as he placed a wineglass, wrapped in a heavy cloth napkin, precisely next to his shoes. He lifted his right foot. When he stomped, the glass shattered like an explosion against the floor.

Abruptly, his arm was around her waist and he was swooping her downward, tango-style, and planting a long, wonderful kiss while their families cheered.

At the restaurant Tim had chosen for the reception, Michal immediately grabbed Ronit to start a *hora*. Leah joined in, then Miranda in her long, flowered hippie dress and Brenda and even Tzipporah, who was six months pregnant, their hair flapping, palms sweating, high heels pounding faster and faster and circling, and then Tim took hold of a couple of hands. But his feet got tangled; he was trying to step behind when everyone else was kicking. After that Yossi bounded into the center of the circle and twirled Ronit so rigorously that her silly veil began to slip. Yanking it all the way off, she fixed it on Michal's hair. At some point, Tim ducked away.

She would have to apologize to him later, for ignoring him.

"I'm next?" Michal asked her. "You'll come home to help me choose my dress, whenever I get married?"

"Of course."

"And the flowers. And the food."

"Yes, yes! But maybe wait until you're a little older?"

"And you come visit us, too!" Yossi declared to Miranda. "Ronit, we will take your friend to climb Masada!"

"And the creek in the Galilee where we always used to play. And Haifa, you must see Haifa. And Jerusalem, *betach!*"

Tim's father toasted his beautiful new daughter-in-law and hugged her. Tim's brother toasted his new sister-in-law the bride and his little brother the groom and soon-to-be business mogul, and pecked her on the cheeks and hugged her. More Champagne. Yossi toasted the United States and Israel and Tim and Ronit and happiness and marriage, and he was so sorry all the relatives in Israel couldn't be with them today but Ronit and Tim had promised they would come to Tel Aviv to visit soon. Maybe for their honeymoon? Laughter. Frowning, Tim mouthed to

Ronit: *Where did that come from?* She kissed him. More Champagne. One of Tim's friends toasted something. Miranda went to the center of the room to raise her nearly empty glass—*Oy va'avoy*, Miranda was drunk. "I've only known Ronit two years—less than two years—a year and a half—but she's already become like a sister. The older sister I never had. I only have a younger sister. So I feel like Ronit is another sister. For one thing, we've been going running together every morning, and I'm going to really miss her. I wish she and Tim could move into my dorm—well, not really. Don't worry, Tim. But my point is, Ronit is a wonderful, special person."

"Miranda, you can sit down now," Tim called out loudly.

THEY MOVED TO TAKOMA PARK, MARYLAND, to a house that had been cut up into four tiny apartments. Their bedroom could barely fit their double bed, a tall wardrobe, and one person at a time going from the bed to the door. The living room was bigger, but the kitchen was only a row of old appliances and four cabinets separated from the living room by a red Formica counter with two tall stools. The slanted ceiling in the bathroom was so low that Tim almost always banged his head.

"You can tell me congratulations again," Ronit announced, perched on one of the kitchen stools next to Miranda.

"Are you getting married again?"

"Ha! No, but it's also good news. I'm pregnant."

"What?"

"I took the test."

"But you just got married."

"Yes, well, we were planning to wait until after Tim finishes at business school and is working for a year or two years, and we have some money. But then, we said, *Lama lo?* Why should we wait so long? What if I can't get pregnant fast? But—" Ronit laughed. "It was very fast."

"So it wasn't an accident? You actually meant to…?"

Miranda hadn't smiled yet, or said congratulations, or hugged her the way Americans were always hugging.

Ronit leaned forward against the counter. "We figured it out. The baby will be born, I think, in the end of March. And I will graduate two months after that. So, number one, I can take the baby to the university childcare center until then." She tapped her right index finger against her left fingers, one by one, counting off the points. "Number two, maybe my mother can come to help…" Her index finger wavered. "Well, probably she can't. Okay. Anyway, number three, we have our student health insurance. Tim asked the university, and it will pay for the doctors and so on. Number four, Tim has to finish this year's courses, and then one more year, and then he'll have his MBA and earn a good income. But for now he won't be making much money. Number five, so, in June, after I graduate, I'll get a job." Running out of fingers, she made two fists. "You're the first person I'm telling, except my parents. You think I'm *meshuga'at*?"

"A little." Because Miranda was sitting straight up on her stool while Ronit was leaning over her elbows, she was looking down slightly at Ronit.

"That's not very helpful."

"It's a big decision…"

"I know it will be hard. But who can be sure what will happen in life if we wait? When you have lived in Israel, you know you can't count on the future."

Miranda had begun twining Ronit's hair into a loose braid; she did it without tugging hard, the way Tzipporah did. "I guess I just think about my mother. She got pregnant with me when she was only nineteen, and it was really tough for her. She had to drop out of college for a few years."

"Yes, but your father died so young. That's why it was tough. Tim isn't dying!" Ronit laughed.

"What does he say about the baby?"

"He's been great, figuring out everything we should do, you know, the medical insurance, and how we can fit into this little apartment. It's just that this is a bad time for him now. His classes are very difficult, and he's not happy at the University of Maryland. You know that he wanted to get accepted to a more famous school. But that will all be better once he graduates and gets a job." Shaking her head free of Miranda's braiding, Ronit sat up from the counter, face to face with Miranda. "I know how much I love my mother, and I want to be a mother very much, too."

Still, Miranda hadn't said congratulations. What kind of a friend was she?

"You'll help me?" Ronit asked.

Miranda hugged her. "*Betach.*"

They walked back and forth along the streets near Ronit's apartment and Judith's house inspecting every stoop sale for old baby toys and clothes. They briefly fingered the onesies and blankets in the infants department of Hecht's, as soft as clouds, though there was no way Ronit could afford any of that.

"Maybe Brenda will shoplift something for you." Miranda giggled.

They read baby books from the library. ("Four months! It's got fingernails!" Miranda exclaimed.) A couple of times, when Tim had to study for an exam, Miranda went with Ronit to the doctor for her checkup.

"I'll speak to the baby only in Hebrew," Ronit promised, "so he'll be able to talk to his grandparents and cousins."

"Can you teach me, too?"

"*Betach!*"

"Shall we take him or her up to the top of the Washington Monument? And the zoo?"

"Sure. And we'll take him running with us, too. Him or her."

"How?"

"After he can walk. Silly! We must plan ahead."

"Oh, in that case, maybe you should be applying to Georgetown for him already. The class of—um—2013?"

"Yes! Oh—better: Ha-Technion in Haifa."

"Medical school too?"

"*Lama lo?*"

"*EHTZ.*" CRADLING TALI, RONIT POINTED UPWARD with her free arm, toward a big, sturdy tree in front of them. Tali moved her head in the same direction.

"What're you saying?" Tim asked.

"Tree. *Ehtz* is 'tree.' And *tzippor.*" A grey-brown blur had landed in a high branch of the tree. "That's your aunt's name, Tali. Tzipporah. Bird," she added, for Tim. "*Tali, tiree hatzippor ba'ehtz.*"

"I don't know why I agreed to give my own daughter a Hebrew name." Tim spoke matter-of-factly while he toyed with one of Tali's pudgy hands. "She's going to get teased all the time."

"Then I'll teach her how to answer back in Hebrew. *Shecket! Teepesh!*"

"Double-declining-balance depreciation," Tim murmured to Tali's forehead. "Ebitda. R.O.I."

"What's that?"

"I'm teaching her to speak business jargon." Tim grinned. "If you can teach her your secret language, I can teach her mine."

Miranda's little sister Lily was tiptoeing toward a squirrel, which was engrossed with a nut or something at the base of an oak tree. She paused a few seconds, took a silent step, stopped. One more step. The squirrel scurried up the trunk.

"They never let me get near them!" Scowling, Lily turned to Miranda, her mouth a thin, taut line.

"They're such scaredy-cats, aren't they?" Miranda wrapped an arm around Lily's shoulders. "I think that's because they don't live in houses with people. Have you ever seen a squirrel in the pet store?"

"A pet squirrel! I'm gonna ask Mommy to get me a pet squirrel!"

Tali was crawling steadily by November. She made her own maze through the two rooms of their apartment, winding around each piece of furniture in the living room, in and out of the bedroom, along the narrow space between the kitchen appliances and the counter, trying to climb up onto every chair, then starting all over. Wherever Ronit was sitting or standing, Tali would halt in front of her with a big smile, showing off her two front bottom teeth, and wait for Ronit to smile back and clap before continuing. Her hair was a silky crown of brown curls.

Even with so much exercise, Tali wasn't sleeping in any regular pattern. She woke up, crying, at all different hours, anywhere between ten o'clock at night and five in the morning, sometimes three or four times. Ronit tried nursing her later, or earlier; for less time or more. She rocked Tali sitting together in the rocking chair. She rocked her in her stroller, in the living room, in the bedroom. She paced around the apartment carrying her. She kept her in the bedroom so that Tim could study in the living room, or in the living room while Tim studied in the bedroom. She sang Hebrew songs, slowly and quietly. "*Heenay ma tov uma nayim, shevet achim gam yachad.*" Again and again. Every time Miranda visited, she rubbed Tali's back and sang, "We Shall Overcome." Some afternoons,

Tim took Tali on long walks, nestled in a carrier against his chest, while he held his book out way in front of him and tried to read.

When her parents came from Israel for a week, Yossi strapped Tali in the car seat of their rented car and she immediately fell asleep while he drove through all the numbered streets of Washington DC and out into Virginia; but as soon as he parked, Tali woke up.

"Tim can't study, because of the noise," Ronit explained. "Because I'm always moving around with Tali. He goes to the library all night."

"Really?"

"His classes are so hard. He worries that he won't pass his exams and get his MBA."

"Did you ask the doctor, about Tali's sleeping problem?"

"Oh, he says all babies are different. They learn to sleep through the night at different ages. What kind of help is that? So I called my mother."

"In Israel? Won't Tim see the phone bill?"

"Yes, I know he will be unhappy, but it's worth the cost! You know what my mother told me? You will love this: She said that I wouldn't sleep when I was a baby, also. Well, I was born around the time of Pesach, so she put some of the seder wine on her finger, and then I sucked the finger."

"And did you fall right asleep?"

"Yes!"

"That's wonderful."

"It's too bad I can't have seder every night with Tali."

For Tali's first Hannukah, Miranda brought eight jelly doughnuts and a yellow party dress like a bright flower, in a box wrapped with blue-dreidel paper and blue and white ribbons. Brenda brought a child-size Santa hat.

A Hannukah Santa Claus? Ronit plopped it on top of the toaster, behind a pile of dishes. Tali would scream if anyone put the hat's tight elastic around her pudgy neck, but Brenda would try to do it anyway unless Ronit stopped her.

The three of them sprawled on the living room carpet with Tali, draping the blue ribbons from Miranda's gift over and around Tali's head like a wreath as Tali laughed and grabbed for them, until Ronit had to get up to make the potato latkes, and Miranda helped her with the grating.

Brenda offered to teach Tali how to count while they cooked; she was a math major, after all. Tim, in the bedroom with the door shut, studied.

When Tim joined them, Ronit lit the candles in her Maccabee menorah: yellow for the *shammash*, and red and blue for the two nights so far.

Tali pointed toward the menorah, squealing syllables that could have meant "light" or "candle."

"You'd better keep her away from that thing," Tim warned.

"Of course I will." Tali was in her high chair anyway, far from the menorah.

Tim began to pour wine for everyone.

"Not me." Miranda covered her glass.

"You're still worried about making drunken toasts?" Tim laughed. "Well, just drink and don't talk."

Seated on either side of Tali's high chair, Ronit and Miranda took turns feeding her mashed banana with a plastic spoon.

"How're your studies going? Is it finals time?" Miranda asked Tim.

He sliced a latke in half on his plate. "All I can say is, after the shitload of work I'm doing, I'd better get at least a six-figure job in the C-suite of Goldman Sachs or Fidelity."

Ronit frowned. "Sea-sweet?"

"Fuck, Ronit, you still don't remember what that means? It's the top echelon—oh, forget it."

Had Tim ever told her what that odd word meant? *Sea-sweet*. What did sweets have to do with a job at a big financial firm? "I'm sorry, your business vocabulary is very confusing."

"Yeah, and I think Hebrew is confusing, but you're always jabbering that to my daughter in front of me, and I don't have the fuck idea what you're saying." Ronit quickly cupped Tali's ears. A little baby shouldn't hear those kinds of words.

"I don't know what C-suite means, either," Miranda mumbled.

"My point," Tim continued calmly, "is that the job market is so fucking competitive, and I'm already at a disadvantage not being at one of the top B-schools—which, I admit, is my fault. I screwed up my GMAT, shit, the timing was lousy, I was getting over the flu, and then there was the wedding—So, fine, but now the pressure's on me double-time to haul ass and get good grades and get a good job and repay the damn student loans." He raised his forkful of latkes toward his mouth. "Not to mention paying for Ronit's long-distance phone calls to Israel."

In addition to the latkes, there was the roasted cauliflower-tahini-pomegranate dish from Leah's recipe that Tim always liked, plus a chickpea-and-tomato salad and store-bought challah. Brenda chewed loudly. Wine glasses rose and descended. Tali gnawed at her plastic spoon.

"Why're you wearing a sweatshirt from Columbia University?" Tim abruptly asked Miranda. "Are you planning to transfer and move to New York?"

"Oh, it's just—I got it as a kind of souvenir of my parents. That's where they met."

"Do people stare at you when you wear it at Georgetown? You could get in trouble wearing another school's emblem on your own campus."

"I don't know…"

"Yeah, no one probably cares. They wear a lot stranger slogans, don't they?"

"I guess." Miranda had flashed Ronit a quick frown, a *what's with Tim?* look.

If only Ronit could signal back to her: *It's just Tim being Tim.* So she stood up, announcing, "And now for Miranda's doughnuts!"

Tim refilled the wine glasses. This time, Miranda nodded *Yes.*

"God, I never eat jelly doughnuts." Brenda broke off a hunk of a second one.

"They're good." Tim licked his fingers.

"Could Tali have a taste of the jelly?" Miranda asked.

Ronit lifted her glass. "Next year in Jerusalem! Oh, I know that's what we say at Pesach, not at Hannukah, but maybe we can make that wish now. Tali's second Hannukah will be in *Yerushalayim*! I will get her a passport."

"I'll drink to that."

"On what money?" Tim slammed his glass down. "On my C-suite salary next year?"

Brenda's and Miranda's glasses wavered.

"Your twenty-four-dollar phone calls every week aren't enough?"

"Tim—"

"You think I just pull hundred-dollar bills out of my ass?"

"We have company. Stop it!"

"They're your friends. I thought you have no secrets, huh?"

"*Shecket*!"

"Speak English!"

Tali screamed.

"Hey!" Brenda shouted. "Both of you! This is, like, really awkward for Miranda and me."

As Tali kept on screaming, Ronit pulled her out of the high chair and ran with her into the kitchen area behind the Formica counter, burying Tali's face against her chest and sliding onto the linoleum floor; anything to block out Tim's shouting. The plastic spoon dropped to the linoleum with a weak snap.

The apartment was finally quiet when Tim walked toward the kitchen area. Crouching, he patted Tali's curls and brushed Ronit's smoother hair. "I apologize, everyone," he called back to the living room, behind him. "The stress of studying and all that. Sit down. Have some doughnuts."

"IT'S NOT ALWAYS SO BAD," RONIT TOLD Miranda on the phone.

"Okay."

"It's just hard for Tim now. It will be better when he has his MBA degree and gets a job."

"Ronit, you're my friend. I want you to be happy."

"Oh, Miranda, I know you do. Thank you. But everybody who is married fights sometimes, *nachon*? It's okay."

"You're sure?"

"Last week, there was a day when it wasn't too cold, so we went for a walk along that long path by the Potomac River, the one that used to be a canal, I think. You know the path I mean? We dressed Tali in her snowsuit and lots of sweaters, and Tim put her in the baby carrier, and it was so nice, Miranda. The river is so wide and quiet and empty there; you don't see all the buildings along the shore that you see in Washington, you know? You can hear birds! And we talked, and we had a good time.

We just have to get away from the bam-bam-bam pressure of his studies."

MIRANDA YANKED OPEN RONIT'S FRONT DOOR and threw her backpack on the living room floor. "I'm going to have to drop out of my history seminar! But if I drop out, I can't graduate in June without those credits. But if I don't drop out, I'll flunk out anyway." Panting, she clutched the top of the sofa.

"Wait. Wait." Ronit grabbed a coffee cup out of Tali's reach.

"The professor hates me. It's impossible. He criticizes everything I do. I swear, he looks for ways to twist my words around."

"What happened?"

The professor had given Miranda a D on her last paper; her second D in a row. So she went to see him during his office hours. "When I explained my thesis, how avoiding the draft in the Vietnam War by going to college was like the rich people in the Civil War who got drafted and paid other people to take their spots, because in both cases, people with money could avoid fighting. You know what he said? He said, 'Then I assume you would eliminate all college scholarships, since scholarships are enabling elitist draft evasion.' What's that supposed to mean? How do I answer that?"

Miranda fell onto the couch, holding her sides as if she had a horrible stomach ache.

Ronit sat down next to her.

"I don't know where to begin. I'm going to fail this class no matter what I do. I can't even focus on my other classes. Am I really that stupid? How did I get through three years of Georgetown if I'm so stupid?" Miranda was curled around her folded arms, shaking her head over and over.

Ronit reached out her arms, and she wrapped Miranda in a hug.

For a long time, they stayed that way. Miranda sniffled, although she didn't actually cry. Gradually, she stopped shaking her head and sniffling, until she finally pulled away. "His office was so weird," she added, oddly.

"In what way?"

"Of course there were a zillion books, all of them very neatly lined up in bookcases. And his desk was neat as a pin, too: an in-box on one side, a pad in front of him, a couple of photos in frames, I guess his wife and kids. Not a pencil out of place. But then there were these stacks and stacks of typewritten pages. I mean, everywhere. On chairs, and his desk, and another table. I asked him what they were, and he said, in a very stony voice, that they were the manuscripts of his last two books. Why would he keep the messy piles of manuscripts instead of the actual books?"

"So who cares about him? I will help you rewrite your paper, and you will get an A, and you will graduate in June—yes you will!—and you will get a great job and a whole new closet of clothing, and after that you can forget about the weird, evil professor."

MARCH WAS TOO COLD TO HAVE Tali's first birthday party outdoors, so her favorite people had to crowd into their apartment— Miranda, Brenda, the two little girls and the boy that Ronit and Tali usually met in the playground, and those toddlers' parents. For the top of the cake, Tzipporah had suggested using tubes of colored icings to squirt pretty designs like hearts and Jewish stars, but when Ronit tried, the hearts and stars all ended up being lopsided circles. Tim tied balloons to every doorknob, chair, and lamp.

"Here's my extra birthday present for Tali," Miranda offered. "Now that she's starting to talk and she'll repeat whatever we say, I promise not to swear in front of her."

"Can you really keep to that?" Ronit asked.

"Fuck no." Tim grinned.

"Test me," Miranda offered. "Oh shoot. Heck. Yikes."

One of the mothers took lots of photos—Tali batting balloons with Tim and Ronit, Tali and her little friends making a mess of the wrapping paper, and everyone hugging and kissing.

CHAPTER FIFTEEN
RONIT
C. 1988-1996

TIM GAVE UP ON THE BIG FINANCIAL FIRMS in January. The recruiters wouldn't take him seriously because his MBA hadn't come from Harvard or Wharton or Chicago or Stanford, he said, so in fact he'd wasted his two years at the University of Maryland, exactly as he'd predicted, trying to study through Tali's crying all night long, and now he was going to have to lower his sights and just apply for a job as a fucking financial adviser at some two-person, no-name retail shop telling Aunt Mabel which muni bonds to buy with her lousy thousand bucks, instead of managing real money—nine, ten figures, trust money and institutional money where you could actually earn decent fees and make decisions. But even those smaller no-name firms never called him back, after the first or second interview.

It was about time Ronit got a job, as she'd claimed she was going to do when she got pregnant, he said.

"Okay, but I can't do it right away. I need to go back to school, for the teaching license."

"Why didn't you major in something useful instead of—what's your bullshit degree?"

"What do you mean, useful? Political science is very useful, to understand how—"

"Just go apply at Peoples Drug Store, for Chrissake. Be a cashier. Be a fucking waitress. Do something. I can't be the only one supporting this family."

She called three childcare centers in Takoma Park and nearby, and within a week she had a part-time job as an aide on Monday, Wednesday, and Friday mornings, and she could bring Tali with her.

Tim shrugged, not looking up from the long list of companies that he was always crossing off and adding to. "Pays shit, I'll bet."

"I don't know. I think it's almost the same as Peoples Drug Store. And with this job, I don't need a babysitter."

"Maybe it would be better if she spent some time away from you. Then she'd learn to speak English."

"Stop that already! She speaks English."

"I never hear it."

"It's baby talk. It's hard to tell what she's saying."

"First you make me have a Jewish wedding. Now you whisper to her behind my back in your secret code."

"I'll teach you Hebrew, too. Okay?"

"No thanks."

BY THEIR THIRD VISIT TO THE National Zoo in the spring, Tali was tugging Ronit and Miranda down the winding path, around the scattered visitors, past the elephants and the cheetahs and the bison and even the giant pandas without pausing, to the Small Mammal House and the glassed-in niche where the big-eared fennec fox was asleep curled up on its stone ledge. For the entire ten minutes that they watched, the little animal slept. Then of course Miranda bought Tali a beige-and-white stuffed fox with adorable oversized ears at the gift shop, because she was always buying presents for Tali. "*Shual,*" Ronit instructed them. Fox.

"I'm going to talk to Tim," she said softly into Miranda's ear at the food court, while Tali fed her fox half of her French fries. "I'm going to tell him we need to go to marriage counseling."

"That sounds like a good idea. Counseling." Miranda held out a flimsy paper napkin to Tali. "Hey, Tali. Does your fox want to wipe his mouth?"

Nodding, Tali rubbed the paper against the animal's face, then kissed its white nose.

"They say a baby can change a relationship between the parents in big ways. And Tim is so stressed-up, because he still can't find a job. You know he wasn't like this when we got married."

"I know."

"You remember when I came back from my second date with him? When he took me to see the Jefferson Memorial all lit up at night, and I was laughing like crazy? Because of the way he just started dancing with me and singing?" It had been like a movie, Tim singing off-key and twirling her around, her clutching his upper arms harder as she got dizzier, Tim twirling her faster, lights of all colors flashing in the sky nearby, until they fell together onto the short, dark grass. They rolled on the ground, a half-turn around, kissing and never letting go. That Tim couldn't have disappeared completely. That Tim had to be somewhere underneath all the unhappiness.

"Do you think Tim will agree to counseling?" Miranda whispered.

No. But it was what all the marriage-advice books said to do.

As soon as Ronit and Tali returned home from the zoo, even before Ronit could get her keys out of her coat pocket, Tim pulled open the door of their apartment and wrapped his arms around both of them together, squeezing them toward his chest. And he laughed. "I've got a job!"

He would only be a financial adviser at a small firm, which was exactly what he hadn't wanted. However, he would have some wealthy clients, and the firm also managed big pension fund accounts, so in a few years he could move up. "Up!" he promised, lifting Tali high into the air.

SUDDENLY, TALI WAS HAVING NIGHTTIME problems again. After Ronit put her in her bed, she immediately climbed out and plopped herself into Tim and Ronit's bed, laughing like a hundred twittering birds. Ronit began lying down half an hour early, letting Tali cuddle with her until Tali would supposedly fall asleep. Then an hour early. Tim stayed in the living room, reading *The Wall Street Journal*, constantly switching channels on TV, rewriting his resume. One night he baked chocolate chip cookies, and when the chocolate smell meandered into the bedroom, even through the closed door, Ronit sleepily came out and found him at the stove with oven mitts. He slid a chunk of a warm cookie into her mouth. She kissed him, chocolate-lipped, and they rested against the Formica counter, drinking milk and eating cookies together while Tali slept.

Tim said the people he worked with were idiots. They'd stuck him with the stodgiest, smallest accounts, which were never going to go for the kind of higher-risk investments that brought in the real commissions that they'd promised him, so how the fuck was he supposed to make more than pennies? He couldn't take it another day. He had to move somewhere that was actually growing, some place like Houston or Atlanta, the Sun Belt. That was the only way he was going to have a chance, not in this shitty city where the only people who raked in paychecks worth talking about were lobbyists.

"Tim, you finally have a job. Please don't quit it yet!"

"I might have to."

"But we need the money."

"So how about you go earn some?"

"I am earning."

"Pennies."

"Why do you always say that about my job?"

"Maybe if I didn't have to keep paying for all your phone calls to your mother."

"I don't—I just need to talk to my mother sometimes."

"Yeah, you sure do need help being a mother, don't you?"

"What?"

"You can't even take care of your own daughter. She hasn't slept decently since she was born."

"That's not true."

"You can't do anything without calling your mother long-distance."

"Don't you—don't—"

"Do I have to pull out the phone so you don't abuse it?"

"What?"

"You can't be trusted. With credit cards, with our daughter, with the phone—I suppose you're cheating on me with some hunky divorced dad at your so-called job?"

She threw her cookie at him. It crumbled onto the linoleum floor; Tim grabbed her arm. She screamed, and he clamped his other hand over her mouth. "Don't you ever," he hissed, "throw something at me."

SHE PUT A NOTE FOR TIM ON THE BED, while he was out with one of his business school classmates who worked in the Maryland state government, who might get him a job. Shoving clothes, toys, and books for Tali and some spare shirts and underwear for herself into her old canvas bag from Israel, she took a taxi with Tali the six miles to Miranda's apartment in Washington.

It was wrong to leave, just like that, without warning Tim. But going to Miranda's apartment wasn't leaving; it was a small vacation. Besides, it was so nearby, and Ronit and Tali would return home in a few days. If Ronit and Tim simply had a little break from each other. If he apologized. If he promised never to grab her that way again. If he got a better job.

Miranda wasn't home. Ronit rang her buzzer four times. She and Tali went for an excursion around the block, skipping over the cracks in the pavement as Miranda had taught them. They sat on the front stoop of the building and counted the people who passed, in Hebrew and English. After that, they named the colors of the cars that drove by, also in Hebrew and English; the most popular color was black. *Shachor.* Ronit read to Tali from her favorite books, the one about the baby bird who wants to find his mother, and Madeline and the other little girls in two straight lines. By noon, though, Tali was whining. "I want Cheerios, *Eema.*" "I'm thirsty." How could she have forgotten to bring food? She'd also forgotten Tali's favorite cup, and the coffee shop she and Miranda always went to, a few blocks away, didn't have booster seats. Ronit tried to wrap her arm around Tali next to her in the booth and simultaneously keep a glass of milk steady with her left hand while spreading cream cheese on Tali's cinnamon-raisin bagel and pouring some Cheerios into a bowl with her right. Tali squirmed, dropping a big hunk of the bagel. "NO!" she screamed. Then she thrust the glass away, and it crashed on the floor, which sprayed the two of them with milk, and she screamed more.

They were back in their own apartment before Tim returned. Ronit shredded her note. After giving Tali a bath, she threw their milk-soaked clothes in the laundry hamper.

NO WONDER MIRANDA HADN'T BEEN HOME: Her job at the Center for Liberal Alternatives was full-time now. "I'm so sorry I missed you and Tali."

"It's okay. I was being stupid, anyway. Running away like a child."

"Will you be all right?"

There was no reason to tell Miranda about Tim grabbing her arm. It would never happen again; Tim had apologized. It was only because of the demands of wanting to be a good husband and father, to provide for her and Tali, he said.

"You know it was so happy at the beginning," she reminded Miranda. "It's just that we fight so much now. About everything. Nothing I do is any good. I don't know how I can live like this."

"Do you—do you want a divorce?"

Divorce.

"Miranda, I'm not ready for that! Tali needs a family."

"But if you're always fighting? And he's always criticizing you?"

"Divorce is a very final step. You can't keep changing your mind, once you say 'divorce.'"

"I know."

"We haven't tried counseling. We've never had a minute to relax about money. When there's less pressure, when Tim has a job he likes and we have more money, things will be better. The way they used to be."

"Do you think so?"

"After you spent so much time helping me pick out my wedding dress? How can I waste that beautiful dress?"

Of course Miranda couldn't see her little smile over the phone.

"Ronit, that's not a reason to stay married!"

"It was a joke."

"Okay."

"But really, I'll earn more, too. I already asked the director of the childcare center if I can work more hours, and she said yes, in the winter. That will help."

Miranda's breath was the sole noise that came over the phone for a moment. "Do you really think it's just about money?"

"Of course it's more than that. But money is a big problem in a lot of marriages."

"Maybe… if you talked a little less Hebrew to Tali?"

"What? That's who I am! You want me to give up my identity?"

"No, I'm—"

"Maybe I should give up my Israeli citizenship, too. That's what you're saying? I should stop calling my mother in Tel Aviv, like Tim complains about?"

"No, of course not."

"Anyway, I try not to talk so much Hebrew in front of Tim. It doesn't help." Neither of them filled the empty air, until Miranda said, "If there's anything I can do. Just ask."

LEAH HAD PLANNED TO COME TO THE U.S. for Tali's fourth birthday, but Yossi had an incident, she said; he fell on the street. Was he dizzy? A heart attack? Complications from the old wound in his leg? Leah had to stay in Tel Aviv with him while the doctors tried to figure out what was happening.

Miranda gave Tali a picture book as her birthday present—a story about a little girl named Hannah who loved gorillas, written in Hebrew.

"You're talking Ronit's secret language with her, too?" Tim snapped.

"*Kofe!*" Tali declared, pointing to the gorilla's picture and bouncing on the sofa. She thrust the book at Miranda. "Read to me, Aunt Randa. Please!"

"Sure—"

Tim grabbed the book. "Why don't you pick something I can read?"

"Daddy! Give it back!" Tali shrieked.

Now that it was spring and the weather was getting beautifully warmer, more like Israel than the U.S., Washington DC opened up for outdoor adventures on the weekends. Ronit, Tali, and Miranda walked all the way around the Tidal Basin, even on the very edge, ducking under branches; and Tali searched for yellow dandelions in the Mall grass; and they rode to the top of the Washington Monument to see the miniature city spread out below them. They sampled the hot pretzels from almost every vendor between the Capitol and the Lincoln Memorial. At the old-fashioned carousel near the Smithsonian castle, Tali inspected all the wooden horses, after which she would sit only on the yellow horse with the red saddle and brown mane. Of course they also had to visit the fennec fox at the zoo. If it wasn't too late, they would end the afternoon at Miranda's apartment so that Ronit could use Miranda's phone to call Leah and Yossi. She didn't tell them the worst parts, like how Tim had yanked her wallet out of her hands and cut up her driver's license. Or the night he'd thrust his fist in front of her face and shook it and shook it until it hit her lip. At least Tali had been sleeping in the other room that time.

In October, Tim was laid off.

His manager said the firm was reorganizing. As a result of the markets' renewed interest in leveraged buyouts and private equity, the firm was shifting its focus to its institutional clients, thus there was less need for retail specialists like Tim. Bullshit, bullshit, bullshit, according to Tim.

"So you have to get another job?"

"Maybe you should get a job."

"Stop saying that! I have a job."

"A real job. Not something playing with babies for ten minutes a day."

"It's more than ten minutes."

"What, fifteen?"

"I work—"

"Fucking playing dolls."

"Mister Big-Shot MBA!"

"What the fuck's that supposed to mean?"

"You brag, oh you're smartypants—"

"Damn straight I am!"

"If we need money so much, why don't you sell your fancy car?"

"I worked hard for that fucking car."

"*Attah lo yodeah*—"

"*Eema!*" Tali screamed, in the doorway.

"Speak fucking English!" Tim's face was next to her nose, from nowhere. Her back was against the refrigerator door. He was going to shove her into it. His breath was spitting on her cheeks. He was too heavy to push away. She pressed her hands flat against his chest, and immediately his fingers were around her wrist, and they were digging into her flesh, and spikes of pain stabbed in a circle around her wrist and up her forearm as if she was wearing a thick, tight bracelet.

"Stop!"

"*Eema!* Daddy!"

Her arm dropped; Tim dropped it. She was gasping deep for breaths while he walked out of the apartment, slamming the door behind him.

The next morning, there was a set of five black-and-blue marks that looked like fingertips exactly where his fingers had been.

BY FEBRUARY, TIM WAS LIVING IN A SMALL house in Adams-Morgan with five university students; Ronit and Tali stayed in the Takoma Park apartment. Tim had found a job, though he wouldn't say anything about it except that it didn't pay much. Their lawyers were working on the divorce. Tim wanted joint custody, but Ronit's lawyer assured her that as the mother and primary caretaker all these years, Ronit had a good chance of winning sole physical custody, which meant that Tali would continue living with her. However, she would have to share decision-making on major issues with Tim.

That would never work. Tim would interpret "sharing" as the right to yell at her for every decision he disagreed with. Whatever Ronit suggested, he would demand the opposite.

Well, her lawyer said, no judge would erase Tim entirely from Tali's upbringing.

What about the violence? When Tim had grabbed her wrist? Threatened her in the face with his fist? Didn't that make him an unfit father?

There were no witnesses or medical records, the lawyer replied.

Ronit had shown Miranda the bruises on her wrist! Didn't that make Miranda a witness?

That was hearsay; legally inadmissible.

And when Tim cut up her driver's license?

He would deny it. Her word against his. Anyway, it had nothing to do with his fitness as a father. Ronit would just have to live with sharing the decision-making with Tim.

"So if I want Tali to have a bat mitzvah? If I want to take her to Tel Aviv to see my parents? Even if I want to buy her a blue coat?" she asked Miranda. "You know what's going to happen."

"He'll say 'no.'"

"And then what do I do?"

Ronit and Miranda rode a few steps behind Tali down the steep escalator at Metro Center, as Ronit scrubbed a wet wipe over and around her fingers, top and under, again and again. "I can't—Tim yells at me even more than when he lived with us. Every time we talk. Every time he comes to pick up Tali. I thought things would get better when he moved out, but he's worse. There are always twenty new things he says I do wrong. And Tali sees it all. I can't do this anymore, Miranda."

"I know."

"Until she's eighteen years old? Thirteen more years like this?"

"Tim won't keep it up for thirteen years."

"How long am I supposed to wait for him to calm down?"

"There must be books you can read. Advice from women who've gone through bad divorces."

"Oh please, Miranda! I should read a book to Tim?"

"I mean advice for you, on how to deal with him."

"All they ever say is, 'Try marriage counseling.' 'Talk things out.' I tried asking him to do that a long time ago." Ronit crumpled her wipe. "I need to get Tali and me away from him."

"Yeah…"

"I need my mother. I need my family."

Tali, at the bottom of the Down escalator, was already jumping onto the Up escalator heading back up past Ronit and Miranda. "Okay, *Eema*?"

"No!" It was too late; Tali had reached the fourth step, then the fifth, climbing the steps herself even as the escalator glided upward. "This is the last time!" Ronit called after her. When she and Miranda got off onto the station floor, she added quietly, to Miranda, "You know that Tali hasn't seen my parents since she was a little baby? Her own grandparents."

"Really? That sucks."

"Since my father had that fall last year, his balance is no good. He can't go on an airplane to come here. And my mother doesn't want to leave him alone."

"Excuse me!" a man's sharp voice snapped from the step behind them.

Quickly, Ronit and Miranda squeezed sideways, to let two tall men in gloomy-hued ski jackets push forward, past them. One man's elbow grazed Ronit's arm.

"I need to take Tali to Israel. It's the only answer."

In Israel Tali could climb up the stubby trees alongside the creek in the Galilee where Ronit, Tzipporah, and Michal had played when they were her age. She could run down the sand on Tel Aviv beach and walk around the old, old stones of ancient Jerusalem, touching the floors that her ancestors might have walked on three thousand years ago. *Sabba* and *Savta* would squeeze fresh orange juice for her from their trees.

"I need my home, Miranda. You understand? You've been my good, good friend, my American sister, but I need to be with my real family now. At least for a little while," she added. "Maybe six months."

Tali had reached the top of her escalator, and Ronit pointed emphatically at the one next to it, heading downward. Waving, Tali hopped onto the moving steps.

"Can you help me, Miranda?"

"Of course. I'm your friend. What do you need me to do?"

CHAPTER SIXTEEN

MIRANDA MUST HAVE GOTTEN ONTO THE WRONG street somewhere. It was supposed to be one left turn and one right turn from the bar on U Street where Brenda had wanted to meet, to get to Route 29, which would take her back to her mother's house. But she'd made those turns, and there wasn't any Route 29 in sight. Unless she'd remembered it backwards, and she was supposed to go right, then left. The sky was so fuzzy. Paddles pounded on her head. She was stupidly grasping the steering wheel of her mother's Subaru as if she was clutching the last rung of a ladder above a sharp drop.

Wait—That was a red light! She just ran a red light. Okay, okay, people did that sometimes. She wasn't driving fast. There were only a couple of other cars on the road.

The street she was on had narrowed to two lanes and started sloping uphill. It was dark and quiet, with an old stone church and a couple of brick townhouses on her right and a huge brick apartment building filling up the left side. Silent cars were parked one after another along both sides. In the apartment building, a hopscotch of yellow lights glowed in a few windows. Brenda had insisted on coming all the way out here, in the middle of Northeast Nowhere; she claimed it was the best bar in the District, the coolest people knew about it, blah blah. Fine. Any bar would be fine, as long as it had alcohol. The only way Miranda could talk to Brenda about Tali and Ronit was if she had at least a glass of wine inside her.

Another traffic light was flashing up ahead, too brightly, like a piece of jade broken into a million sparkling shards.

Broken, like everything else.

Tali was dead. Six years ago Tali had climbed up a set of monkey bars and now she was dead. Six years ago she would have been almost six years old; maybe the monkey bars were in the park, or maybe it was the playground at her school. It had rained. Maybe it was March, her birthday month. It was a rainy March Saturday, six years ago, and Tali was wearing her yellow rain slicker. Tali climbed the monkey bars in her yellow rain slicker, six years ago. And she called out to her girlfriends, "I'm going to climb to the top. I'm going to climb the highest!" Six years ago she climbed to the top of the monkey bars and counted all the cars she could see below her.

Tali was dead. Tali was dead and she would never count Lego buildings from the top of the Washington Monument again. Tali was dead and Ronit had been living alone in Tel Aviv without her all these years. Tali was dead, and Bill was cheating on Miranda's mother, and Russ might lose his job, and Miranda might lose her job if she pushed too far, and the wedding caterer would cancel if Miranda didn't pay him, well so what, who wanted a wedding anymore? Tali was dead—

There were too many cars, all of a sudden.

There were too many streets crossing up ahead.

STOP!

A car horn blared.

A second horn.

There were cars coming from two different streets on her left and two more on her right, and someone was honking, and another car was flashing its brights, and there were too many different traffic lights—six, eight, twelve? how could there be so many all at once, and was the signal for her lane red or green? Could she make a right turn? The paddles were pounding on her head. The stupid steering wheel wouldn't turn—a car was coming toward her, its lights like angry eyes—TURN! Turn—But her hands wouldn't hold on—

There was a horrible, crashing, scraping shriek all around.

She jerked forward.

The car stopped.

THE POLICE OFFICER AIMED HIS BIG FLASHLIGHT at the

Subaru, its dark blue hood jammed diagonally into the driver's side of a beigeish car as though it was a leech clamped onto its victim's neck. The other car was about the same size as the Subaru—four doors, hatchback style. Scattered on the asphalt around both vehicles were long sharp glints of dark-blue and beige metal, clear plastic shards of headlights, broken glass; the other car's rearview mirror was flopped on the ground next to the Subaru's front tire like an abandoned toy. A few lingering wisps of smoke still drifted up from the Subaru's engine, into the stinging cold air.

A car inched past Miranda and the policeman.

"How did this happen, ma'am?"

"It was confusing…"

The policeman glanced around. The three wide streets and six corners were docile now.

It was probably the kind of little accident that looked worse than it actually was. All the broken glass. Not worth a cop's time; if she could just answer his questions and get him to leave quickly, could she avoid a ticket? How big a ticket could it be? "You know, it's a multiple intersection?" she asked him. "With a lot of confusing streets, crossing together? And it's nighttime?" *And I was upset because my friend's daughter is dead.* Something was sharply hurting near her left shoulder and her neck. "And I'm not familiar with this neighborhood at all. I was looking for—well, I guess, Route 29?"

"Route 29?" Behind the politeness, the cop's voice veered between astonishment and condescension. "Route 29 is pretty far away from here, ma'am."

"As I said, I'm not, you know, really familiar with this area."

The policeman kept shining his flashlight slowly around her mother's car and through the windows, as though he might find a dead body underneath or a bag of drugs hanging out of the bottom of one of the doors. He wasn't much taller than Miranda, with shoulders way too broad for his height and hair cut close to his scalp. Finally, he stepped onto the sidewalk, gesturing for Miranda to join him.

"Ow—!" As she stepped onto the curb, the pain from her shoulder shot down her arm.

"Are you all right, ma'am?"

"Yes." Maybe the cop would be more sympathetic if she was injured. On the other hand, it might make the accident seem worse. Which version would be better for her? There wasn't any wetness on her neck or the outside of her coat; her collar didn't smell of blood.

Apparently, the cop had already lost interest in possible injuries. "Did you have any passengers?"

"No."

"Was there anyone in or near the other car?"

"No. I mean, not that I saw."

"Pedestrians?"

"No."

"Have you been drinking tonight, ma'am?"

Oh no.

Why was he asking her that?

He wasn't close enough to smell any wine on her breath, was he?

Drunk driving was major. People lost their licenses for that. But she wasn't drunk. Just one glass. Plus a little of the second glass. Of course she had to tell the truth, to a cop standing right in front of her mother's banged-up car. "I had a glass of wine with my friend. A couple of hours ago." She wasn't drunk. She was speaking perfectly normally; she was standing without wobbling. All she had to do was keep control of herself and keep talking as she was doing, and persuade him.

In the fuzzy darkness, beyond the glow of the nearest streetlamp, it was impossible to see the expression on the policeman's face. Still, he wasn't writing anything down or grabbing for the handcuffs on his belt, so what she'd said couldn't be too bad.

"Do you take any prescription medications?"

"No." At least that was an easy question.

"Did you use any controlled substances?"

"No."

"May I see your license and registration, ma'am?"

"It's my mother's car, actually. I don't know where she keeps the registration…"

Now the cop was writing something. Taking her license, he walked bow-legged to his squad car, which was double-parked a few cars behind the one Miranda had hit. No doubt he was checking her name and the Subaru's license plate against the police department's database, just like in *Law & Order*. Would a misdemeanor conviction for disorderly conduct at Dulles Airport seven years ago show up in the search? So what! She was being paranoid. The case was over, finished, she'd paid her fine and done her community service—But what if his database was as thorough as the FBI's and he found her original kidnapping arrest?

When he returned, he brought a few traffic flares. Squatting, he placed them around the Subaru.

"Ma'am? If you could come with me to my car?"

To his car?

He couldn't be arresting her just like that. For what? It was only a fender-bender.

Without speaking, they headed down the sidewalk, single file, Miranda in front. Each step prompted another little shot of pain near her neck, but it felt much better if she hugged both arms around herself. Just before they reached the squad car, the cop took a few long strides backwards, away from Miranda.

"If you could walk toward me in a straight line, please," he said, "alongside this curb, with your arms at your sides—"

Oh no, oh no, he was actually doing it to her: the drunk-driving, walk-in-a-straight-line test.

"Starting with your right foot," he was saying, "please place your right heel directly in front of the toes of your left foot, and then repeat that with the other foot. And then continue in that pattern, counting the steps as you do them. Please do that for nine steps."

But she wasn't drunk! She was walking normally. She was talking like a rational person. The cop had no right. She could refuse to take the tests. She could ask for a lawyer. Russ would know the laws. No, she couldn't refuse; that would definitely make the cop suspicious.

She was wearing black leather pumps with short heels. She moved her right foot forward. It quivered—just a little! Her heel found the toe of her left shoe, bumped it, then steadied itself firmly on the concrete. "One!" She could do this. Next, the left foot. Forward, down, heel to toes. The pain was still nagging her neck, or maybe it was closer to her collarbone, and her left shoulder was weirdly hanging down lower than her right, but those body parts would have to wait; she had to focus on her feet, not her shoulder. "Two." Then the right foot. Then left. Then right—Wait! Where was her right foot supposed to go? It hit the ground, but it was nowhere near her left foot. Okay, okay, she would just slide it over until it was in place. One step; she'd messed up one step. That was all. Did she have to score 100 percent? Anyone would be nervous in this kind of situation, and stumble. It was nighttime. The sidewalk probably had ruts. Her shoulder hurt. She had to keep going. Left foot. Right foot; don't waver again! Left. Right. "Nine!"

"Thank you," the policeman said. "Next, keeping your right foot on the ground, please turn around in a series of small steps, and then return to where you were, walking in the same manner."

Turn. Circle. Nine steps back.

"Now, if you could, please, with your arms at your side, lift one of your feet about six inches off the ground, whichever foot you choose. Six inches is about the length of my flashlight. Can you see that? So, please lift that foot this high, with your toes pointed upward, and stay there for thirty seconds, while you count 'one thousand one, one thousand two,' and so on, until I tell you to stop. Please keep your eyes on your foot the whole time."

One-legged, without holding onto anything for support? She wasn't a flamingo.

No. She couldn't argue with him.

What if the people inside the nearest brick townhouse were gawking out the windows? Sneering. *Drunk driver!*

She lifted her left foot. Was it six inches up? "One thousand one. One thousand two—" No! Her foot had crashed down to the pavement. Of course it wanted to be on solid ground. She lifted it again. If only she could grab something for balance, even just to put her arms out ballerina-style; even for a few seconds. "One thousand three." Her right leg was shaking. "One thousand four. One thousand five." She was a robot. She kept counting.

"Thank you. And now—" He had come toward her, so that he was standing maybe two feet away, under the streetlight, and he held a pen vertically up at face level. His face had no expression. "Please stand with your feet together and watch the top of this pen as I move it back and forth. Please do not move your head. Just follow it with your eyes."

He moved the pen side to side, and again, and again, and then up and down, and again, and she watched it, and then he slid the pen into his pocket.

He returned once more to his car, this time opening the passenger-side door. When he reappeared, he was carrying a small, black, rectangular box, barely bigger than his hand, with a clear plastic tube sticking out.

"If you wouldn't mind, ma'am. Just blow into the end of this tube. Steady breaths, as if you're blowing out a birthday candle."

NO! No no no no this was it, this was the breath test, this was the serious one. No....

She could refuse now! Could she? She could delay a few seconds by taking the deepest breath imaginable, as though she were about to dive underwater and hold her breath until this monster went away. A few more seconds for the alcohol to dissipate. One glass of wine.

Her lungs rose inside her chest, she opened her mouth, and she glued her lips to the hard plastic of the tube. After seconds and seconds, it beeped. The cop took it away.

For a few more seconds, while Miranda's shoulder and collarbone throbbed, and a slight cold wind shivered down her neck, and she hugged herself again, the policeman looked at the little box and then wrote something in his notebook. "You have a blood alcohol level of zero-point-zero-eight," he finally said.

Which meant?

"You are under arrest for driving under the influence of drugs or alcohol in the District of Columbia."

His mouth was moving.

Under arrest. Driving under the influence. But she hadn't taken drugs. It was only a glass of wine. She wasn't hearing right. She wasn't going to be handcuffed, she wasn't going in the back of the squad car to the police precinct, she wasn't going before a judge, not again; she was a health care analyst at a respected think tank. She was working with an important Senate committee! She had hundreds of followers for her restaurant reviews on District Foodie! The cop was saying more things. He was taking her to the station. She had ten days to request a hearing. She had a right to an attorney.

No, this wasn't happening, not again. That was seven years ago. That was a different Miranda. *You are under arrest.*

But officer, my friend's daughter is dead!

He was putting her hands behind her back.

No no no no, she would call a lawyer; they would plea bargain. She wasn't going to jail. This wasn't happening. The metal snapped around her wrists.

It was heavy.

It was pulling down her left shoulder, and it hurt. It really hurt.

The cop's hand was on her right elbow. He was nudging her to move.

But the Subaru—they were leaving the Subaru, glued to the other car! Her mother's Subaru. She would have to tell her mother.

She couldn't tell her mother, not on top of everything else her mother was coping with.

She would have to get someone to bail her out.

If she was really arrested.

The cop was guiding her downward, bending her into the back seat of his car. Ow! Her shoulder banged the doorframe.

Her shoulder was screaming. She was being arrested. Tali was dead. None of this was happening. She'd never met Ronit for coffee.

But she was sitting in the back seat of a police car, with a metal grill and a policeman in front of her. She had drunk more than a glass of wine this evening, which was way beyond what she ever drank. And every second, she was moving closer to the police station.

The cop was speaking into his crackling police radio. Reporting her arrest. Miranda Isaacs, white female, age thirty-two.

Okay: She would find a lawyer. She would ask Brenda to bail her out. Again. She would go to the ER for her shoulder. She would tell her mother some kind of story about the Subaru. She could say that she'd driven into a parked car—stupid, stupid, she was so sorry. She hadn't been paying attention. There'd been too much traffic. She would pay for all the repairs. She would pay for a rental car for her mother.

Maybe she wouldn't need to put up bail. Maybe the police would let her out on her own recognizance, as a longtime District and Maryland resident with a steady job. A clean record, at least for the past six years.

But if she had a broken arm, or a dislocated shoulder, or something else that needed a cast, something she couldn't hide, then… She would say that she took a bad fall while she was running.

And if worst came to worst, and she had to stay overnight in jail until she could be arraigned, like after Dulles Airport seven years ago, well then, she would tell her mother that she hadn't come home last night because she and Russ had decided on an impulse to take a motel room for a night. Giggle, giggle. And then she'd broken her shoulder… falling out of the bed?

Except she's need a better explanation for Russ.

But she'd told Russ that she had lied to him only that one time, about the kidnapping. She'd told him he could trust her.

She couldn't keep on like this, all the secrets and stories! She'd crashed the Subaru into a parked car, but she'd hurt her shoulder running. Or did she break her arm in the car crash? Was that before or after the night in the hotel? Not to mention that the bathroom plumbing in her and Russ's apartment was supposedly broken, and also the kitchen sink; or was it the bathroom sink? And she had never told Russ that she'd gone to visit his parents. And what had she said to Mort about giving the bus riders' names to Scott? She couldn't keep everything straight.

She had to. Just this one more story. This truth was too awful to share with anyone.

CHAPTER SEVENTEEN

"IT'S ONLY ABOUT TWO HOURS FROM BUFFALO to Toronto," Clement Anderson explained, his slow voice echoing through the speakerphone console on Scott's desk. "But we had to drive to Buffalo first, from our house, you see, to get to the bus. That's another forty minutes."

In Mr. Anderson's background, his wife murmured something.

"Closer to an hour," Mr. Anderson corrected.

The office was still stuffy, and the one-armed cactus in the black tub was still bent over as if it would fall down any moment. This time Scott was sitting in his chair, thank goodness, so Miranda sat, too, across the desk from him. Pushing her list of names toward him on the desktop, she pointed to the third line. Clement and Delia Anderson, ages seventy-two and seventy, respectively. Retired foreman at the Trico windshield-wiper plant; housewife. Prescriptions: Zocor and Plavix.

Scott glanced at the paper while he reached for a folder near his elbow. Even after ten minutes, he still hadn't asked why Miranda had her left arm in a bright blue sling.

Voices came and went outside the closed door of the office, and Scott chomped on his gum and read whatever was inside his folder, and through the speaker Mr. Anderson said some words tinged with static, and Mrs. Anderson said more words in a higher pitch.

How much do you use your car? the lawyer had asked Miranda. *You should assume you'll lose your license for six months.*

"…senior center, Delia."

"No, it was the receptionist. At the cardiologist's office."

"Was it the receptionist now?"

Scott was underlining something. "And you have…?"

"Have?" Mr. Anderson asked.

"Your conditions. Your medical conditions. That you need to fill prescriptions for."

"Well, the doctor says I have high cholesterol, so that's the Zocor. And then he says I need to be watching my blood pressure."

"Because of your heart attack," came Delia's voice.

"Yeah, yeah, I had a little something last spring. So that's why I get the Plavix."

The DUI remains on your criminal record for fifteen years, which will be available to any potential employer should you seek a new job.

"That wasn't so little, Clement. Why are you always saying that? Miss Isaacs, you remember how we talked about it on that bus ride when you came with us? The doctor says it's a good thing I was home and I found him in the kitchen. Clement, you remember what the doctor said."

"And I'm doing everything he said, aren't I? I'm taking this Plavix now."

"You should stop eating so much bacon and all that grease."

How had this conversation gotten so out of control? The Andersons needed to quit bickering, immediately! They had completely lost Scott's interest, and if that continued, he wouldn't want to hear any more of her witnesses or anything from her at all. "Mr. Anderson," Miranda broke in. "Can you tell Scott what you and I talked about on the bus: How much money do you figure you save by filling your prescriptions in Toronto?"

"Well, now. Let me get that for you."

There was a silence on the speakerphone. Scott jotted a note on another page in his folder before closing it and reaching for a second one.

"The Plavix, it's costing three hundred twenty-two dollars for three months if we buy it at the Walgreens here. So when we went to Toronto, we paid a hundred ninety-nine. Well, a hundred ninety-eight and ninety cents. And the Zocor, that was—"

"Three twenty-two versus one ninety-nine?" Scott interrupted. "You saved more than one-third of the cost?"

"Well, I guess that's true. If that's what you calculate."

"Would you be willing to come to Washington to testify about that?"

HER LAWYER SAID:

She should expect to ultimately shell out thousands of dollars— for his fee, of course, plus the criminal fine, assuming she didn't get the charge dropped—which wasn't going to happen; and repairs to the Subaru, repairs to the other car, definitely a lawsuit by the owner of that car, medical costs—she did say she'd sustained injuries, didn't she?—and then there were the nickel-and-dime bills, for drunk driving classes, an ignition interlock device, impounding her car.

And if she charged those thousands to her credit card and her past-due balances kept building, then her credit score would suffer. Badly.

In addition, according to the law, she could be sentenced to up to one hundred and eighty days in jail. Of course, that was unlikely for a first offense, but she would most certainly be on probation for six months. The courts took DUI quite seriously.

THE INSURANCE COMPANY SAID:

Yes, they'd heard from the owner of the other car. They were in discussions with the owner's insurance company.

It was premature to discuss any impact on Mr. and Mrs. Higgins's policy.

THE ORTHOPEDIST SAID:

The X-rays showed a diaphyseal midshaft clavicle fracture, or in layman's terms, a fracture of the collarbone. Ms. Isaacs's activity must be strictly limited, for probably three to four months. To start, they would want to immobilize the shoulder area by keeping the affected arm in a sling, bent at a ninety-degree angle. She might also need to sleep sitting up for a brief time. Would Ms. Isaacs describe her pain as severe? She could certainly take over-the-counter pain medications such as ibuprofen, naproxen, or acetaminophen, although of course these should be used in moderation.

HER MOTHER LOOKED AT HER OWN LAP for a long time before saying: It was too late at night to talk.

THE MECHANIC AT THE AUTO SHOP WHISTLED.

NOW SCOTT WANTED MORE EXAMPLES. The worst hard-luck cases; the most talkative and charismatic; those who'd seen the biggest savings; the ones—if any—from the committee members' home states. Not that he would promise that he'd actually use any of them as witnesses or in the written report.

"We figured how I might skip some of my prescriptions, you see?" said Paul Lauterbach, who lived all the way out in Elmira. "We're thinking, if I could get a bit more exercise, if I cut back on the waffles and whatnot, maybe I wouldn't need the Lipitor but every other month. So then we'd only have to pay for my wife's metformin, for the diabetes, for that month."

"It was a long day, on that bus. Tell you the truth, I'm not sure we could do it again."

"They're criminals, the drug companies, the doctors, all of them! They're all in cahoots together."

This kind of fracture pretty much heals itself, Ms. Isaacs, but it does take time. Twelve weeks is not at all unusual.

"No, no, I'm sorry. Between my husband and myself, we've got nine prescriptions, and the V.A. only covers two of his. And then Medicare, no, it doesn't cover drugs, does it?"

"I don't know, doctors just keep prescribing and prescribing, but do we honestly need all those drugs?"

Theoretically, again, Miranda, the law says you could be fined as much as a thousand dollars for a DUI first offense, but it's more likely to be just a few hundred dollars. Less than seven hundred, I'd say. That's the least of your worries, honestly.

"In fact, Miss Isaacs, my wife and I actually drove up to Toronto ourselves, about five months after that bus trip where we met you. Yes, ma'am. It was an awfully long trip, and we were pretty tired, you bet. To be factual, my wife doesn't drive anymore, so's I had to do it all myself. But three months is just three months. My wife runs out of those pills after three months, and I didn't see anyone organizing any more buses."

Once the pain diminishes, and you are able to move the shoulder joint somewhat, then we'll begin physical therapy, strengthening exercises, that sort of thing. The goal is always to avoid surgery, if possible.

"Then, for the Nexium, I'm paying a hundred and eighty six in Canada, and that's three hundred thirty-five here. And for the Fosamax, that's a hundred and thirteen in Canada—Is it all right then if I round off the pennies?"

"To tell you the truth, I wasn't feeling so certain whether the bus would make it. When that driver missed the exit?"

LILY PUSHED OPEN THE DOOR TO TED'S ROOM: "Three friends of mine want to come to the Iraq march with me. They're going to make signs. You're coming with us, right? Can you walk with your arm in that thing?"

IT WAS BRENDA'S FAULT, FOR letting her order that second glass of wine. Wasn't it a friend's responsibility to help out another friend? To realize when a friend needs help? Friends don't let friends drink and drive.

THE ORTHOPEDIST SAID: "No running, certainly. Walking is fine in moderation, but why would you want to be walking and standing for an entire day?"

"I DON'T KNOW HOW IT HAPPENED, Mom. It was stupid—beyond stupid. Irresponsible. I'm sorry. I just—I just got confused by the intersection, and my hands slipped on the steering wheel... I'll pay you back for every penny of the car repairs. And the rental car."

"You damn well will pay," her mother replied. "Shit, Miranda. It's something I'd expect from Lily, not my thirty-two-year-old daughter. Smashing my car."

"HEY, I'VE BEEN THINKING about your question," Lily said in the hallway outside the bathroom. "What a twelve-year-old girl might like for her birthday."

What?

Miranda backed up against the hallway wall. "What?" she whispered.

"Don't you remember? You asked—"

"Yes!"

Tali wouldn't want anything for her birthday. Tali wouldn't have a birthday.

"I was thinking about a choker, because everyone's wearing them now. You know, like lacy, or beaded? But that's too boring. She probably has five of them anyway. And then I saw this bracelet in the Goodwill store; I think they call it a charm bracelet? It has lots of dangly things that are supposed to symbolize stuff or remind you of stuff. So I thought maybe you could get a charm bracelet in one of the tourist places with charms of famous sights in the District, like the Washington Monument and the White House. So she could remember living here, and you."

NO, OF COURSE IT WASN'T BRENDA'S FAULT.

MORT HOVERED IN THE DOORWAY OF HER OFFICE: "I got an email from Scott, at the Senate committee. He thanked me…" Frowning, Mort scratched the back of one ear. "He thanked me for providing some witnesses for the committee's public hearing on drug prices next month. Do you know anything about witnesses?"

"Sure. Uh, don't you remember, in our report last winter about prescription drugs? We included some of my interviews with the seniors who travel to Canada to get their meds more cheaply. Those are the witnesses."

"But how did the committee learn about that report? I didn't think that was one of the reports we sent them."

Because I told Scott without exactly telling you. No, she couldn't confess that, too; she couldn't cope with one more crisis or one more confession in her life. Russ. DUI. Tali. Collarbone. Car. "Scott was looking for witnesses for the hearing, so he asked if we had any." It was almost true.

"I see. You should have listed it on our roster of congressional requests and projects, Miranda. I can't have everyone going off on ventures I don't know about."

Yes, she should have done that. And she should have tried to persuade him more openly. The Center was Mort's baby, as Jean had said.

Mort went on, "It sounds like it will be fine. Scott said he thinks the testimony will be very effective. But please update the roster." He nodded as he left her office.

RUSS EMAILED: "DO YOU WANT TO GO out on another date Saturday night?"

IF CONGRESS ACTUALLY PASSED LEGISLATION some day, maybe Mr. Zelniki wouldn't have to go to Toronto for his wife's refills every three months, and his cousins in South Bend wouldn't have to drive all the way to Windsor, Canada. The Andersons might be able to save the same one hundred and forty-four dollars right at their neighborhood Walgreens. Mr. Lauterbach wouldn't be forced to skip his own medications, in order for his wife to get the diabetes drugs she needed.

That was what Mr. Lauterbach did for his wife. He risked his health, so that she could stay alive.

They'd been married fifty-five years last June 22, he'd said.

The Andersons had seven grandchildren and two great-grandchildren, and Delia nagged Clement to quit eating so much greasy food because she wanted him to live long enough to play with those great-grandkids. The Laceys with their sweaters that almost matched, who finished each other's sentences and held hands like teenagers, they joked that their marriage was so old, it qualified for Social Security. The Lauterbachs had been high school sweethearts who got married the Sunday after graduation. That was what true love was, decade after decade: Dedication. Sharing. Shared taste in clothing. Taking care of each other.

And trust, Russ had said.

Her mother and Bill must have thought they'd had all that. For twenty-two years they'd stuck it out, learning to tolerate the other person's annoying mannerisms, Bill's clunky slowness, Judith's constant little awkward movements. Thinking, presumably, that their marriage would last forever.

If a husband discovered his wife had been arrested for kidnapping seven years earlier and had never told him—could a marriage survive fifty-five years after that beginning, no matter how many hours the couple spent visiting history museums together and running across the Arlington Bridge?

What if the wife also failed to tell him that she'd been arrested for DUI, four months before their wedding?

Could the wife even keep such a huge secret for fifty-five years? How many more supporting secrets would that require? Hiding her anxiety every time she went to court until the process was over. Staying calm when *Law & Order* ran a show about drunk driving. Explaining all the expenses that would be eating up her paycheck. Not to mention the lies about the broken collarbone and smashed Subaru. Ongoing, endless years of lies, big and small. It would be like walking down the aisle dragging two fifty-pound balls and chains behind her.

But if she told Russ the truth, that would be a three-hundred-fifty-pound ball and chain. Criminal record. Credit record. License suspended. Probation. Arrested. Again. How many secrets could a marriage survive? How many arrests could a marriage survive? Could a husband trust a wife who lied twice—but only twice? Or three lies, if Miranda counted the fact she'd gone to see his mother behind his back, but did that have to count as a lie, too?

UNLIKE THE REST OF THE BUS RIDERS, THE LACEYS came to Scott's office in person, because they were visiting their daughter, son-in-law, and brand-new granddaughter in Wheaton. Bernard Lacey wore a burgundy cardigan sweater over a plaid shirt, and he held his tan golf cap in his lap. Jane Lacey, seated between Bernard and Miranda, wore a purple sweater and exuded a combined scent of lilac and spearmint. She unlatched her pocketbook nearly every time her husband spoke, as though she was prepared to produce a document to support him.

"Would you be willing to come back here to Washington?" Scott asked them, writing rapidly in a notebook.

"To come back?"

"Yes. To testify in front of our committee, to tell the members what you've just told Ms. Isaacs and me."

"Oh." Jane and Bernard turned exactly simultaneously toward one another.

"Would we be speaking in, uh…"

"…in public?" Jane finished.

"In the newspapers?"

"Is that a problem?" Scott demanded.

"I'm not sure if we…" Bernard began.

"…would really want to do that."

"The reporters wouldn't quote every witness in their newspapers," Miranda said quickly. "They wouldn't have the space, for one thing. But the important thing is that the senators would be listening to you. They need to hear how high drug prices actually affect people, every day."

"Well, that's true."

"It certainly does affect us, every day."

"You would be doing a public service," Miranda added.

"So that's a yes," Scott said.

"You should wear those sweaters when you testify," Miranda told the Laceys. "It looks great, the way you're a matched pair."

Jane and Bernard glanced at each other's sweaters.

"She knitted them," Bernard declared, squeezing Jane's hand.

Jane blushed.

"Really?" Miranda leaned closer. The stitches marched, row after perfect row, like neat, long lines of Greek columns intertwined with braided vines of thick rope. "They're beautiful."

Jane pointed toward Miranda's sling. "You need to take care of that broken arm of yours, Miss Isaacs."

CHAPTER EIGHTEEN

THE CROWDS BEHIND MIRANDA PROPELLED HER out of the Metro car as soon as the doors slid open, like popcorn shooting out from a popper. They mobbed the station's small platform: grey-haired, pony-tailed, frizzy, bald, braided, bearded, earringged, tall, short, fat, thin, chattering, bobbing, wearing ski jackets and wearing T-shirts, carrying backpacks and carrying babies in slings and most of all carrying signs. "No War for Oil" "Impeach Bush" "Stop War/End Racism" "War Kills Peace" They smelled of coffee and fried eggs and too-strong, flowery perfume. Their voices echoed off the waffled grey walls as they flowed toward the turnstiles.

Hugging her left arm in its sling tight against her chest, Miranda used her right shoulder to lever some space between the two people in front of her. "Lily! Wait there!" she called out.

She drew her left shoulder closer against her torso as someone pushed past.

Just beyond a scrum of bodies and next to the escalator stood Lily, in a lemon-yellow down vest and red overalls, along with her three friends, whatever their names were. One was stick-thin with purple hair and a purple plaid shirt; one wore a blue knit cap over curly brown hair and carried a placard that read "Stop Bush's Stupid War," with a peace symbol in the O of "Stop"; the third, her hair tumbling around her shoulders in dreadlocks, had a dark-green jacket and a bright pink sign, "War Is Bad For Me and My Cat," that swayed dangerously close to a few heads.

"How many people do you think are here?" Lily was suddenly next to Miranda.

"In this Metro station? I don't know. A couple hundred?"

"They said there were a million people in Australia," offered a man nearby.

"In Rome, too."

"A million?"

"I wish I was in Rome."

"Do you think anyone will get arrested?" Lily asked.

A chant began, partway down the escalator: "Hey hey, ho ho, Bush's war has got to go!"

Outside the Metro station, the swarm absorbed Miranda, Lily, and the other three girls and moved them down Twelfth Street, past the hulking EPA building and its massive marble towers on their side of the block, and the towers and balcony and thick stone walls of the Old Post Office and IRS on the opposite side, marchers filling the street and its wide, pebbled sidewalks. From the direction of the Washington Monument, invisible two-and-a-half-long blocks away and around a corner, words spurted out from a sound system in broken, staticky sets, and people cheered.

A couple of helicopters hovered in the dull blue sky, one up near the Capitol, another near the Monument. The weathermen were predicting a blizzard, but it wasn't expected to start for another ten hours or so, long after the march would be over.

Lily's purple-haired friend disappeared.

Then the dreadlocked girl with the cat sign.

What—Alien abductions? The Rapture? Fainting?

No; both girls reappeared. They'd just bent down for a second, maybe to tie a shoelace.

At the corner of Constitution Avenue, even more people squeezed onto the sidewalk, from every direction, with kids, dogs, American flags, peace flags, wheelchairs, strollers, and more signs, until there was barely two inches between bodies and no one was moving. The orthopedist was right; Miranda shouldn't have come. It was going to be nearly impossible to protect her shoulder.

But how could she miss what might be the biggest mass action to take place in the United States since she was a little girl, and more important, the closest she might ever get to glimpsing what her parents' life had been like? All these people, cheering and chanting and marching together, believing—for that one moment of solidarity, regardless of what might happen later—

that their sheer numbers could stop a war.

Directly in front of Miranda and the four girls, a short line of people was linking arms and singing. Someone pushed her from behind, and Miranda's right shin banged into a concrete planter box. Through the static, the voice over the loudspeaker had gotten angrier.

"When are we going to do something?" Lily demanded.

"I can't hear what they're saying."

"I'm hungry. Can we go get hot dogs?"

There was louder applause; the angry speaker was finishing with a rising shout. Another one was introduced.

"My feet hurt," the girl with the purple hair muttered. "I need to move."

"Can you crouch down at all? Does that help?" suggested Miranda.

Lily nestled against Miranda's right side, and Miranda wrapped that arm around her.

"Tell me we're stopping the war by doing this," Lily grumbled.

"We're stopping the war."

"Come on. By standing here?"

"If enough people gather in enough protest marches, maybe. That's what Mom and my dad did, back in the Sixties."

"They did more than that."

"Sure; they organized the protests, for one thing. But most people back then, all they did is exactly what you and I are doing right now. Go to rallies. Write letters. When the numbers add up, the politicians notice."

"Bush won't." Lily shifted slightly away from Miranda. "He wants to go to war in Iraq no matter how many people die, because he thinks he can do it better than his daddy did."

"You're probably right," Miranda agreed, "but he also wants to get re-elected next year. I don't think he could ignore protests that were as widespread as they were against Vietnam."

"If we started to climb the White House fence and got arrested, that would really stop the war."

"I wouldn't try it, Lily. The jail cells probably smell of piss."

"I'm hungry," Lily's friend repeated.

At last the crowd was, almost imperceptibly, inching forward. A group in front chanted "The people/united/will never be defeated!" while a group to the left declared "This is what democracy looks like!" as the voice from the stage announced something.

"Cops!" one of Lily's friends shrieked.

Over at the intersection of Constitution and Fourteenth, a few policemen waited next to sawhorses, their legs planted far apart in firm Vs.

"They're going to beat us up!"

"Don't shout," Miranda whispered to Lily. Several marchers were frowning at them. "They're just blocking traffic. It's what police always do at protests."

"Not at the civil rights protests Mom went to. The cops beat up the marchers!"

"This is different. Everyone's got dogs and babies."

"Yeah. Look at that guy! He's juggling." The girl with the "Me and My Cat" sign pointed behind the five of them.

It was true: In a small circle of cleared space, a man in a light grey jacket was juggling three things that might have been metal bowling pins. Was there a political message in juggling? He kept the pins going in an oval-shaped loop.

"All we need is a lion-tamer and a trapeze—" As Miranda began to turn to Lily and her friends, someone ahead of her stopped abruptly. Miranda stumbled against that person; pain ripped through her shoulder; she flung her right arm around her left and clutched the arm and sling against her chest; the woman behind Miranda fell against her. They staggered. The woman slipped to her knees on the concrete. Miranda grabbed someone's arm and stayed upright.

"Are you okay?"

Miranda and a man who smelled of onions helped the woman stand up.

"Yeah, yeah. It's nothing."

Miranda looked back toward Lily and her three friends.

Who weren't there.

Not even tying shoelaces.

"LILY!"

There were people in navy-blue windbreakers and people in black down jackets, people with ponytails and with cascades of curls. There were people with babies in backpacks and people with dogs on leashes. There were people guzzling from water bottles and people holding hands. There were people with placards and people with cameras, and all of them kept pushing her forward.

"LILY!"

"One two three four, we don't want your daddy's war"

"The people/united/will never be defeated."

There was no one in a lemon-yellow down vest and no one with purple hair and not even a sign declaring "Stop Bush's Stupid War" with a peace symbol in the O of "Stop."

"LILEEEEE!!"

Shoving desperately with her right arm and shouting, Miranda got herself to the far edge of the crowd with enough free space to pull out her cell phone from the canvas bag on her right shoulder.

Hey. It's Lily. If you're friendly, leave a message!

"It's Miranda. I'm here, sort-of near where the juggler was. Where are you? Call me right away!"

Further in front of her, the marchers were heading up toward the Capitol, spilling onto Madison Drive and the pavement next to it and the Mall's winter-shriveled expanse of grass.

If you went with Lily, I'd feel a lot more reassured. She'd promised her mother: She would watch out for her sister.

But Miranda couldn't have been distracted more than a minute by the juggler and the stumbling. How could four teenage girls have disappeared into thin air so fast?

"This is what democracy looks like."

"LILY!"

The red-and-blue umbrella of a food cart waved limply at the base of the American History museum plaza, up ahead. Of course! The girls were hungry; they were buying hot dogs. Water. Ice cream. At the cart, there was a bald man, a heavy woman with a little boy… No Lily.

No phone message from Lily.

Maybe the girls had stopped into the museum for the bathroom. Miranda dashed past the food cart to the museum's walkway—*No running!* the orthopedist had said—She slowed to a fast walk, up the few marble steps, onto the broad plaza, and quickly to the security line. The guard poked around inside her canvas bag with a stick.

The bathroom on the first floor had six stalls, three sinks and two big mirrors. No Lily.

The bathroom on the second floor had four stalls, two sinks, two mirrors. No Lily.

The museum was vast and full of people and rooms with corners. Lily could be anywhere. Or not in the museum at all. She could be looking at Clara Barton's original ambulance, a small covered wagon with a red cross on the green frame. An antique hand-pumped fire engine. Would Lily want to wander through the exhibits? A giant locomotive made of metal and wood from 1831, resting on a section of an old bridge. No, none of this would interest Lily. She'd want colors and fabrics and clothing and designs that jumped out at her. Maybe she and her friends had gone to see the First Ladies' dresses, just like Ronit and Miranda had embarrassingly loved to—

First Ladies.

The White House.

No.

If we started to climb the White House fence and got arrested, that would really stop the war.

Lily might just try it.

Miranda ran out the exit from the museum on the Constitution Avenue side.

Hey. It's Lily. If you're friendly, leave a message!

"Lily, it's Miranda again. CALL ME! Where ARE you?" Down Constitution, onto Fifteenth Street. Past the grassy Ellipse, vending trucks lined up along the curb as though preparing to march in their own parade; plenty of hot dogs and Cokes for Lily's friends if they were here. Past the tall Old Ebbitt Grill and the stern columns of the Treasury building. The chants of the marchers were a faint rumble, blocks away. Left onto Pennsylvania Avenue.

Of course there were no ambulances or fire trucks with red lights blazing in the road in front of the White House.

Secret Service agents in black uniforms were positioned at half a dozen spots along the White House's spiked fence, as usual. One agent held a leashed dog. Tourists took pictures posed against the famous backdrop. A pair of Jehovah's Witnesses stood silently next to a display of pamphlets, and a man with a grey beard held up a long sign declaring "No War for Oil." Was he AWOL from the protest, too?

Miranda bent over for a moment, holding her sling steady, to gulp deep lungfuls of air.

Lily wouldn't actually have tried to scale the fence. She was impulsive and overdramatic, but she wasn't foolhardy. Still, she might have stood close to it and shouted, figuring that she was accomplishing something.

As Miranda approached the nearest guard, his shoulders tightened.

"Hello." She had to smile pleasantly, like a tourist. "Have you seen four teenage girls, maybe within the past half-hour? I'm looking for my sister."

"Were they in a tour group?"

"No, no. They just—you know teenagers, they just had this spur-of-the-moment inspiration. To see the White House. One of them has purple hair"—Miranda fake-groaned—"I'm sure you'd remember her."

"No, ma'am. I haven't seen four young ladies by themselves."

Then where was Lily?

Back at the march? Calmly flowing along with the crowd, picking up her friend's fallen sign? Fighting with a policeman and getting arrested? At a different museum, other than American History? Shopping? She and her friends could have wandered up Twelfth Street to Hecht's, seeking out odd items to mix and match. A red-plaid flannel shirt. A green T-shirt with Mickey Mouse on it. A flowered tablecloth.

It was impossible to search the entire city of Washington DC. If Miranda searched one section of Hecht's, Lily could be in another. If she went into one cute little bakery, Lily could be in a different one a block away. *If you went with Lily, I'd feel a lot more reassured.*

Would Lily have abandoned the protest and gone home? Maybe it was that simple. The four girls had gotten bored and hungry, or they wanted to call their other friends and they needed to recharge their cell phones, so they'd headed back to Silver Spring. They weren't four years old, after all. They knew how to ride the Metro and how to phone 911; they knew not to get into strangers' cars. They had intended to go to the march with or without Miranda, and they were perfectly capable of returning to their own houses without her. They were simply too irresponsible to tell her what they were doing.

Her mother answered the phone.

"Mom? Is Lily there?"

"What do you mean? Isn't she with you—" Her mother didn't wait for

Miranda to reply. "YOU LOST LILY?"

"I just tried her cell."

"Try it again!" her mother snapped.

It was nearly four o'clock. More and more people were straggling away from the Capitol, where the march was supposed to end; letting their signs drag, wandering in clusters of two and four and five across the Mall. What could Lily and her friends have been doing for five hours that hadn't shown up on the radars of the police or the hospital emergency rooms that Miranda and her mother had called so far? The museums would close soon, and before long the blizzard would start. The Metro would be mobbed. The buses would be stalled until the streets were plowed.

Miranda's shoulder throbbed, and feet ached from walking, walking, walking. Her stomach was barebones-empty. She needed one of those hot dogs that Lily's friend had wanted.

"This Land Is Your Land" rang out on her cell phone.

But it was only her mother again. "Call Georgetown Hospital. I'm calling Sibley as soon as we hang up."

"Okay."

"And call me on the home phone—Don't call my cell! I'm keeping that line clear for Lily and hospitals."

"Okay."

"Fuck, Miranda, you don't know the other girls' names?"

"I'm sorry. It was kind of—"

"We should be calling their families. We're responsible for those girls."

"Maybe they're on Lily's school lists?"

"How the hell do you lose four teenagers?"

"Mom, they're sixteen years old. They know how to get around the District."

"Not in those crowds!"

"They can find the Metro—"

"You said you'd keep an eye on them."

Up ahead on the Mall, cheerful music blared from the old carousel.

The carousel where Tali always rode a bright yellow horse with a red saddle and brown mane and tail.

"You sit on the grey horse next to me, Aunt Randa, and Eema, *you sit on the*

white horse or the blue horse. And I bring the picnic."

"Okay. Where are we going on the horses?"

"To visit Sabba and Savta in Israel."

Lily wasn't dead! For heaven's sake, just because she wasn't answering her phone did not mean she was dead like Tali.

But Lily was definitely missing, and Miranda had definitely promised her mother to keep track of her.

How could she constantly mess up like this? Drunk driving. Losing Lily. Kidnapping Tali, if she wanted to go back that far in her past. Where was her brain? Her mother had counted on her, exactly because she couldn't rely on Lily. Even if Lily had taken the Metro to the District half a dozen times before, it was different today with all the crowds, and she could well have gotten confused or even lost her phone, especially if her friends were even less familiar with the streets than she was. Miranda was supposed to have been watching for all of that.

The sky was flint-grey now, ready for snow. Was there any place in all of Washington DC left to search? Maybe Lily was at the Metro station, heading home. Maybe Miranda should just ride the Red Line, from end to end. Maybe Lily was in the basement of the American History museum, and the cell phone reception there was lousy. No, no, and no. Stupid stupid stupid.

"Mom? Have you heard anything?"

"Fuck it, Miranda, it's my fault, not yours. I've been planting these romantic fantasies in Lily's mind ever since she was born. Mommy and Jerry storming the halls of Columbia. Mommy and Jerry ending the war in Vietnam. Mommy and Jerry getting arrested at the Democratic Convention. Every Great Cause, every protest, every picket sign and every time anyone sang 'We Shall Overcome,' filling her brain with the nobility of mass marches. What did I think I was doing? Of course Lily wanted to go to this march and stop the war in Iraq singlehandedly, just like Mommy and Jerry."

What?

"This is what fucking happens, Miranda. They don't accomplish anything. A crazy kid goes to an anti-war demonstration and gets in trouble and gets arrested and so what? It's all bullshit. Does the Vietnam War end? Not till years later. Do the police stop beating up people? Hell no. No one pays attention, the politicians do what they were always going to do, and now God the fuck knows where Lily is."

"You think it's wrong for Lily or me to join a protest march?"

"I have to call hospitals. I don't have time to talk."

All of a sudden, her mother had completely changed her story about her own history of political protests, just because Lily had temporarily gone missing at one? All of a sudden, her mother and father were wrong to have risked arrest protesting the unjust war in Vietnam and the horrible conditions of farmworkers in the California grape fields and police brutality at the Democratic convention in Chicago? What did her mother wish she and Jerry had done instead, stayed home sewing needlepoint pillows? No, that didn't make any sense. She couldn't mean what she was saying. She was just frantic at this moment and blaming anything within sight. Lily had gotten lost at an anti-war demonstration, therefore all demonstrations were bad.

Miranda's phone played "This Land Is Your Land" again, and it was her mother again, and this time she was laughing and crying simultaneously. "She's okay. She's okay. She's at the ER. It's just a—She broke her toe."

THE WHITE-LIT PEDIATRIC EMERGENCY room smelled weakly of rubbing alcohol. A toddler screamed somewhere; a metal cart clacked again and again as it rolled along the floor. Doorless cubicles encircled the central nurses' station, each containing a single bed, a short steel cabinet, and a plain wooden chair. In one of the cubicles, Lily sat at the edge of the bed, her feet resting on a metal stool, talking with her friend in the blue knit cap.

"Mom!" Lily shouted, wriggling awkwardly but quickly on the bed, toward the front of the cubicle. "Miranda!"

Their mother sank onto the bed and wrapped Lily in a tight hug.

"You found me! We got so lost, and my foot hurt like shit. And we missed the end of the march!" The two smallest toes of Lily's left foot were taped together with thick white surgical tape.

"Sweetie, are you okay? What happened?"

"I think Lily banged into something," the friend replied. "Like, one of those big concrete road blocks?"

"And it really, really hurt," Lily added.

"She couldn't walk."

"We had to, like, limp to the hospital. It took forever."

"Yeah, because we didn't know where the hospital was."

"And we never got to the Capitol or any of the speeches!"

Their mother hugged Lily again, shaking a little, while Miranda squeezed the lower part of Lily's arm that wasn't being hugged. "Mom and I tried to call you."

"Oh, shit. I forgot. My phone ran out of charge."

The tip of Lily's baby toe, where it peeked out from the tape, looked swollen and red, although none of the toes seemed to be bent at any weird angles. Their mother touched one finger to the tape. "What did the doctor say?" she asked. "What are we supposed to do for follow-up care?"

"I'm not sure. But I have to wear this boot-thing when I walk." She pointed to a chunky black contraption on the floor that looked like a weird combination of a ski boot and a Teva sandal. "And I can't go to school for a couple of days."

"Okay. Don't worry." Their mother hugged Lily yet another time. "As long as it's nothing serious, that's what matters. I'll ask the doctor myself."

Miranda was still ridiculously holding Lily's arm. She let go. It was only a broken toe. Broken toes could be fixed, just like broken collarbones. Lily wasn't crying; she was probably happy to miss school. Her friends could sign the surgical tape on her foot and draw funny pictures with markers. "How did you get lost?" she demanded. Her voice was too harsh; she took a breath, then continued more slowly and softly. "We were all there, all of us together, watching the juggler. What happened?"

"The juggler?"

"At the Mall. You and your friends pointed him out. Remember?" How could Lily forget? That was how it all had started. "With the big metal bowling pins."

"Yeah, right."

"Tanya was hungry," the friend interjected. "She really wanted a hot dog."

"Yeah. And she said she'd seen one of those food trucks on Constitution, right behind us. We just thought it would take a minute. We'd come straight back and you'd be there, Miranda, where we left you. No one was moving anyway."

"But there wasn't a truck where Tanya said."

"So we tried to go back to you, but I didn't know exactly where you were. With all the people everywhere."

"And then Tanya and Cass went home. They said they were bored."

"Can you believe it? Bored at, like, the biggest protest march we've ever seen in our lives?" Lily reached for Miranda's hand. "I should've found a way to phone you, I'm really sorry. You, too, Mom. It was just like, so hard to even move around. And we were trying to listen for what was happening, and decide whether we could keep going with the march—And we didn't think it would all take so long with the hospital. I'm sorry."

"Have you talked to my parents?" the friend asked. "I guess I should call them. Can I use your phone?"

Miranda handed hers to the girl.

"Did you see the march on TV?" Lily added. "Do you think Bush saw it, too?"

"I hope he did," their mother replied.

"Do we still count as four of the million people who were there? Even if we left early?"

"Yes. You count. You absolutely count." Their mother laughed.

"It was worth breaking my toe!"

"I don't know about—"

"Yes it was! Wouldn't you do it, too?"

"My activist daughters who are going to stop the war in Iraq and change the world. I'm proud of you." Their mother pointed at the friend's placard, propped upside-down against the steel cabinet. "Great sign. 'Stop Bush's Stupid War.' We always had such serious signs back in my day. We could've used more fun."

"Next time I'm going to make a sign," Lily declared.

"Maybe next time, I'll march with you." Their mother laughed again. "Just don't break any more bones. You two girls, with your collarbone and your toe, I swear."

"I'll go find a doctor," Miranda offered quickly.

The clacking cart had disappeared. All three nurses at the central station were on phone calls, and the toddler was still screaming.

Now their mother thought that Miranda and Lily were wonderful activist daughters after all? Now she was back to her old self; now it was good to be out in the streets demonstrating against the government and maybe even worth breaking a toe for the greater cause, and their mother was proud of her own history again? In fact, the next time there was a big protest, she might even join it? Forget what she'd said before, on the phone?

Through the window behind the nurses' station, snow hadn't started falling yet. Maybe the predictions about the blizzard would be as unreliable as everything else.

CHAPTER NINETEEN

SUNDAY:

With her unslinged hand, Miranda dragged a stainless steel chair from the kitchen into her mother's bedroom and closed the door. She twisted her hair into a long banana curl at the side of her neck, let go, and twisted it again. And again and again and again. For twenty minutes, or thirty minutes, however long she talked, her voice kept going, and she twisted her hair while her mother stretched out on top of the queen-size bed, propped against the headboard, the pages of *The Washington Post* she'd been reading fanned out next to her on the dark-green duvet, silently flexing and unflexing her toes in their red socks.

"I can't go on play-acting and keeping a dozen secrets from you, Mom. I'm sorry, I know you have too many of your own problems to cope with. And I'm not asking you to take on my baggage. But how can I keep on every day la-de-da 'oh the bathtub plumbing in our apartment'? 'oh, I only hit a parked car, I'm fine'? I can't juggle it all anymore. I'm tired of making up stories and hiding things from you. I'm sorry. I'm sorry about not telling you the truth. I'm sorry about losing Lily. I'm sorry about what I did to the car. I don't blame you if you've lost all trust in me."

For too long, after Miranda stopped talking, her mother lay in the wide bed, flexing and unflexing her toes. "Shit. Wow," she finally said. Pulling herself upright, she wriggled around until she was sitting at the side of the bed, facing Miranda, her feet flat on the floor. "It's hard to believe any of this. I don't know where to begin. Shit. Is your collarbone healing okay? The way the doctor expects?"

"Yeah."

"All right. At least you weren't hurt any worse than that. But kidnapping?

Drunk driving? Miranda, that's serious."

"I know."

"You don't even like to drink. I don't understand how you could be so dumb, Miranda. Certifiably dumb." Her mother crossed her arms while she exhaled. "You could have killed someone driving drunk, do you realize that? Manslaughter! As it is, your driving record's going to be shit for a long time, even if you don't go to jail. It's going to shadow you for years. And I need to talk to our insurance agent. You had no right to keep that from me, Miranda; it's Bill's and my policy. It's in our names. If the insurance company drops us—"

"I'll pay the premiums. You can take me off the policy."

"And the repair bill? And the other car's repair bill? And my rental car? And the legal fines? Where are you going to get the money for all that?"

"I'll—I'll get a cash advance."

"Do you have a lawyer?"

Across the hall, there was a bang as Lily's bedroom door opened, followed by the dull, off-kilter thudding of her footsteps, limping, in the direction of the bathroom. Heavy thud. Light thud.

Her mother looked toward the thuds, while she rubbed the flannel of her shirtsleeves against her biceps. "And Ronit's daughter…"

Aunt Randa, guess what? Eema got *a squirting thing that makes roses for icings, so we're going to make cupcakes with yellow roses.*

"It's awful," her mother said.

"Yeah."

"I know you loved that little girl."

"Yeah."

"For Ronit… Like a knife stabbing her in the heart, every day. From the minute she wakes up and remembers."

The rigid way Ronit had held onto the spoon while she talked in the coffee bar. The flatness of her voice. How she walked out the minute she'd said what she wanted to say, without waiting for one of the American hugs she hated anyway.

"How old was her daughter?"

"Five or six. Depending on when, exactly…"

"They were living in Pittsburgh?"

"Yeah."

"That's not far away from here. A few hundred miles, I think."

"I don't know."

Did Tali still have soft, brown curly hair back then, when she fell off the monkey bars? Had she lost her front teeth? Did she still insist on wearing only yellow clothing?

"For a mother… If you or Lily or Ted—"

"Don't go there, Mom."

Miranda reached out, and for a while they sat with Miranda's hand wrapped over her mother's, until her mother let go and shifted in her seat. "But I don't understand how you could—Kidnapping, Miranda? How could you possibly agree to something like that?"

I can't do this anymore, Miranda. I need my family.

"I didn't see it that way. I just wanted to help Ronit."

"But you must have realized that you were breaking—"

"Okay, Mom. Can you stop now? I've gotten enough of that lecturing from Russ."

"And you should! How do you think—"

"Stop!"

Her mother bit down on her lower lip and turned her head aside, as though her whole body had to participate in throttling further criticisms of Miranda.

When had the room gotten so cold? Just ten minutes ago she'd been comfortable enough in her cotton jersey. Now goose bumps were scampering up and down her arms, and even the stupid sling was shivering. She hugged her left arm tighter, until the shaking halted.

"I'm glad you told me all of this," her mother said, when she finally turned back.

"Really? Glad to know how much I've messed up?"

"Glad to know what's actually going on with you."

Her mother was looking at the floor. Maybe there were no more words to say. *I love you anyway.* Miranda had told her mother nearly everything. She didn't need to get into all the stuff about Russ.

"I know you wanted to be a supportive friend to Ronit," her mother abruptly continued. "When a friend asks for help, sometimes a person doesn't stop to think. They just act. And then it turns out that the end result has repercussions they never envisioned."

"Is it a little like being a good mother, the instinct to help a friend?"

Her mother frowned. "How?"

"Like the instinct to protect your child? You see the tiger coming, and you throw yourself in front of the child. Like that. You do whatever your friend asks. You do whatever it takes to protect your child, without thinking." Or like kidnapping the child to get her away from a terrible father, but she ends up at a playground in Pittsburgh.

"Not exactly." Her mother bunched her shirttails together.

"I don't understand why Ronit didn't tell me about Tali. All these years."

"It was probably too painful for her to talk about. Didn't she say something like that at the coffee bar? How she couldn't even put the words on paper."

"But I might have helped her. Like you said, she was only a few hundred miles away. I could have flown to Pittsburgh, and I don't know, cried with her. Listened to her. That would have been a lot better way to be a friend, instead of sending stupid birthday presents to Israel every year."

"Neither of us can really understand how painful it is for Ronit or what might help her ease her pain."

"Now she's shut the door forever."

"People keep secrets for all kinds of reasons, Miranda. To avoid hurting other people. To protect their jobs. Who knows why? After all, you didn't tell Russ about the kidnapping." Her mother was speaking faster and faster as she went on. "Sure, some people do it to cheat or get away with crimes, but I don't think that's the majority of cases. Sometimes I think people just get so used to their public version of the truth, if they've been doing it for a long time, that they forget the secret they've been hiding."

From the hallway came Lily's limping thuds, returning to her bedroom. Grace Slick's voice pounded out for a few beats from her open doorway, before the door slammed: *And if you go chasing rabbits…*

"Can I ask a trivial question about the kidnapping a moment?" Her mother added. "I'm confused about something. How did Ronit's husband find out that she was planning to take their little girl to Israel?"

"Oh, Tim bragged about that. Afterwards, I mean." Now her mother was dropping the criticism entirely? She was done talking about drunk driving, kidnapping, and everything else Miranda had done wrong, and now it was just a daughter and mother sharing an anecdote, like normal people? The real test would be if she let Miranda borrow the car again. "There was a long stretch of time, seven or eight months, that Ronit and Tim had to stay in Washington after we were arrested, to finish up all the arrangements with the divorce and whatever, and that's when he told Ronit how he arranged everything, and she told me." Miranda twisted her hair into a banana curl again. "He said he'd kept a copy of the mailbox key when he moved out from their apartment in Takoma Park, while Ronit and Tali were still living there. So he used to read Ronit's mail all the time, and he saw the airplane tickets when they were mailed to her. And then he had a friend from business school who worked in the Maryland attorney general's office, so he asked that guy, I guess, to use his influence to send police to the airport."

"He stole her mail? That's a federal crime."

"Well, he's a horrible person. He claimed he put everything back in the mailbox, so she never had any idea that he did it."

"But how did he open the envelopes without Ronit realizing it? Was it the way they do it in bad detective novels, steaming open an envelope?"

"Actually, in his case, it was freezing."

"What?"

Miranda stretched out her legs, until her feet almost hit her mother's. "Apparently, if you leave an envelope in the freezer for a few hours, it kind-of pops open. Then you re-glue it. It's supposed to be a lot easier than steaming."

"Shit. I never want to mail a letter again, if it's that easy to break into the envelope."

"I'm sure the FBI was reading your and Dad's mail, back in the Sixties, right?"

Next to the closet, the radiator finally hissed into action, though it would still take minutes before little waves of lukewarm heat would start to melt into her skin.

"Oh…" Her mother hiked her glasses higher on her nose. "We weren't that important for the FBI to pay that much attention to us."

"Why do you belittle yourself? You two were helping to organize major demonstrations. At Columbia and Chicago, and with the farmworkers. When I think about everything you two and Grandpa did, and all I do is talk to old people about their prescriptions."

"And that's important work. You could change health care policy in the U.S."

"I'm a drop in the ocean, Mom."

"Now you're the one belittling yourself. Just because you were an idiot and got arrested for drunk driving, that doesn't mean everything you do is idiotic." Her mother was actually smiling a little now.

"Even losing my sister?"

"That was careless, not idiotic."

"Okay, Mrs. Social Worker. I'm a part-time careless idiot."

"You're not so bad. As long as you never drink and drive again."

"Never! I'm never drinking again."

"All right."

"Or driving."

"You don't have to overdo it. Just drive safely. And no more kidnapping."

Her mother was getting up, so Miranda stood, too, and they awkwardly hugged one-armed, Miranda leaning her right side toward her mother while angling her left side away. "I'm angry with you because I love you. You know that, right?" her mother asked, from inside the hug. "I'm terrified that you could have killed yourself driving, or gone to jail for years for kidnapping."

"I know. I love you, too. And I deserve the yelling-at, anyway."

"So when are you moving back in with Russ?"

Miranda pulled away. "You're kicking me out?"

"Don't be so melodramatic. I love having you here, but this isn't your real world. Haven't you both had enough time to think things over? You have a married life to build now."

Not yet.

I'm not telling you everything, Mom.

I haven't told Russ about the DUI, for starters.

MONDAY:

"Miranda? Can I come in?" Her mother was already pressing Ted's bedroom door shut behind her. "We need to talk."

"Did something happen?"

What else could have gone wrong now? Russ had called, and her mother had mentioned the drunk driving. The Steinmanns had called to complain about Miranda's rude visit. The court had sent a notice that she was to report to jail immediately.

"I haven't been completely honest with you, either," her mother said.

Now it was her mother on a chair, and Miranda on the bed.

"What you said yesterday, about secrets, and mothers protecting their kids… You and Ronit. You and Russ. And Lily, all fired up to get arrested or break every bone in her body to fight against the Iraq war, just like Jerry and I did; so she thinks. And you, too. You're doing such good work in your job, but you feel like a failure if you're not on the front lines stopping a war. All of that. It's been, well, prompting me to do some thinking. I should have…" Her mother curled all ten fingers together into a single, intertwined fist. "We need to talk about your father."

CHAPTER TWENTY
JUDITH
C. 1968-1970

AS SOON AS THEY EMERGED FROM THE SUBWAY at Broadway and 116th Street, there was a fence of tall iron spikes topped with small golden crowns. A massive stone-and-brick building stood at each end, and two towering statues of figures in Roman robes guarded the front. Behind the fence, three walkways stretched into the invisible distance, separated by strips of greenery and lines of well-spaced trees. And from somewhere deep beyond all that came a tinny voice and the faint echo of cheering.

"…LISTEN, PENTAGON …university RACISM…"

"It's Columbia University!" Marilyn screamed.

"Where's the tear gas?" Kim demanded.

"What does tear gas smell like?" Judith asked.

"If we didn't have to go to dumb high school today," Kim added, "we could've been here already."

"Let's go find where they took over the buildings!" Holding aloft the three tulips she'd carried around the whole day at school, Marilyn strode through the nearest opening in the fence and onto a path of diagonal red bricks, with Kim immediately behind. Judith ran past a cluster of people in jeans to catch up.

Crowds spilled from the three walkways into a rectangular plaza. The tinny voice was coming from a guy holding a bullhorn and standing on a tiered marble staircase at the left side of the plaza, which led up to a big domed building with a row of Greek columns.

"…no longer be part of the military-industrial-UNIVERSITY complex…"

The sky looked like any April afternoon sky, as blue as Cinderella's dress in the Disney cartoon, dotted with a few cotton balls of clouds. The air smelled like cigarettes and cut grass and pizza, but nothing that could be a poisonous gas.

Clearly, the people who crowded into the plaza weren't high school students. They wore jeans and sandals, the boys had beards and hair to their shoulders, and they blew perfect smoke rings from their cigarettes. Some of them applauded the speaker with the bullhorn whenever he paused; some shouted: "Ho, Ho, Ho Chi Minh/NLF is gonna win!" Some drifted away. Some talked and laughed with each other, not even tossing a glance at the speaker on the staircase. Some of them—the ones not in jeans—were probably reporters and photographers from the newspapers, aiming their cameras or scribbling in small notebooks that definitely were not big, fat, high school three-ring binders. A few of the people in jeans were thrusting mimeographed white flyers at everybody going past them.

"So what do we do now?" Judith asked. It was almost four-thirty. She was supposed to be home for dinner at six, and it would take more than an hour to get back to Brooklyn.

"Just think," Kim pointed out. "Someday we'll tell out grandchildren we were here. When students took over their own college! When the revolution began!"

"Is anyone thirsty?"

"Should we ask somebody what's happening next?"

From her book bag, Marilyn pulled out a small six-pack of Fig Newtons and passed it around. The three girls sat down on a stone bench at the bottom of the tiered stairs. The tulips had fallen to the pavement near Judith's shoes.

"President Kirk, we know you can see us!" the speaker with the bullhorn shouted.

Part of the crowd cheered.

"We know you can hear us!"

Cheers.

"We're here on your front steps!"

"Louder!"

"I'm leaving," Marilyn announced. "I've got a lot of homework."

"Homework!" Kim retorted. "We're seniors, we don't have to do homework."

"Nothing's happening here anyway. Are you guys coming with me?"

"What's supposed to happen?"

"I don't know. It just said on the news that students took over the principal's office or something. When else are we ever going to see students kicking out their own principal?"

Someone stopped in front of them, holding out a sheaf of white papers. He had shaggy dark hair like the Beatles and brown eyes, and the arm proffering the papers was skinny. "We're going to try to keep the sit-in going all night again in President Kirk's office, so we need supporters here on the plaza. Can you come?" His voice was deep and cheerful.

Stay all night here, on the Columbia campus? On the ground? As though Judith didn't have to be at her parents' kitchen in Brooklyn for dinner by six o'clock or at Erasmus Hall High School at eight o'clock the next morning; as though she, too, was a college student who could cut class as easily as she flicked her cigarette lighter.

The guy had already pivoted away, waving his flyers at someone else.

"Is there something I can do now?" Judith asked quickly, jumping off the bench.

"Judith? Where are you going?" Marilyn called.

The guy turned back toward her and smiled. The smile beamed across his face and widened his mouth, revealing teeth as perfectly white as a dentist's advertisement but a little crooked. Up close, his eyes were a rich, almost liquid brown. Almost like chocolate icing. "Sure. You want to give out some of these flyers?"

She could stand next to him, working side by side with a college student with beautiful brown eyes.

But she had to get home for dinner.

"And we're not leaving until you kick out the Pentagon warmongering researchers! And we're not leaving until you give Morningside Park back to the people who really live here!" the speaker on the steps continued.

"Do you need any supplies? Like, I could bring—um, blankets?" Her cheeks were broiling; they probably looked as red as blood. What a completely idiotic thing to say. "For the sit-in?"

However, the guy didn't groan or guffaw. In fact, he nodded. "That would probably be cool, but none of the people running the sit-in are here. I don't know what they want to do, except for these flyers. If you want to help?" He immediately swirled toward the path where two boys in denim jackets were approaching, his skinny arm outstretched, waving a clutch of white paper.

What would she tell her grandchildren? *I listened to part of a speech at the big Columbia University protest in 1968 and then I went home for dinner.*

"I can help you with flyers. I just need to make a phone call."

MARILYN AND KIM HOVERED NEXT TO HER, at the phone booth on Broadway.

"Why are you and your friends at Columbia University?" Mom demanded from her end of the line, in Brooklyn. "You're going to City College next year. That's what you said you wanted."

"No, I'm just here for—um—an hour? I just—with Marilyn and Kim."

"Hi!" Marilyn and Kim shouted toward the receiver.

"Don't you have homework?"

"Listen, Mom, I'll only be home an hour late. Maybe."

"But what are you doing at Columbia University?"

Judith glanced at Marilyn, then Kim. They shook their heads rapidly. But what did they expect her to say to her mother? "It's, um, a kind of— thing. Like a protest?"

"What?"

"I've got to go. I'll be home by seven."

"Why did you tell her about the protest?" Kim shouted at her, after she hung up. "She'll freak out when she sees the news on TV and realizes you were there."

"What else could I do? Make up a story?"

STICKING OUT HER ARM, HOLDING SLIPPERY pieces of paper, trying not to drop any of them, trying to get people's attention, all the people rushing by and none of them wanting to be bothered, the papers wrinkling and slipping to the ground and that would be littering and she had to bend to pick them up, and her arms were aching from sticking rod-straight out in the air, and her fingers were black from the ink that smeared as she sweated.

JOIN US!! the flyers said at the top, in large, handwritten letters. *SIT-*

IN. HAMILTON HALL! Join the hundreds of students, faculty, news media, rock bands. Plus …. a captive Dean Coleman. Don't miss it!

There was a moment when the guy with the chocolate eyes and shaggy dark hair said, "I'm Jerry," and she said, "I'm Judith."

The plaza was emptying; the bullhorn had been quiet for a long time. Judith and Jerry headed to the lines of trees and the three pathways near the subway entrance, offering flyers to everyone they passed. Who refused, or limply took one, glanced, shed it. And finally, she had to ask Jerry: "Doesn't your arm hurt?"

"Like shit." He laughed. "You want to take a break?" He pointed toward the iron-spiked fence in front of them.

As they meandered south on Broadway, away from Columbia, Jerry walked with his hands shoved into the rear pockets of his jeans so that his elbows stuck out like chicken wings. He looked back and forth constantly, his head tilted slightly upward, at the huge brown and red and white apartment buildings around them. At 110th Street, he paused by a newsstand. "Are you thirsty? I'm getting a Coke."

"Oh…" Was he offering to buy one for her? Did that make this a date? Boys paid for everything on dates, but maybe that was only the rule for high school. Maybe college guys who were protesting against the war in Vietnam didn't follow ordinary dating rules.

"We can share," he added.

No high school boy would have been that sensitive, that mature.

Jerry held the can out to her, before even taking a sip himself. The aluminum was freezing. He kept his fingers on his half, and they didn't touch hers.

They ambled back uptown toward Columbia, but Jerry stopped just outside the fence and seated himself on the low curb, his legs extended into the street. Judith sat, too, and tried to tug her white miniskirt so that it covered more of her thighs. Only inches away, while they both watched the traffic in front of them, Jerry's face was as close and exposed as an actor's on a huge movie screen. No acne. No shaving nicks. No sickly smell of aftershave like Daddy. His faded denim jacket had a hole just below the right shoulder. His hair was silky-looking, and it had traces of lighter brown mingled with the dark. One loose eyelash rested on his cheek—one delicate little crescent of brown-black thread.

She set the Coke on the asphalt by her feet. "Do you go to Columbia?"

"Nah. I used to go to Cooper Union."

"Used to?"

On the street in front of them, cars of all colors and sizes rushed, honked, and swerved around each other.

"When I was a kid," Jerry said, in his deep voice, "I wanted to be an astronaut, I guess like every red-blooded American boy in the early Sixties, especially in Iowa, where I lived. Sputnik. John Glenn. JFK promising we'd go to the moon within the decade, right? And one of the college majors they recommended for astronauts was engineering, and Cooper Union is one of the best engineering schools in the country. Plus, it's free. So, being as my mom doesn't have much money, it seemed like my path was all carved out for me, when I got accepted. But last fall, after I got to campus, Judith? The whole world had changed. How could I sit in a classroom and study hyperbolic orbits and escape velocity, while the world was exploding around me?" Hunching forward, he reached across Judith's legs for the Coke. Brisk footsteps passed on the brick walkway behind them. "People are dying in Vietnam; American soldiers are killing innocent people, dropping napalm on kids, mothers, grandmothers, whole villages, every day, for no reason, have you seen what it does to people's bodies? It burns their skin off! Like strips of a goddam onion. Can you even think what that must be like? And LBJ is flat-out lying to us. Goes on TV and lies about body counts and 'light at the end of the tunnel' and all his bullshit, there's no light for the folks in Vietnam, is there? And then Martin Luther King gets murdered. The greatest man in America. This is a guy who was willing to go to jail, who went straight up to the racist cops and sheriffs and bus drivers and he didn't yell, he was always peaceful, right? Who was just trying to get the same rights for people with black skin as for you and me. Basic human rights. After they murdered him, I had to get out of the ivory tower and do something. And we are: We're making a revolution, Judith. We've already forced LBJ to give up running for a second term, and whoever gets elected president next will have to end the war. Don't you feel it? Just look around—" He aimed the Coke can back toward the tiered staircase, out of view far behind them

—"Look at what we did here today. The Columbia administration knows that they can't go on helping the Pentagon with their secret weapons research anymore."

"So…?" This guy, Jerry, was a college dropout. That was what her parents would say. *Dropout* was not a compliment for them. "What are you going to do instead of college?"

"I haven't figured that out yet. Okay if I finish the Coke?"

"Yeah. Go ahead."

He leaned back his head and took a long slurp before cramming the empty can between his feet. "For now, I'm going to stay here at Columbia and work on the sit-in, right? For a few days, anyway. And then I might go to California to help the grape workers with their strike. Have you heard about that at all? It's unbelievable, they get paid almost nothing, less than a dollar an hour, and they work twelve hours a day, fifteen hours, without even any water to drink—and it's over ninety degrees in the summer—and did you know they have to piss in the fields, because the damn owners of the big farms won't give them portable toilets? They've got this amazing leader named Cesar Chavez. Don't buy grapes, by the way."

No grapes? But grapes were healthy. Or at least healthier than Hostess Twinkies and potato chips.

"But you know what I really want to do? I want to get a motorcycle and just go around the whole country, from one protest to another. Or—don't laugh at me, okay?" Picking up the Coke can again, he rotated it against his other palm. "I'm thinking of working on Bobby Kennedy's campaign."

"Why would I laugh? He's against the war, isn't he?" No, but Daddy said that Bobby Kennedy was a spoiled rich kid, like all the Kennedys, who thought women would vote for him just because of his good looks.

Jerry was nodding rapidly. "Right. And he's the only politician who really gets what black people are going through. What the poor are going through. What King was trying to do. I think he really would change the System, even though, I know, he's a millionaire who's part of the System. But he's different. I think with Bobby, maybe we have a shot at making genuine change through electoral politics." He glanced at the Coke can, then rolled it into the street.

"So you're going to campaign for him?"

"I don't know. I'm trying to decide where I can do the most good. There's so much shit going on, right? It's hard to know where to start."

"How about—are you going to go back to school?"

"Sure. Eventually."

"You could transfer to City College!" Oh God, that was so dumb; she sounded like she was chasing him. Boys were supposed to do the chasing. She bent forward to nudge her book bag closer to her feet. Maybe that would look casual.

"Do you go to City College? Cool. What're you majoring in?"

"Well, actually, I'll be starting there in the fall. I'm just, um, still in high school. Now." God, what was she saying? That was the end of any future Cokes for sure; Jerry would never want to talk to a baby from high school again. Why hadn't she pretended she was a freshman at City College? He would've believed her.

But in fact, he put out his hand, and when she stared at it, he laughed and drew her hand off of her lap and shook it. Once. "You're only in high school, and you're already so aware of what's happening in the world. How Columbia is participating in the Pentagon war machine. That's great, Judith. Now you've got to go to your high school and inspire everyone."

His hand was dry. Strong.

Then he let go, resting back on his elbows. With his lower lip thrust out, he spit a sort of "psst" noise. "And all of my plans will be bullshit if I get a letter from my friendly neighborhood draft board."

Oh no. That was the big one. That was the knife that the boys in Judith's class would be facing in two months, it would march in front of them at graduation, gleaming sharp and deadly, or at best they might delay it by going to college like her brothers: Vietnam.

"What are you—what are you going to do? How do you—?" she stammered.

"They don't give deferments for organizing against the war that they want you to fight in."

"How about deferments for helping the grape pickers strike?"

Jerry burst out laughing.

She'd managed to come up with a joke that made him laugh!

"Too bad I can't get deferred that way," he went on, still smiling for a moment. "My strategy for now is to keep moving around enough that I'm always ahead of the draft board. Then they can never find me to send me the notice."

"Does that work? Legally?"

"I'm not sure. So my back-up plan is to re-enroll in Cooper Union and get my student deferment reinstated. Or should I apply to City College?" He was grinning; teasing.

"That's okay if you want to stay at Cooper Union. They might have better deferments." She could tease, too.

"And my next back-up to the back-up—or, I think it's my first back-up—anyway, I registered in Iowa. They say that in the farm states and the South—outside the big cities, right?—so many guys actually volunteer, that the draft boards fill their quotas and never need to drag in anyone else."

"Oh. I didn't realize that."

"I don't know if it's true. So—" a shrug. "My fourth plan is Canada. Like everyone else."

The blue sky, peeking over the top floors of the apartment towers, was fading into white and pale yellow, the first washed-out hints of sunset. That meant, probably, that it was after six o'clock. Which meant that Judith had better get onto the subway that very instant, even though she couldn't possibly be home by seven. Mom and Daddy were going to be furious.

What if she cut all her classes tomorrow? What if she took the subway back here to Columbia by herself to help with the sit-in? But what if she was caught? Anyway, what would she do, wandering around Columbia?

Nevertheless, just what had happened today would be a story to tell her grandchildren, like Kim had said. *Did you ever hear of that famous labor organizer Jerry Something, who helped the grape workers in California get toilets? I shared a Coke with him once.*

A heart couldn't break after a single can of Coke.

"I'd better go," Judith declared. It was supposed to be a perky tone of voice. It needed to be perkier. "It's a long trip home to Brooklyn, which is where I live. And I've got homework to do. I still have to get that high-school diploma."

What did she want Jerry to say in response? *Don't go!* And then what?

"Are you taking the subway to Brooklyn?" he asked. "You want to walk to 110th with me, instead of getting on here? I have to head that way anyway."

"You're not going back to the plaza? To the protest?"

"Nah. Giving out flyers is bullshit."

Once again, they strolled southward on Broadway, Jerry's hands in his pockets. They kept far enough apart that even her book bag didn't touch him.

"Judith," he stated, like a pronouncement, as he sidestepped a woman with a dog. Judith sidestepped after him, taking an extra skip-step to keep up with him. "That's such a formal name. You're never Judy?"

"Every Judith is Judy."

Jerry laughed. A second time she'd made him laugh! He licked the tip of his index finger and held it up in the air toward her. *Score one for you.*

"Also, I'm named for my grandfather," she added. "Jacob. So I kind of want to honor him by using the full name." That was such a weak explanation. "He was a protester, in a way."

"Oh yeah?" They were at 111th already, only a block from good bye at the subway station. Halting, Jerry relaxed against a light pole. "Tell me about your grandfather Jacob the protester."

"I mean, I don't know if you'd exactly call him a protester. He probably wasn't. He was just a poor orphan in Russia, and he wanted to marry my grandmother, who was wealthy—that's what my father says —and that was a scandal. Her family kind of exiled him to America. But he saved up money for ten years, until he had enough to send her a boat ticket, and she waited for him all that time. So she came to New York and married him after all. So that's why."

"Ah! Your grandfather Jacob fought against the capitalist class system."

"Oh. I never thought of it that way." Grandpa Jacob: He could have been giving out flyers at Columbia, maybe. "And my dad, Seymour, was an actual protester. He used to be a union organizer."

Pushing himself off the light pole, Jerry tugged something out of his rear pocket. It was one of the white flyers. From a different pocket, he took a pen. He set the flyer against his thigh while he quickly wrote on it, then ripped the paper lengthwise in two and held out the smaller piece to

Judith. "This is my friend's phone number. I'm crashing in his studio for a few days. What's your number?"

He wrote it down on the piece of the paper that he'd kept, while she stuttered.

Then his lips were on her lips.

They pressed. A little bit wet. Smooth, not chapped or anything. Tasting of, well, Coke.

The kiss ended quickly.

He waved and headed across Broadway, west toward wherever he was going.

CHAPTER TWENTY-ONE
JUDITH
C. 1968-1970

EVERYBODY LOOKED LIKE HIM.

There were hundreds of people jammed into the Columbia plaza on Saturday, even more than earlier in the week. They all looked twenty years old, and they were all wearing jeans; a lot of them were skinny, and most of the guys had shaggy dark hair.

They sat on the grass and the stone benches and the side staircases leading to the rest of the campus or just milled around. They smoked cigarettes and ground out the butts on the brick pavement, but they weren't as excited as they'd been the day Judith had first come; they didn't laugh as much or chat casually. A few people tried to start singing. Heated voices sparked out of little clusters. On the tiered staircase where the speaker with the bullhorn had been—the staircase up to Low Memorial Library, according to the newspapers—there were now four organized rings of people: an outer ring of protesters wearing red armbands, scruffy denim shirts, and black T-shirts, at the bottom of the stairs; then a ring of adults with tweed jackets and white armbands; a ring of short-haired guys wearing blue armbands, some of them in jackets and ties, some of them with bulging muscles showing through their shirts; and the last ring, the one closest to the building, a solid semicircle of police, arms crossed on their chests, belts heavy with guns and clubs.

Kim glanced right and left. "Should we ask some guys for a cigarette?"

"Why? Did you start smoking?"

"To look at their faces, dodo. To see if we see your boyfriend."

"He's not my boyfriend."

"Give me a back rub?" Marilyn asked Kim, and Kim pressed her fingers against Marilyn's shoulders and down an inch.

"This is dumb," Judith muttered. "Let's go."

"Don't you want to find him?"

"No! I just want to get out of here."

He might not be on the campus at all. Or even in New York City. He could be in California, peeing on the grapes with the farmworkers.

"If he wanted to see me, he could've called, like a normal date."

"That's high school rules," Kim scoffed. "In college, girls can call boys."

"I don't know the college rules yet."

SHE TOOK HER FINALS. SHE GRADUATED. Police had broken up the sit-in at Columbia a week after it began, dragging protesters out of the president's office and beating them with billy clubs. Students also staged major demonstrations in France and other countries. She worked at Uncle Morris's stationery store three days a week.

"HEY, JUDITH-NOT-JUDY," THE DEEP, CHEERFUL voice said through the pink Princess phone in Mom and Daddy's bedroom. "It's Jerry. From Columbia back in April."

As though she knew a million Jerrys.

"Hi." At least her voice didn't crack. "How are you? Were you arrested at Columbia? When the police beat up everyone?" *Pigs;* she was supposed to call them pigs, not police.

"Nah, they mainly arrested the leaders and the guys who'd been staying in President Kirk's office. I wasn't there. How about you? Are you okay?"

If only she could've answered: *In fact, I spent the night in jail.* Something dramatic…"No. I wasn't there, either."

"Listen, I'm sorry I haven't called before now. I've been—well, I guess I could give you a lot of excuses. Busy and traveling and all that, but the fact is—Shit. I've been in California, working on Bobby Kennedy's campaign. Going door to door trying to get people to vote for him. I'm an asshole, right?"

"I don't think you're an asshole."

"Thanks," and it was as if his voice was smiling over the phone, loosening up for an instant, "but I sure feel like one."

"At least you were doing something, trying to get him elected. That's more than most people do."

"And where did that end up? He's dead, too."

"Were you with him? When he, um. Got shot."

"At the Ambassador Hotel? Nah, but I was watching it on TV with a lot of other volunteers from the campaign, and that was pretty tough, Judith. To be surrounded by people who'd poured their time into the cause, for weeks and weeks, who believed in him like I did, and at first he won the primary, right? And then, just when we're cheering and celebrating and starting to think that he was honestly going to do it, to be nominated— Then to see the faces on the TV change, all of a sudden. Like a light going off—Hey, I'm sorry for dumping all this on you. But listen, I'm in New York again. You want to get some pizza?"

She told her parents that she was meeting some friends for pizza in Manhattan. *Some friends. One friend.* It was close enough to being true.

"What friends?" Mom asked.

"From school. You don't really know them. We're going to talk about college."

"You have to go all the way to Manhattan for pizza?"

"I'll be going to school in Manhattan next year anyway."

The pizzeria was in Greenwich Village, where all the hippies lived and took drugs. But it looked like any pizza restaurant in Brooklyn, with a huge four-shelf steel oven in the back, a row of cracked red-vinyl booths along each side of the room, a large plate-glass front window, and posters of the Coliseum and the Leaning Tower of Pisa on one wall. From the counter, Jerry carried two flimsy paper plates with a slice of pizza on each and grease leaking through the bottoms, one plate balanced on top of a can of Coke. Sitting down across from Judith, he popped the pull-top on the Coke and twirled the metal ring around his index finger.

His tangled brown hair was still shaggy, maybe a little longer since two months ago; his eyes were still as rich as chocolate. His teeth were still dentist-white and a little crooked. Tufts of dark hair pushed out over the round neckline of his black T-shirt, and long skeins of muscle pulsed down his skinny arms as he brought his slice of pizza toward his mouth, then back to the paper plate. He drew his lips together to suck some grease off of his fingertips.

"I guess you've graduated from high school by now?"

"It must seem silly to you, to talk about high school."

"No." Somehow, he managed to frown and smile at the same time, furrowing his brow while his mouth tilted up at the edges. "Just the opposite. You cared enough about the shit that was happening at Columbia, the weapons research they've been doing and the racist gym they wanted to build, to come all the way from Brooklyn and support the sit-in. Shit, when I was in high school, like I told you, the only thing I thought about was going to the Moon."

She needed to drink some of the Coke, because her throat was way, way too dry to form words.

When she finished, he removed her straw, set the pop-top opening directly against his lips, and took a long swallow. Then he replaced her straw.

So if she drank straight from the can now, would she taste the tomato and cheese from his lips?

"I'm going to Chicago soon," he announced. "Why don't you come with me?"

Chicago, Jerry said, would be the next big action. The Democrats would be holding their presidential convention in Chicago at the end of August, and the political bosses had already decided they'd nominate the war criminal Humphrey, who was LBJ's vice president, now that Bobby was killed, so people were organizing the biggest demonstration ever —MOBE, SDS, the Yippies, Women Strike for Peace, everyone, thousands of people, twenty thousand maybe, they were going to show up right there at the convention, in front of all those politicians and all the TV cameras, to make it clear that this was not a true democratic choice. That there was no real difference between Humphrey and Nixon, because they both were part of the Establishment that got the U.S. into Vietnam. The cops in Chicago were notoriously violent, worse than the ones at Columbia. So it would be heavy. But the organizers were trying to keep it all peaceful, although the Yippies were being kind of ridiculous, they were going to nominate a pig for president, but that was hardly violent, right? And MOBE was seeking to go the full legal route, official permits and everything. Some people wanted to confront the cops with music and flowers, which was probably bullshit symbolism, flowers versus guns. But hey, why not? "Your grandfather and your father would be proud of you, if you come."

"That's not fair!" Giggling, she wagged her finger at him. It was as if the Coke was full of booze, not caffeine, getting her drunk on carbonated bubbles and Jerry's words. "You can't use my grandfather and my father to make your point."

"Okay. Just come anyway."

"How? I don't have any money."

"I have a motorcycle now. You can ride for free, and we'll camp out."

"You're nuts."

He had to know that she couldn't. To even picture telling Mom and Daddy: *I want to ride on the back of a motorcycle to Chicago with a twenty-year-old guy I only met once and we'll probably get arrested.*

But what would it be like, to ride with Jerry on his motorcycle? She'd have to wrap her arms around his waist, to hold on. To rest her hands on the thin cotton of his T-shirt. To feel his stomach muscles underneath the shirt tense and relax as he breathed. To nestle her cheek against the nape of his neck, where it was probably soft.

And what would it be like, to be with Jerry and twenty thousand fellow protesters, marching and holding up banners under the very noses of President Johnson and Vice-President Humphrey? Side by side with Jerry, fighting for justice, like Daddy always said.

"Come on. We'll change the world." He smiled at her as he stroked a circle along the edge of the Coke can where his mouth had just touched.

"I'll think about it." That was true. She would undoubtedly think about it a lot.

"Okay. Here's an easier question: Have you seen *2001* yet? Do you want to see it this weekend?"

A movie. They were dating.

He walked her to the subway, his hands shoved into his rear pockets the same way as in April when they'd left the rally at Columbia. At the subway entrance, he paused. With his hands on her shoulder blades, he pulled her a little closer to him, and he stared at her, and his lips lingered for a long time. He did taste of tomato and cheese.

PROBABLY HE'D SPEND A WEEK AT THE Democratic convention in Chicago, Jerry said, as they wandered, swinging hands, in and out of the cross-cutting streets in the West Village after the movie, and then he would decide where to head next. For sure there would be plenty of action around the presidential election, but he still wanted to return to the grape workers, too. Their conditions were worse than he could describe, slaving in the summer heat without drinking water and toilets, breathing in pesticides every day. Their kids, scrawny and staring. The shacks where they lived, with dirt floors and cardboard boxes for furniture. The boycott was growing. "Come with me."

"I can't."

"Why not?"

"You know I can't."

"We'll camp on the beach in Big Sur."

"Big Sur?"

"It's in California. It's beautiful."

"I can't."

"Even if we get arrested at the convention, you'll be out before school starts."

"Oh that's certainly tempting. If we get *arrested*?"

He only laughed and swung her hand up toward a red door in front of them. "Here."

They were facing a three-story, red-brick row house on a side street lined with similar two- and three-story, red-brick row houses, all of them silent behind their tall bare windows.

"Where?" she asked.

"It's my friend Larry's cousin's apartment, where I've been staying. But he's away this week. The cousin." Jerry tugged a key out of his jeans' front pocket.

Into a man's apartment?

She wasn't even eighteen yet.

She couldn't keep saying no.

She would just—just for half an hour. Just for a cup of coffee. A glass of water.

"I have to be home by eleven," she whispered.

"You will be," he whispered back. "I can take you on the bike."

It didn't mean anything if she kept her clothes on.

He wrapped one arm around her, while they sat on edge of the purple suede couch in the living room of his friend's cousin's apartment, and then his lips were on her neck. Gently. Like fluttering butterfly wings.

"Jerry—"

"Are you on the Pill?"

"NO!"

"It's okay. I've got condoms."

"No—that's not—"

He withdrew his face from her neck. But he didn't stand up and leave. Instead, he stroked her hair, symmetrically, starting on both sides at the top of her head and sliding down to her cheeks. "You're a virgin." He said it; he didn't ask.

She nodded. God, she was a dumb little girl. No, she was a good girl.

"Whatever you want, Judith. It's cool. I would be honored to be your first time."

Oh God.

Could there be a more beautiful way to do it, for a girl's first time? Could any man be more sensitive?

"Granddaughter of Jacob the anti-capitalist protester," he added.

That wasn't fair.

But they were in a revolution. They were throwing out the old, like Kim said, like Daddy said, throwing out the rules that had led to Vietnam and the horrible conditions of the grape workers. Only uptight bourgeois girls waited until they were married.

THEY SAW EACH OTHER ONCE MORE BEFORE HE LEFT for Chicago, when they rode his secondhand Harley to Coney Island. She brought Daddy's camera and took a picture of him, his hair blowing a little, propped on the bike, laughing.

THE SKY IN THE PICTURE POSTCARD WAS A Milky Way swirl

of purple, red, and gold. Below the swirl, a turquoise ocean crashed into jagged black cliffs. *Hi from Big Sur, California!* was printed diagonally across the photo in red.

The postmark was September 25. Next to Judith's address, Jerry had written: "Spent almost a month working for the grape boycott. Talked to a lot of customers at Safeway grocery stores in Oakland. They're usually nice, but it's so damn hard to get people to care. Driving down the coast now. Beautiful, right? Peace and love, Jerry."

The handwriting was in black ink and classic script with all the proper loops and curves for the capital T, D, and O. Even Mom, with her teacher's training and her practice filling in crossword boxes, didn't form letters that perfectly.

Not that Mom, luckily, had seen the card. Of all days, thank goodness, thank goodness, Mom had asked Judith to bring in the mail that day.

The postcard didn't say where Jerry was going next, or if he was coming back to New York, or when, let alone whether he planned to re-enroll at Cooper Union. "Down the coast." The Pacific Ocean coast, presumably. How far down? To Mexico? Could he escape the draft in Mexico?

Did "peace and love" mean "love"? Or only, "peace, love, good vibes, and rock and roll"?

HE WAS IN NEW YORK TWO WEEKS AFTER HIS postcard arrived. He'd never actually made it to Chicago for the Democratic Convention, and now it was way too late to re-apply to Cooper Union. He got a part-time job driving a DeCamp Lines bus from New Jersey to the Port Authority Terminal in Manhattan and back and forth, four hours per day Monday through Friday, the morning rush-hour shift. He had to wear a shirt with DeCamp stitched on the left-side pocket, but they let him have his own boots and keep his hair long if he tied it in a ponytail, he said. He rented a narrow room in a falling-apart clapboard rooming house in Union City, with a hotplate and a shared bathroom and a twin-size bed on a black metal frame. His arm muscles under his DeCamp shirt hardened from gripping the extra-large steering wheel that was nearly horizontal instead of vertical and maneuvering the huge, heavy bus onto the on-ramp for the Lincoln Tunnel. He smelled a little bit of gasoline and the coffee he was always drinking.

Sometimes, after his shift, he met Judith at City College between classes. Sometimes she cut class to see him. Sometimes they got pizza or took slow walks around Manhattan. Rarely, they saw a movie. And sometimes they went to his apartment in Union City for the whole day, as long as she was home in Brooklyn by six for dinner. (Or eight or nine or as late as eleven o'clock on the weekends, if she told Mom and Daddy that she was going to a lecture at school, or studying with friends, or seeing a movie with friends, or the subways were messed up, or any of the explanations she could invent; after all, she was eighteen years old and in college now, and she shouldn't be obliged to account to her mother and father for how she spent every minute of her day.) A lot of evenings, Jerry went to meetings. They were strategizing about how to protest the war, then how to protest Nixon's election. He couldn't make plans or dates with Judith, because plans implied that the world was predictable, unchanging, going on as it had always been going, and that was the last thing they wanted, wasn't it? The whole point was that the world had to change. Opportunities and inspiration were not predictable. So people had to grab whatever moments they could. They grabbed love, because who could predict when love would come around again? "Is that really what you want, Judith? A life you can write down on a calendar?"

Marilyn went with her to Planned Parenthood, where they gave her a prescription for birth control pills, no questions asked.

"Can I call you Jude?" Jerry said. It was from the new Beatles song. "Would Grandpa Jacob mind if you had a nickname?" And he sang the first few bars to her, as they snuggled on a bench by Wingate Hall, softly and off-key. *Hey Jude, don't let me down/ You have found her, now go and get her*

Then in April he went to Washington DC, to protest the war directly in front of Nixon's window, he said.

SOCIOLOGY CLASS. WORLD HISTORY CLASS. Sit on the bench by Wingate, eat an apple. Watch the thermometer inch up to 70 degrees. European lit class. Was any of that going to change the world, as Jerry was doing?

Sure, and how much had he actually changed the world, with all of his sit-ins and grape boycotts? Nixon got elected. The U.S. was still fighting in Vietnam.

But Jerry didn't give up. He was protesting right in front of the White House!

Was he still there? Holding a sign in front of the White House for two entire weeks?

And if not, where was he?

Wake up in her parents' apartment. Ride the bus to Uncle Morris's store. Hit the cash register keys. Take the money. Flirt with the guy from the deli next door who always hiccupped. No, don't bother. Go home to her parents' apartment.

Go to a rally against the war. Bring a handkerchief soaked in vinegar in case there was tear gas. Shout. Chant. Less than two hundred people. None of them Jerry. No tear gas.

She quit taking the Pill. Jerry was maybe in Washington DC or maybe God knew where, and he might return God knew when, or maybe never, and the Pill was full of dangerous chemicals and it made her disgustingly bloated.

She switched her major from history to social work. If she couldn't change the world, she could at least change a few people's lives, one by one.

She quit using eyeliner, even though without the black outlining, her eyes would appear boring and watery brown. But eyeliner was part of the old bourgeois definition that said girls had to do fake things to make their bodies "beautiful." Like plastic surgery. High heels. Padded bras. They should rely on their natural beauty to shine through instead.

The spring semester ended. She worked in Uncle Morris's store full-time.

She went to the movies with groups of kids from school. She saw "Midnight Cowboy" twice and "Easy Rider."

Two men walked on the Moon.

No postcards from Jerry.

Hit the cash register keys. Take the money. Give back money. Put the package of paper in a paper bag.

`THE WARMTH IN HIS VOICE WAS SO STRONG, HE COULD have been right next to her in Mom and Daddy's bedroom, not on a telephone somewhere miles away from the Princess phone. She could have kissed the phone cord all the way up and back.

Her legs shook, and she sat down on the bed. "Where are you? Are you still in Washington DC?"

"Nah. A much more boring place. I'm in Iowa."

"Iowa?"

"At my mother's house."

"Is it a farm?"

His laugh danced over the phone line. "You know, I think she's the only person in this damn state who's not growing corn. Nah, she's a waitress in Des Moines. Somebody's gotta feed the business lobbyists and the government big shots who live in this city, right?"

It was a tiny house far outside the center of the city, just one bedroom, a kitchen, and a living room. He slept in his sleeping bag on the living room floor, but that was okay. His parents had moved to Iowa after World War Two because his father wanted to get out of Minneapolis, then his father couldn't find a job, and then he left when Jerry was a baby. Now his mother, Malka, worked two shifts as often as she could get the hours. But the good part was that she got to take home a lot of leftovers whenever she worked the closing shift, like extra bread if there was too much for making bread pudding. She had a lot of medical bills to pay off from surgery a few years ago, when she had breast cancer.

Three minutes, the operator cut in.

"Shit, I've got to hang up. This is on my mom's phone bill. But I want to hear about you. How's Brooklyn? Are you taking any classes that're teaching you anything?"

He would be coming East in a couple of days. There was going to be a big demonstration in October—a different kind of protest, a moratorium against the war, to stop the country from conducting business as usual. "I'll call you when I get to New York."

They could live together, in his little room in Union City, or wherever he found a place. With her job at Uncle Morris's store, and if he could resume his old job at DeCamp, they could pay the rent, buy food, and organize protest rallies together. (Though they'd probably have to become vegetarian. Meat was too expensive.) If he got back in time, they could go to the concert upstate that everyone was talking about in Woodstock.

Not that she actually suggested any of that to him. Living together. Being vegetarian. Making plans.

Not that she could ever say to Mom and Daddy: *I'm living in sin and having sex with my boyfriend, who's a college dropout and drives a bus.*

"WELL, ACTUALLY, JUDE," JERRY SAID, "I'VE been arrested. Can you, uh, bail me out?"

In her parents' bedroom, Judith pressed the pink telephone receiver tight against her ear. "Arrested?"

"I know I'm asking a lot of you, to call like this." Even on the phone from a police station, his voice still was—dammit!—warm and sexy. "I was arrested during the moratorium this morning. Um, so can you come to the Manhattan Criminal Courthouse? Near City Hall?"

Manhattan Courthouse. City Hall. Did New York have a city hall? There was a pencil in the drawer of her mother's night table, but the only piece of paper was the newspaper page with the crossword puzzle. Judith tore off a corner and tried to write "Manhattan Courthouse" until she ran out of room after "Cour."

"I don't know how much the bail will be or when exactly I'll be arraigned, but it's supposed to be within twenty-four hours of when I was arrested, which would be around noon, I think, tomorrow. So it would be good if you could get to the courthouse, um, maybe, tonight? And, uh, if you know a lawyer? Basically, well, if I don't make bail pretty fast after the arraignment, they'd probably send me to the Tombs."

"What?"

She had to grab the receiver, to press it back against her ear.

She had to shut the bedroom door, before Mom heard her, out in the kitchen.

"Jude?"

He was in a police station somewhere, maybe he was handcuffed, maybe he'd been beaten up; he would go to jail if she didn't help. How could she argue with him? But it didn't make any sense. "Jerry, I don't understand. How could you get arrested? It was a nonviolent moratorium. I was there with some friends from my class. We were just walking. There were school kids."

"Well, yeah. Um. Mostly. Listen, I probably shouldn't talk about this on the phone here, right? The police phone? Um... But if you could?"

Find a lawyer? Find money for bail? Sit around a courthouse all night with criminals? Keep him out of the Tombs?

"I don't know who else to ask," he said quietly.

Everyone had heard the horror stories about the Tombs jail. Old, dark, filthy. Lice-ridden, flea-ridden, walls smeared with shit, floors flooded with sewage, inmates constantly punched and knifed. Six men in cells built for two; drug dealing, suicides, gangs, and guys like Jerry would be prime targets. Everyone would hate him, the guards and the other inmates alike. Draft dodger. Hippie. Long-haired hippie faggot draft dodger.

"How much would you—How much would bail be?"

"I don't know. Maybe a few hundred? Less than a thousand, I'm pretty sure. It depends on the judge. And on the charges."

"Could your family help?"

"How could my mom get here from Iowa in time? And my dad disappeared years ago. I told you that. And I don't really know anyone besides you in New York. A few guys at the bus company, just to say hi. The guys in the Movement, yeah, but two of them were arrested, too, actually."

There was a scraping sound from Jerry's end, and some dulled voices.

"I don't think you need the whole amount of the bail in cash. I don't know, really. I'll find out more at the arraignment, I guess. I'll offer my bike as collateral, but I don't think it's worth much." The more he talked, the faster his sentences flowed. "You know you'll get your money back. It's just to guarantee that I'll show up for the next court hearing, and then they give you back your money."

To spend all night and half the next day in a courtroom in downtown Manhattan. Missing her classes. And find a lawyer. And bring a few hundred dollars. Even if she wiped out her bank account, with her earnings from Uncle Morris's store, that was less than a hundred dollars, and it was supposed to go for books and subway fare and school supplies and clothing. Marilyn would be in the same boat. Kim? She never had money. They didn't know any lawyers.

There was only one place to ask.

And they wouldn't have a few hundred extra dollars lying around.

"Jude? Are you really angry?"

"Sorry. Um, sorry. I'll see what I can—I don't..."

"I don't know what to say. Thank you. You're the most incredible person. I'll explain more when I see you."

"Okay."

"I won't skip out on you, Jude."

His voice could just melt down her neck.

"I'll make it up to you. Good night, sweetheart. Thank you. Thank you."

So, Mom and Daddy, I have to go out after dinner because I need to sit around a courthouse in Manhattan all night and tomorrow morning. And I also need a few hundred dollars. It's for my boyfriend the dropout who's been arrested and oh yeah, we've been having sex.

Daddy, it's for my boyfriend, and he got unfairly arrested, Daddy, because he was protesting the Vietnam War!

Yes, Jerry was fighting injustice, but how the hell did he manage to get arrested in a nationwide nonviolent protest? Millions of people all over the country had marched peacefully against the war. Even Mayor Lindsay lowered the flags to half-mast in solidarity; cars drove around the streets with their headlights on to show support, everyone made the V-for-peace sign, everyone was laughing and in a good mood, and Jerry managed to do something dumb. What did he do? Hit a cop? Smash a police car? Goddam him. All right. She couldn't leave him in a filthy, crowded, shit-smeared, lice-ridden jail with drug addicts and criminals who hated draft dodgers. She'd get the bail money somehow. She'd, yes, she'd ask Mom and Daddy. She'd tell them—she'd tell them as little as possible, without completely lying. *He's just a friend. He's a guy I've been dating.* She would bail Jerry out of the Tombs. But that was IT, goddammit! No more pizza. No more movies. They were finished. He thought he could come and go as he pleased, show up, kiss her, zoom off to California, zoom off to Washington, come back, ask her for hundreds of dollars—And if it wasn't this arrest, then the next time he showed up in New York maybe he'd be drafted, and then he'd be running off to Canada—No, he was wrong, life could be planned, and there was nothing so terrible about trying to plan a little for the future.

Jerry could make his revolution without her from now on.

CHAPTER TWENTY-TWO
JUDITH
C. 1968-1970

MOM SCOWLED AT THE *NEW YORK POST* CROSSWORD puzzle, spread flat on the yellow Formica table in front of her. Suddenly, smiling with pursed lips, she filled in a long series of squares using her sharp pencil.

"When will Daddy be home?"

"Five-thirty, I suppose, like always. Maybe six."

Damn, why couldn't Daddy get off work earlier? Why couldn't he be retired?

"He might stop at Uncle Irv's," Mom added, rapidly printing some more letters, "to watch the end of the World Series game, if it's still going on."

"Why?"

"The Mets are playing."

Damn double damn, the Mets had better win. And fast. "Can I help with anything? With dinner?"

"No. It's all set."

Whiffs of brisket, fat, and onion drifted from the battered tin pots on the stove. Three white dinner plates, three forks, three knives, and three glasses were laid out on the Formica table, along with the salt-and-pepper shakers shaped like little chefs, salt in a white toque, pepper in black. Taking one piece in each hand, Judith began gliding the shakers to and fro so that they bumped and retreated, bumped and retreated. Then she switched to making swirls.

Mom erased a few squares.

Judith let go of the shakers and reached for her history textbook. The War of 1812. Another pointless war: The Americans keep trying to invade Canada. The British burn Washington DC. The peace treaty leaves everything the way it was when the war began. Someday high school history books would write about Vietnam. *I once dated a guy who helped end the Vietnam War.* Her chair squealed on the linoleum floor as she kicked it back from the table. "I'll make a salad."

"Why? We have string beans."

What else was there to do? She straightened the forks and knives next to the plates. The TV news wouldn't be on yet. Maybe Walter Cronkite would talk about people who were arrested at the antiwar moratorium.

"You're very nervous tonight, Judith."

"I'm fine."

Was that supposed to be the beginning of the kind of Big Mother-Daughter Talk they'd never had before? *How are your grades? Are you pregnant?*

Walking to the stove, Mom stirred the two pots, and the kitchen was abruptly engulfed in steam. And then, thank God, keys jangled at the front door. "Helluva game, did you hear?" Daddy laughed. "Swoboda made an unbelievable catch, saved the damn game."

Thank God again. The Mets must have won.

"So you heard there was that big protest today? Against the war," Judith began, as they sat down and Daddy dunked a forkful of egg noodles into the brisket juice on his plate.

"Did you go? Did she tell us she was going, Bessie? Good for you, Yudeleh." He turned to Judith. "How many people were there?"

"Well, the thing is…"

Daddy slurped while he chewed.

"So, one of my friends, he's really active in all these protests. Like for the grape workers in California? With Cesar Chavez? So, well, it's really a bummer. He got arrested…"

Frowning, Daddy aimed his fork toward a hunk of meat. "I thought they said on the radio it was peaceful."

"The thing is, he might have to go to jail."

"This isn't your *meshuggeneh* friend Kim, is it?"

"No, no, it's, um, someone else. And he needs someone to go to the courthouse in Manhattan right away with a few hundred dollars for bail."

"So?"

Mom was chewing. Daddy was now ripping apart a small roll.

If only they could read her mind and answer Yes, without being asked.

"So—could I borrow…?"

"Borrow?" And then Daddy did read her mind, and he slammed the rest of his roll onto his plate. "You're asking for how many hundred bucks, for what? Some *schnorrer*?"

"He's protesting the Vietnam War, Daddy!"

"I can protest the war without paying hundreds of dollars."

"But they'll beat him up at the Tombs!"

"Why is this worth hundreds of dollars?"

"It'll be less than a thousand dollars."

"Why should I help some schmuck get out of jail?"

"If you want to protest the war," Mom added quietly, "you can help your brother instead of a stranger."

The brisket still smelled of onions and gravy-roasted fat. The thin aluminum chair legs still wobbled on the linoleum. "What do you mean, help my brother? Which brother?"

Mom pushed away her plate, although several chunks of brisket remained. "They ended the draft deferments for graduate school students, starting this semester. David could be drafted."

"Oh shit."

"Watch your language!"

They both stood, Mom and Daddy, and Mom carried their two plates to the sink and turned on the water, and Daddy went over to the refrigerator and then to the window and then back to the table.

Forget about Jerry. What was he, to Judith? They had to save David. How could money protect David from being drafted if he'd lost the grad-student deferment? Well, maybe Mom and Daddy were saving to send him to Canada. Maybe it was for lawyer's fees. Maybe the draft board could be bribed. Whatever they planned, David was her brother, and Jerry was just, like Mom said, a stranger.

"Why do you care whether this boy goes to jail, Judith?" Of all people, it was Mom, not Daddy, who had taken a chair and moved it closer to Judith. Her dark brown hair, still free of grey, was brushed into waves around her face. Her apron had a pattern of little blue teapots and frying plans.

"Well, because…" Because why? Because he had long hair and he'd get beaten up in jail, or worse. Because she could circle her fingertip among the dark hairs that peeked out from the top of his T-shirt. Because he truly, passionately wanted to stop the Vietnam War and help the farm workers and do more good things to make the world better. Because when he kissed her on her neck, or behind her ear, or on her shoulder, or on her breast, or on the inside of her thigh, her body exploded.

"He's your boyfriend?" Mom's voice was even-keeled.

"NO! No…"

"I can't imagine you'd ask for money unless he means something to you."

Suddenly Daddy was looming over her. "Have you even been going to your classes at all? All those nights you say you're studying late—"

"Seymour, calm—"

"All of a sudden this Mr. Protester you never mentioned before, now you want hundreds of dollars for him. Who is he? Why does he ask you for money? You think I'll like him just because he's against the war?"

"No!"

"You think I'll pay his bail like that, I have hundreds of extra bucks lying around, why not? Why don't I give out money to every schmuck who says he's against the war?"

Why didn't they get out of her face? They were blocking all the air, and making her eyes wet, and nothing she said would be the right thing, so forget the money, forget going to the courthouse. She held up her hands, palms out; if they would just go away from her.

But Jerry could get killed in the Tombs.

"He's fighting the war, Daddy," she whispered, gulping. "He has no one else to ask."

I'm never going to see him again.

She was panting. Her heart and lungs were heaving, as though she was running away from a galloping, ravenous lion. "They hate war resisters in the jails. The cops. The guards. All of them. The pigs." Her vocal cords, somehow, dragged the words up from somewhere.

She ought to stop. Shut up. Mom and Daddy would never give her the money. They had to save David. And they had to pay Michael's grad-school tuition next year, and they had to help Jonathan and Adele with the new baby. She didn't want their money; she didn't care about Jerry. She would probably never see him again anyway. As soon as he was out of jail, he'd be zooming off to California. Canada. Iowa. She couldn't spend all night hanging around a courthouse. She had homework to do. She should leave the table. But her cheeks, dammit, were wet.

What was a jail cell like? Was it actually covered with shit? Would Jerry have to sleep on a bare, hard bunk? Would they cut his hair off? What did the prisoners at the Tombs wear? They didn't—oh shit. Handcuffs? And those feet things? Ankle irons? Chains?

Goddam Jerry goddam him goddam him.

"You're paying it back." Daddy's voice was slow and tired, as if it was coming from the far end of the apartment. "If I do this. You're paying me back, from your paycheck from your uncle's store." Then the voice was louder, immediately in front of her face again, his thick grey mustache almost brushing her nose. "And so is this Mr. Protester. You tell him that. Every cent of it, he's repaying me; even if he skips town and forfeits his bail, he's repaying me. With interest!" He straightened up heavily. "I'll call Morris and Irv. They might have some cash from their stores. And one of us can go to the courthouse. You're not going to that place at night, Judith."

"Are you still dating that boy?" Mom asked.

"No." She wasn't. She was never going to see him again, once she got him out of jail.

Daddy lumbered over to the yellow phone that was mounted on the kitchen wall next to the refrigerator. He hooked his index finger into the round dial and rotated it, and it screeched. Then the dial swing back with a bing. Then the next number. Then back again. Seven times. Screech. Bing. Screech. Bing.

HE RETURNED, ALONE, SCRAPING HIS SHOES ALONG the thin living room carpet, a little before noon.

"Daddy!"

Slowly, he shook his head. He hung his coat in the closet by the front door. He fell into the old Naugahyde recliner that smelled of dried sweat, pushing it a little ways back.

"Is he—?"

"Out of jail? Yeah. The bail bondsman took our cash and your Aunt Sophie's engagement ring as collateral."

"Sophie's ring?" Mom demanded, looking up abruptly from her crossword.

"She'll get it back. You think I'd cheat my own sister-in-law? But the bondsman keeps ten percent of the total bail as his fee." Pressing the recliner as far down and back as he could, Daddy exhaled a long, fat breath. "The judge wouldn't let your friend out without bail because he doesn't live in New York and he doesn't have family here. No community ties. Maybe the judge is a Republican and hates anti-war protesters, I don't know."

"Did you see Jerry?"

"Yeah."

Was he beaten up? Was he ….?

"How much will it cost us?" Mom asked.

"Did he seem—did he—like he's okay?" Judith asked.

"He could use a shave," Daddy replied to Judith. "Does he always look like that?"

"I mean… Did he seem hurt?"

"Yudeleh…" Daddy released another breath. "No, he was fine. I didn't notice any broken bones."

"Did he say what he was arrested for?"

"It's been a long night, Yudeleh. We didn't have a big conversation."

"What did it look like? The jail."

"Enough questions. What are you doing home? Didn't you go to school?" Easing forward, he spoke to Mom. "The boy wanted to thank us, in person. I invited him to dinner tomorrow."

"Tomorrow? Shabbos dinner?" Mom asked. "Why?"

Tomorrow? In person?

All right. Jerry wanted to thank Mom and Daddy. That was very nice of him. But that would be the last of Jerry. Besides, there was the blind date on Sunday night with Marilyn's cousin who was studying American literature at Brooklyn College.

JERRY WORE A NAVY BLAZER AND A PALE-BLUE button-down

shirt, and he'd tied his hair at his neck in a ponytail.

Jerry owned a blazer and a button-down shirt?

He brought a bouquet of some kind of pink flowers, which he held out to Mom at the door. "I can't thank you enough," he said. "You saved my life."

Jerry?

He pecked Judith on the cheek and shook Daddy's hand, repeating his thanks. By then, Mom had walked away.

Who was this polite, nicely dressed person?

As always, Mom circled her hands three times around the Shabbos candles and then she and Judith covered their eyes while they said the blessings together, but Judith peeked through her fingers. Jerry was standing next to Daddy, his head properly bowed, his hands loosely clasped in front of his—well, actually, in front of the fly on his trousers. But that was where hands would naturally fall, wasn't it?

Jerry offered to help carry the serving platters, but Mom waved him off.

Jerry and Daddy sat at the Formica table while Judith hurried back and forth from the stove, snatching the platters of food from Mom, lingering as she set them down at the table. Roast chicken. Roasted potatoes. String beans. There were no black-and-blue marks on Jerry's face or neck, no scratches, no visible bandages.

Mom had left Jerry's flowers lying on the counter.

"And how about Swoboda's catch in the fourth game?" Daddy asked Jerry.

"Yeah, I heard about that."

"He was almost lying flat on the grass! I'm telling you, Jerry, he dove into that grass like it was a swimming pool."

"But do you think it's more than a one-year fluke? Can the Mets keep going for the long haul?"

"Well, they'll never be the Dodgers, but they've been getting better in the last couple of years."

Jerry was a baseball fan?

Finally, all four of them were seated, and Daddy and Jerry continued.

"You know we're bombing Cambodia now?" Jerry asked. "That's what people are saying."

"We should be getting the hell out of Vietnam, and instead Nixon goes into another country! The man's a madman."

"I bet he's invaded more countries, too, and they're just keeping all of it secret." Jerry's chin was shaved so smooth, if Judith ran a finger across it, she probably wouldn't feel a single dot of stubble.

"The way they've been lying to us about everything, sure. Where's that light at the end of the tunnel?"

"And more people keep getting killed."

"But," Daddy said as he leaned forward over his plate, toward Jerry. "Here's my question. Why can't you do all that, protest the war, march against Nixon, and still go to college?"

"I agree. I plan to go back to school."

Did he? Really?

Mom continued slicing her chicken.

"In my day, I would've given my left arm to go to college—You notice I say the left arm, not the right one. Because I'm right-handed. I'm not that stupid, to give up my good arm. But my point is, who could afford college back then?"

"I get what you're saying, Seymour. You think I'm throwing away an opportunity that I don't appreciate."

"Exactly!"

"But I feel like I can't—life can't—just go on, business as usual. That's what Nixon wants us to do! You know, pretend everything's fine, while they're killing thousands and thousands of people in Vietnam."

"And how does it save anybody's life if you drop out of school?"

"Because now I have the time to work on organizing."

"Organizing?"

"We're building a movement, Seymour. A lot like you were doing, when you were organizing for the unions."

"It's not the same thing at all! You don't know what you're talking about. I was building something long-lasting."

"So are we."

Daddy pointed his fork at Jerry. "You ever hear of the Triangle Factory fire? In 1911, here in New York, at a clothing factory; a hundred forty-six people were killed. Because the factory owners locked those girls in. Deliberately locked the doors. To prevent stealing, so they said. And that wasn't all. The fire escape led to a blocked airshaft. There weren't any sprinklers or fire doors. So when the fire started, those girls were trapped. And you know what? A lot of that was completely legal. Yeah, the laws didn't protect workers, and the owners didn't give a damn. All sorts of things you take for granted today—child labor laws, minimum wage, basic safety standards—those are the kinds of things a union fights for, laws and collective power so that working guys have something on their side to counteract management's power. That's the strongest kind of organizing you can do within the capitalist structure. That's what I call building for the future."

"And I'm thinking about the future from a different point of view, Seymour. What kind of a society do we have if our government can keep invading countries for no reason—secretly invading them, right? If we let our government lie and keep us in a war the public doesn't support? If we let Nixon get away with this, what will the next president do?"

"So what are you building?"

"A movement. We're opening people's eyes. We're galvanizing them. And then, with this energy, we're putting more and more pressure on Nixon so he can't ignore the public voice. Look at how many people came out for the moratorium this week, all across the country."

"And if Nixon doesn't listen to you?"

"We get more people. We try something else."

"And you get arrested again?"

Jerry grinned. "Hey, Seymour, that's not my five-year plan."

"What did you get arrested for?" Suddenly, Mom spoke to Jerry.

Daddy laid down his fork. So did Judith.

Sitting properly upright, Jerry focused his chocolate eyes on Mom. "I know it was intended to be a nonviolent protest. And that's how I started out the day, too. But after a couple of hours, when you're walking along, and everyone's chanting, and it feels good, and the cops are pretty much waving you by, and soon you're talking to the other marchers about ordinary stuff, their kids and their jobs and their favorite pizza places, and you're laughing—Well, it feels too nice. As if we're just out for a stroll in the park, right? What am I doing here, when people are dying in Vietnam every second while I'm marching and talking about pizza?

When people are dying in Vietnam because Americans are shooting them and napalming their villages?" He was talking straight to Mom, never turning his face away. "Every footstep I took, every nice moseying-along footstep, someone was dying hideously because of something my own government is doing. I couldn't walk like that any longer. I needed to do something more—more serious. Something that would make a bigger statement. Does that make sense?"

Finally, Jerry shifted his attention toward Daddy, for a second; then back to Mom. A few strands of dark hair had come loose from the ponytail and were clinging to his neck.

"So what did you do?"

In fact, it had been in the *Post*, one paragraph fairly high up in the main story about the moratorium, although Jerry's name wasn't mentioned: Four people from SDS were arrested for breaking into the president's office at NYU, where they smashed windows, threw furniture around the rooms, and painted slogans. They claimed they were protesting the fact that NYU allowed ROTC to recruit on campus, which made it complicit in the Vietnam War machine, they said. According to the newspaper, NYU officials hadn't determined, as of press time, whether any important papers were missing.

Jerry had been charged with second-degree criminal mischief, which was a felony, plus third-degree trespass and third-degree criminal tampering. He'd gotten a court-appointed lawyer at the arraignment, but now he was sharing a pro bono SDS lawyer with the other three arrested protestors.

"You'll get your bail money returned," he added. "I promise you I'll make all the court appearances. I won't run off and leave you holding the bag."

"They don't refund the ten percent fee," Mom replied.

Mischief. Trespass.

Jerry's big, serious protest against the war and injustice. He threw furniture.

"Well." Daddy rubbed his lips with his napkin. "I don't agree with what you did, to be honest, Jerry. Sure, we've got to stop Nixon. But what's the point of breaking windows at a college?"

"Judith, come help me get dessert," Mom ordered.

While Mom boiled water for instant coffee, Judith grabbed a few star-shaped sprinkle cookies out of the cookie jar and dumped them on a plate.

At nine-thirty, Mom said it was getting late and Jerry had to leave.

"I guess you're going be watching that draft lottery, in a few weeks?" Daddy asked, as Jerry placed his chair neatly against the table.

"Yeah, unless I get a miraculous deferment before then."

"You shouldn't have to watch that by yourself. Come have dinner with us. Judith's brothers will be here. The two youngest, David and Michael, they've got to worry, too."

"It's late," Mom repeated.

It was Judith's role to accompany Jerry to the door and say, "Thank you for the flowers, good-bye." At the threshold, however, he gently tugged her out of the apartment, into the building's hallway and behind the half-ajar door.

He cupped his hands around her cheeks. Then he eased her face closer to his.

He smelled of the apartment, of Mom's roast chicken spiced with paprika and onion powder, of coffee.

There was ink on his fingertips. Still stained, from the fingerprinting at the police station?

"Jude…" It was one whispered word, stretched out a little, a single word filled with warmth, like a thermos. "You've been a saint, putting up with my craziness. A Jewish saint. Can I see you this weekend?"

No. I have a date.

The terrazzo floor in the hallway beneath their shoes had a beige base, inlaid with tiny bits of green and yellow.

"I promise I won't get arrested again before then."

He strolled his fingers through her light-brown hair as he sang, softly, *"Hey Jude, don't let me down/You have found her, now go and get her…"*

AT THE DINER, MARILYN'S COUSIN ORDERED A chocolate milkshake and a hamburger for each of them. "Oops," he apologized, a moment afterwards. "You don't keep kosher, do you?"

"You go to City College?" he asked, while the busboy filled their water glasses. "Isn't that pretty far from Brooklyn?"

"Do you like the Beatles?" he continued, after the waitress brought the burgers.

"So you're majoring in social work?" he asked.

"What are your hobbies?" he also asked.

"Revolution," she replied.

He frowned. "What do you mean? Is that the name of a card game?" Then he guffawed.

ON MONDAY EVENING, DECEMBER FIRST, THEY sat on the plastic slipcovers of the plaid couch, and on the recliner, and on the two chairs with yellow cushions and thin aluminum legs that Michael and Jonathan carried into the living room from the kitchen. David and Michael came from their apartment up in Washington Heights; Jonathan came from his apartment in Queens, though Adele stayed home with the baby. Seven sets of eyes stared at the TV set, nestled inside a big wooden cabinet opposite the sofa. Mom didn't even bring her crossword puzzle.

The grey-haired congressman on the TV screen reached his arm deep into the tall glass cylinder, stretching so deep that his white cuff and the sleeve of his black suit jacket rode up from his wrist, and he pulled out a small plastic capsule. And someone announced: September f—

NO!

—ourteenth.

Yes! Yes, yes, it was okay! They were safe. David's birthday was September first, not September fourteenth.

But another arm was already inside the cylinder.

April twenty-fourth.

December thirtieth.

They sat on the recliner and the couch and the kitchen chairs, and they didn't move. No one spoke. No one even uncrossed their legs. They stared at the TV screen, as a hand reached into the cylinder, and a voice called out a date, and a hand reached in again, and a voice spoke again.

By number fifty, Judith's fingers ached from clutching the front edge of her chair.

By seventy-five, she dared to glance quickly at the others.

What if they'd missed it? What if the voice had called David's or

Michael's or Jerry's birthday way back at number twenty and none of them had heard it?

Michael's birthday was the first to be snagged. February tenth. Number two hundred sixteen. That was probably safe. The experts were saying that people with birthdays above two hundred in the lottery probably wouldn't be drafted. Even Nixon wouldn't need that many soldiers as cannon fodder. Michael grinned around the room, a little feebly. "I'm taking the bullet for you guys."

David came in at two hundred twenty-five. Hell of a lot better than number one. He let out a real laugh.

Jerry: An unbelievable three hundred thirty-eight.

And suddenly everyone, all of them, even Mom, they were all jumping up and running one to another, hugging the first one nearby, then hugging the next, crying, laughing. Mom kissed and hugged Michael, then David, then Michael again, then David again. Daddy hugged them. Mom hugged them one more time. Jonathan hugged them. Jerry kissed Judith. Daddy slapped Jerry on the back. Judith clutched Michael and David. Michael, David, and Jerry shook hands. Daddy got out a bottle of bourbon. Oh God, oh God the world was good, it was safe, they were all safe, no one was going to Vietnam, they were the luckiest family in the world.

SHE SAT ON MARILYN'S BED, IN MARILYN'S BEDROOM, next to Marilyn, just inches away from Marilyn, their thighs almost touching, and Marilyn stared at her. She nodded.

"Two months," she managed to say, her voice croaking as it came out of her throat.

Ridiculously, she wasn't nauseous. It was merely that her throat was clenched up.

"I just got the results. From Planned Parenthood."

CHAPTER TWENTY-THREE
JUDITH
C. 1968-1970

MARILYN'S BED HAD A COMFORTER WITH A FADED pattern of pink and yellow flowers. On a bulletin board nearby, she'd thumbtacked her class schedule, a couple of glossy magazine photos of Mick Jagger, and an oversized postcard reproduction of a Degas painting of two ballerinas in billowing white skirts half-collapsed on a bench. Three stuffed animals—a fuzzy brown dog, a pink bear, and a white rabbit—rested against her pillow.

"Weren't you on the Pill?" she asked.

Judith pressed her palms against her stomach. "I quit when Jerry went to Washington DC last spring."

"And you didn't restart—?"

"I broke up with him… I thought I did… It just kind of happened again. After the draft lottery."

Marilyn exhaled.

"I can't tell Mom and Daddy!"

MOST GIRLS CHOSE ONE OF TWO OPTIONS, the counselor at Planned Parenthood had said: Give the baby up for adoption. Marry the father.

There might be two more options: Abortion. Raise the baby alone.

Or no options at all.

"Abortion is illegal in New York State," Judith told Marilyn. "There's a bill in the state legislature to make it legal, but who knows if it will pass, and in any case, it would be too late for me."

"But you hear about…things." Marilyn faltered. "Women go to Puerto Rico…"

"Great, thank you. And are you offering to pay for my plane ticket?"

"Could you ask…?"

"Who?" Ask her parents? Oh, sure. Now that they'd gotten back the money that they put up for Jerry's bail, why wouldn't they be thrilled to hand it straight over to their daughter who'd screwed up again by having sex with the hippie dropout? "And the hospital bill? And the doctor fees? And are you offering to miraculously get my parents' permission, too, while you're at it? Since I'm not twenty-one yet."

Of course Marilyn just sat, like a lump on the bed. As useless as the damn ballerinas on the postcard: Were the ballerinas going to give her answers?

Ask her brothers? Tell them their unmarried baby sister was knocked up? Steal from Uncle Morris's cash register?

Marilyn placed a palm over Judith's hands.

"Pennyroyal tea," Judith said. "Parsley and cohosh tea."

"What?"

"Tansy tea. That's some of the stuff women've tried. To get rid of it. I read it in the library."

"Oh yuck."

"They probably don't work. They just make you sick."

HEY, JERRY, YOU'RE NOT GOING TO BELIEVE THIS.

Would he smile? Would the smile get wider, until it showed his a-little-bit-crooked front teeth?

Would he hug her?

Really? I'm going to be a dad? No shit!

Jerry?

His own father had left, years ago. Wouldn't Jerry like to fill the emptiness, to be the perfect dad he'd never had?

Maybe he'd sing to the baby. "Hey Jude." "Rock-a-Bye Baby."

Would the baby have his thick, dark hair and his chocolate eyes?

Would he want to name the baby Cesar, for Cesar Chavez? Or Bobby, for Bobby Kennedy?

Would they carry the baby to demonstrations, strapped to Judith's back like an Indian papoose? But what if there was tear gas? What if Jerry got arrested again? What if he wanted to go back to California to help the grape workers? Could two adults and a baby even fit on a motorcycle?

MAYBE IF SHE GOT ANOTHER TEST AT Planned Parenthood, it wouldn't be true.

"HOW ARE YOUR STUDIES?" MOM ASKED as she pushed open the bedroom door. "Please set the table. Dinner is in five minutes."

Studies?

Mom couldn't see anything yet. Could she? Was that why she'd opened the door without knocking, to stare at Judith's belly before Judith had a chance to hide it under a baggy shirt? The belly looked the same as it had last week and last month and two months ago, a slight pudginess just from ordinary eating. Soon the weather would be warm enough to wear her Indian-print blouses, which were so loose that they'd cover any bulge, at least for a few months. But weren't mothers supposed to have some sort of sixth sense, especially when it came to their daughters and pregnancy, a mystical instinctive ability to gaze into their daughters' faces and know that they were pregnant?

Mom? Mystical?

But what if she really could sense the truth?

Abortion
Adoption
Marry Jerry
Raise the baby alone

HE WAS ON HIS MOTORCYCLE, GRINNING, one long leg stretched to the ground, shaggy brown hair blowing in the breeze. His smile that melted ice and sent the leaves swirling to the heavens with excitement.

Where were they when she took the photo? Greenwich Village? No, the street was too empty; maybe Coney Island. She should have included more of the scenery, so she could remember. She should get a frame for it.

One leg on the ground, holding him in place, steady, balanced. But the other foot was cocked back, already on the pedal. Raring to go save the world.

IN HER PARENTS' WEDDING PHOTO FROM 1942, Mom had dark wavy hair, dark eyes, dark lipstick, and a short gauzy veil, and she wore a satiny long-sleeved dress with a train that pooled in a circle around her feet. Daddy had a tiny black mustache then, and his curly hair was dark like Mom's. They didn't look at one another. She was seated, he stood behind her with a hand poised on the back of her chair, and they gazed somberly at the camera. It was because the war had just started, Mom had explained; it was no time for giddiness. They'd married in a rush before Daddy went off to basic training.

"I HEARD ABOUT SOMEBODY…" Marilyn began.

They were whispering, even though their heads were barely six inches apart as they leaned across their table in the diner.

She should order milk. If she wanted a healthy baby. If she wanted a baby. If she got a Coke, would that kill the baby?

"She went to a place," Marilyn was saying. "Here. In New York."

Although the air in the diner was hot and steamy, the skin on Judith's face was suddenly cold. Her cheeks. Even her lips. But not her palms, they were sweaty.

"To a doctor?"

"I don't know."

"It worked?"

"I don't know."

"I'm already nine weeks."

There were stories. Back alleys. Not even real doctors. Infections. Dirty, bloody, fake doctor-white coats. Coat hangers. Hemorrhaging. Blood and blood and more blood.

Douching with Lysol. With Coke. With Comet cleanser. Swallowing a gallon of castor oil. Falling off a horse.

Who the hell had a horse?

Abortion
Adoption
Marry Jerry
Raise the baby alone

THEY COULD SQUEEZE INTO JERRY'S ROOM IN Union City. She

would learn to cook vegetable stews on the hotplate. She would buy cheap, bruised vegetables. She and Jerry would rock the baby to sleep singing "Hey Jude" and "We Shall Overcome," and the baby would sleep in a dresser drawer, which they'd make all cozy with soft blankets and pillows. It would be late summer or early fall when the baby was born, so they would take long walks all together. They would show the baby the plaza at Columbia where they'd met, and City College, and the pizza place in Greenwich Village where they'd had their first date, if Jerry remembered which pizzeria it was. Coney Island. The movie theater where they saw *2001: A Space Odyssey.* The courthouse where Daddy and the uncles had waited for Jerry's arraignment? Well, never mind that.

Yes, Jerry would have to postpone college, as she would. But he could earn a decent salary at DeCamp. Sometimes they'd go with him for a few stops while he drove the bus. They would sit directly behind him—Judith with the baby in her lap—and he would wink at them in the rear-view mirror. She'd rub his shoulders. She'd hold the baby's soft little cheek against his neck, and Jerry would squirm a little, as if he was being tickled, and the baby would trill with baby-bell laughter. With his charges from the NYU break-in plea-bargained down to a couple of misdemeanors and his community service done, Jerry only needed to finish paying off the seventy-five dollar fine. With his nice high lottery number, there was no risk that he'd get drafted. They could have a solid family life.

Until he went off to join the grape pickers in California.

Or the next protest march in Washington.

Or Chicago.

But if she loved him.

If she loved him, and he loved her, they would work it out. That was what people did, when they were truly in love. They compromised; they found ways to make things work. He would learn to stay in one place and change diapers.

That was what a girl did, when she accidentally got pregnant. The boy "made an honest woman out of her," and then the two of them put on a phony show for the world: *Oh gee, what a surprise, I got pregnant so quickly, we've only been married a month... Oh my gosh, the baby came three months premature.* Okay, fine, no one would be fooled—certainly not Mom and Daddy—but after a couple of years, after Judith went back to school and then got a job as a social worker, who would know the true story or care? They could fudge the baby's birthday, and the baby would never realize.

Jerry might be a little intense and disorganized, with his head in the clouds, but he was also a decent human being, and he would do the right thing.

AND WHO WAS SHE KIDDING, TO EVEN PRETEND that there were truly any alternatives?

Adoption?

To go through the next seven months, her stomach bulging bigger and bigger, squeezing into a few baggy pieces of clothing that she might scrounge somewhere, kicked out of school, everyone staring at her, Mom and Daddy furious, ashamed, disgusted—and then toss her baby away to strangers?

To go through the next seven months, gritting her teeth, ignoring the little kicks and signs of life inside of her, turning her head away whenever she saw adorable toddlers or moms with their baby strollers, to be merely a—a—a can of Coke, carrying a soda for someone else to drink?

Abortion?

Just how did she think she would pay for this jaunt to Puerto Rico? Or Europe, oh sure, why not? With the eighty-three dollars in her savings account? She couldn't go to Mom and Daddy and Uncle Morris and Uncle Irv again, not after they'd already bailed Jerry out of jail. Jonathan and Adele didn't have enough money to take care of their own baby, on Jonathan's starting-out accountant's salary. David was in grad school, and Michael was graduating in June, so which brother would have a secret bank account in Switzerland? Ask Kim and Marilyn? What kind of despicable cockroach mooches off friends when they're as poor as she is?

Or she could go to a filthy room, in a dark alley somewhere. Where she might bleed to death or die of an infection.

Abortion
Adoption
Marry Jerry
Raise the baby alone

RAISE THE BABY ALONE?

If Jerry didn't want the baby? If he wouldn't get married?

"Like—*The Scarlet Letter*?" Marilyn stammered.

They both stared at Judith's chest, where there was now only a faded denim Army-Navy surplus shirt, but where the scarlet A would be.

"That was three hundred years ago," Judith insisted. "Nobody thinks like that anymore. It's the sexual revolution. Free love. The Pill."

Except that her family and all their neighbors definitely still did think like *The Scarlet Letter*.

If she didn't marry Jerry, she couldn't possibly afford an apartment of her own, no matter how crummy and tiny. And therefore, she and the baby would have to live with Mom and Daddy. Glowering at her in disgust every day. Hiding her from the relatives at seders and Rosh Hashanah dinners. Maybe refusing to utter the baby's name. *Slut. Trash. Bastard. Bringing shame on our family.*

We should never have bailed him out of jail. I told you, Seymour.

If he was still in jail, he couldn't have gotten her pregnant.

She might as well be wearing a scarlet A.

Abortion

Adoption

Marry Jerry

Raise the baby alone

And decide now.

If she was going to somehow have an abortion, she was running out of time to do it safely. But if she was going to continue the pregnancy, she was also running out of time, because her belly would be poking out in a month or so, which meant Mom and Daddy and the whole world would know. Which also meant Jerry would know.

Which meant get married. Now.

Or not tell him. Break up. Now.

Never see him again?

Never kiss him again?

She was ten weeks pregnant.

AT THE BUS STOP, HE WRAPPED HIS BARE HANDS around her wool mittens, the bitter February night wind tossing his hair and the streetlight gleaming on his face. Bouncing on his heels, he grinned. "It's almost spring. You ready for a big trip?"

I'm pregnant.

"I don't know…"

"Are you worried about school? I bet you can take a semester off."

Shit, he was so—so goddam bouncy. "No, I know that."

"So? You want to head west?"

Judith kicked the toe of one boot against the square base of the streetlight pole. How cold was it? They'd predicted a little above freezing tonight. Enough to make a person's cheeks sting. "It's just so—I thought we were kind of daydreaming when we talked about California. The beach. Not for real."

"But shit, Jude, isn't that what life is about? Being spontaneous. Being alive to possibility. Catching your dreams as they fly past you. Do you really want to just sit around and take final exams and earn your paycheck every week?"

He was such a boy. Even his hair, waving around as if he was a kid who refused to use a comb.

"Don't you want to go back to school?" *Don't you want to stay in one place for a while? Until your child is born?*

"Probably. Later. Once I see how things are doing. Cooper Union isn't going anywhere." Still tightly holding her mittened hands, Jerry stretched backwards, as far as his arms would extend, as though it was just her grip that was keeping him from falling. "The world is changing, and we can move with it." He pulled himself forward until he was more normally upright. "Don't worry, we wouldn't go till April, when the weather's better for biking and camping, and my fine'll be completely paid off, and I'll have some money saved. We'll camp at Big Sur. Swim in the surf. Eat fresh guacamole. Hey, you want to visit the supermarkets in Oakland where I used to talk to shoppers about the grape boycott? Maybe the boycott office has some work we can do." Laughing, he strummed her cheeks with his icy fingers. "Or we can skip the supermarkets. But seriously, Jude, I want to share all this with you."

"Can't—?" She coughed. *Can't you share New York with me? Can't you take the money you've saved and use it for baby clothes?*

He kissed the tip of her nose.

His lips were so cold. From the chilly air.

IF ONLY HE WOULD STICK AROUND. SOMETIMES. For more than two weeks. If only he would quit worrying about the goddam grape-farm workers. If only he would settle down, and drive his goddam bus, and go to school, and be there to change a few diapers and—and understand that being a good father was another way to change the world. If only he could be someone completely different than he was.

JERRY…

They would be lying face to face in the narrow bed in his room, their bodies sinking a little on the left side where the mattress sagged, his arm around her, his lips brushing circles on her nose and cheeks. She would be wrapped in the differently sweet smells of his sweat and Coke and toothpaste, and maybe a little diesel gas.

There's no pressure, Jerry. No obligation.

His body would tense, at that point. As soon as one person says "no pressure," the other person knows that means there is pressure.

But you have a right to know…

I want to keep it. I think I want to.

Of course you can go help the grape workers.

As often as you want.

Of course you can go to the demonstration in Washington. Even if you get arrested again.

Give him a chance to do things right. It was his baby, too. Tell him the truth, get the marriage license, make everything look legit. Shove the damn license in Mom and Daddy's faces. Give Jerry a chance to actually see the baby—his baby. To fall in love with the baby. To take responsibility. And then, if marrying him truly was a mistake, then get a divorce.

NO.

No, goddammit, goddammit, GODDAMMIT, if only it could be Yes.

Grandma Sarah had waited ten years, until Grandpa Jacob the anticapitalist rebel had enough money to send her a boat ticket.

Mom had married too soon, because Daddy was going off to fight in World War Two, and their marriage was so obviously a mistake.

Mom had been the same age as Judith then, when she married too soon.

Jerry would always be her first time. She would always remember him. He was passionate and smart and sexy and caring and so beautifully full of ideals, and maybe they'd been a little bit in love. Probably. But he was not the man she should marry for the long term. And therefore, it wouldn't be fair to open that door, to put the guilt trip of her pregnancy on him.

I'll look for you, Jerry. I'll look for you on TV when they show the next march against the war, and when they show the grape workers winning a contract for better pay. And when they show people being arrested at those marches, I'll look, too. Who knows, maybe I'll even see you on TV when you're inaugurated as president someday.

Even without Jerry at her side, she wouldn't be alone. Mom and Daddy would surely let her and the baby—their own grandchild—live with them. She could be honest with them, and they wouldn't stay angry or embarrassed for long, not in this day and age, not with their own daughter and grandchild.

She and the baby would live in her bedroom. Mom would teach her how to cook, and the apartment would be filled with the wonderful smells of roast chicken, onions, sweet carrots, and chocolate cake. The baby would grow up with a whole family nearby—two doting grandparents, three doting uncles and (eventually) their wives, and a slew of cousins. Daddy would take him or her on long excursions and subway rides, just like he'd taken Judith, to Inwood with the Indian caves and the old glaciers that looked like humungous slabs of melted rocks, and to the building that had been the Triangle shirtwaist factory. With all that help and support from her family, Judith would eventually be able to return to school and get her degree. And she would sing the baby to sleep with "We Shall Overcome" and "Hey Jude."

Truly, Jerry was making the decision easy for her, by zooming off to California before her belly was big enough to notice. She could simply tell him that she wouldn't go with him because she wanted to stay in school. To him, it would just seem like all the previous times he'd invited her and she'd refused and then he'd disappeared. But this time, if he returned to New York and phoned her, she would no longer be available. *I'm seeing someone else*, she could say. Gently. He would never have to know the truth.

And she would wait, and eventually her Mr. Right would come along.

With his own dreams, and worth waiting for.

"But what will you tell the baby?" Marilyn asked.

Judith rubbed her sweatshirt where it rested against her stomach. Even though there was nothing really to rub yet, soon enough there would be.

"I'll tell the baby all the good things that are true about Jerry. About how we met at Columbia, and how his eyes were like chocolate icing, and his big wide smile. And his dreams. About how he really, truly wanted to help the grape pickers and stop the U.S. from dropping napalm on the moms and children in Vietnam, and how hard he worked on Bobby Kennedy's campaign. Because I want my baby to dream, too. But I think, Marilyn… I'll tell the baby we were married."

"Wow." Marilyn rubbed her own ring finger, as she stared at Judith. "How will you do that?"

"I guess I could buy a cheap ring at a jewelry store. I don't know, but I just think it'll be easier that way. Not to get into all the shit about how Jerry's irresponsible and I didn't believe he'd stick around. Why should I tell my kid bad things about his own father?"

"And besides, your kid might blame you, if he knew the truth. You know? 'Why did you send my daddy away?' "

"Shit, I didn't even think about that. Yeah, that makes it more important, to say that we were married. We were married, and Jerry loved the baby very much, but… maybe, he died tragically in a car accident while I was pregnant? Or soon after the baby was born? Some story like that."

CHAPTER TWENTY-FOUR

AS SOON AS MIRANDA EMERGED FROM THE SUBWAY at Broadway and 116th Street, there was a fence of tall iron spikes topped with small golden crowns. A massive stone-and-brick building stood at each end, and two towering statues of figures in Roman robes guarded the front. Behind the fence, three walkways stretched into the invisible distance, separated by strips of greenery and lines of well-spaced trees. A few people strolled from the three walkways onto a rectangular plaza.

At one side of the plaza, just beyond the tiered marble staircase leading up to Low Library. sat a stone bench.

Was it here, near this bench? A guy with shaggy hair like the Beatles and brown eyes like chocolate icing gave a piece of paper to a high school girl. Was it a different bench? Was there no bench at all?

Well, one fucking thing was for sure: That guy with sexy hair and sexy eyes had never been shouting into a bullhorn on the tiered staircase, rousing the crowd to revolution.

Leader of the student uprising at Columbia in 1968. Arrested. Organizer of the marches at the Democratic Convention in Chicago. Arrested again. Main speaker at a peace rally in defiance of the illegal denial of a permit. One more arrest. Pivotal figure in Bobby Kennedy's campaign, the grape workers' strike, the 1969 antiwar moratorium, countless other protests for justice and peace and human rights, with Judith at his side; FBI files up the wazoo, no doubt. Certainly on Google?

None of it. Not a single fucking thing was true except that once there was a guy named Jerry Isaacs. Or maybe Jerry Isaacs wasn't even his name, maybe that was as fake as everything else and Judith was still lying.

A guy on a secondhand Harley, one leg stretched to the ground to prop him in place, leaning slightly into the handlebars, wearing jeans with ragged cuffs and short boots, with a wide grin, aviator sunglasses, and dark, shoulder-length, dramatically windblown hair.

Had Judith noticed yet that the sacred photo was missing from the oak credenza at the bottom of the staircase in her house? Too bad.

Hell, maybe the photo wasn't even Jerry at all. A stray guy Judith took a picture of one day.

Miranda smashed it against the stone bench.

She smashed it, and the glass splintered, and shards shot all around the bench and onto the concrete pavement and on her ankle boots and maybe on her wool coat, and she was holding a heavy silver frame with a photo half falling out and jagged edges of glass clinging to the rim. And her right thumb, suddenly, hurt.

She jumped away from the bench. With her sleeve, she brushed rapidly at the front of her coat and at her sling. She wiggled and shook, and she hopped away from the pile of scattered glass bits at her feet, but she needed a tissue or a paper towel, something to wipe the fragments off her clothing more thoroughly. Small splashes of red fell on her coat. Immediately, she dropped the frame and the photo onto the pavement, among the pieces of glass.

When she wrapped the cuff of her sweater over her thumb, the cuff blossomed red.

Fuck them, fuck them, fuck both of them, and fuck Tali, too, she could say fuck all she wanted, Tali was dead anyway. She kicked the goddam stupid frame and the stupider more goddam photo with her boot heel until the photo tore against the pavement. Grabbing her black shoulder bag and pressing her sling against the front of her coat, she half-ran up the marble staircase. Low Library, that imposing building with all of its Greek columns at the top of the stairs, must have bathrooms inside, and bathrooms would have soap and water and paper towels.

A minute up the staircase, however, she stopped and turned around.

The campus was spread beneath her like her private realm. The marble stairs cascaded down to an expansive landing laid out in concentric squares of alternating red bricks and white cement. A few steps below that, the three walkways that had begun at the iron gates continued across a rectangular plaza. Past the plaza, two long lawns rolled majestically toward another mammoth, columned building that faced straight at Low Library from afar, like a pair of huge bookends. Small streams of people moved steadily along the walkways and the plaza in both directions.

If she had been Jerry Isaacs, standing just where she was standing, shouting through a bullhorn:

"President Kirk, we know you can see us!"

"And we're not leaving until you kick out the Pentagon warmongering researchers!"

If only it had been him.

His shaggy dark hair blown by the wind, his jeans with ragged cuffs, his eyes and his smile that could melt a high school girl's nervousness. *"I started to leave the protest today to get a can of Coke with a pretty high-school girl, because my arm hurt from giving out flyers. But I came back. I came back to join the sit-in at President Kirk's office, I came back to give speeches until my voice was hoarse, I came back at the risk of getting arrested, because I knew that future generations will view us as role models for changing the world. Even if we don't succeed immediately, if something is important, you stick to it."*

The Jerry who had never existed.

That was what Bill had meant, wasn't it? *"Why don't you Google your Saint Jerry sometime?"* He didn't mean that Miranda might find news articles about all sorts of dramatically destructive things Jerry had done—killing policemen, blowing up buildings, calling for a riot. No. He meant just the opposite. She would find nothing, because Jerry had done nothing.

Which meant that Bill had known the truth. Which would have made it even worse for him, living every day with Saint Jerry's photo on the oak credenza, and Judith spinning out fairy tales to Miranda and even Ted and Lily, and Miranda throwing those fairy tales in his face. Nevertheless, he'd kept Judith's secret for her. And when he'd rescued Miranda from the police, after she was caught shoplifting the glitter pens, he'd kept her secret, too. He wasn't the one who was a jerk.

No, he was still a horrible jerk for cheating on Judith.

But her thumb was stinging badly, and a little blood had begun dripping again. Miranda speed-climbed up the rest of the stairs and past the Greek columns, tugged open the outer glass door, then a heavier second one, and after that her boots were clicking on the orange-red-and white marble floor of a small, high-ceilinged vestibule. Up four short steps, she could go left or right, so why not left? Just beyond a doorway, a wooden sign finally promised

"Ladies Room, one flight down" next to a staircase with a black marble floor, and she clambered down as rapidly as she could, holding the railing while she squeezed the cuff of her sleeve tighter around her bleeding thumb.

A girl was already in the ladies' room—a student, presumably, maybe eighteen, with jeans and long blond hair, drying her hands. Miranda could ask her: *Have you ever heard of the big protest here in 1968, when they took over the president's office? Have you ever heard of Jerry Isaacs?* The girl glanced at Miranda, dried off, hoisted her backpack. To her, Miranda must seem like a weird Lady Macbeth with a broken arm, taking forever at the sink as she leaned over and hopelessly tried to scrub the tiny splinters of glass out of her thumb and palms. She scrubbed with water, with soap, with wet paper towels, but there was only cold water, dammit, she needed some sort of antiseptic. Or hot water and Band-Aids, at least. What would happen if she couldn't get the splinters out? They probably weren't dirty. Her hands would hurt, but the cuts wouldn't get infected.

That was a thought: Leave the splinters in—grit her teeth, ignore the stinging pain—and when her train rolled in to Washington at midnight, go to the emergency room, maybe the ER at Sibley Hospital, the same one where Lily had gone. Stay there all night, until it was time to go to work.

And tomorrow? Hang around the Center until Mort finally left for the evening, then sleep there? The townhouse had five bedrooms, according to Mort; at least one of them ought to have a bed. Unless Mort was already living in the place. Which seemed likely, come to think of it. No matter what time Miranda arrived in the morning—even the three days she'd come in at six o'clock to work on the bus-rider lists for Scott—Mort was always at his desk, with his cold coffee and croissant. And it would be impossibly awkward, to bump into Mort while she was brushing her teeth in the second-floor bathroom of the Center's townhouse at ten at night.

All right, then forget about the Center. There were relatively cheap hotels where she could stay on the outskirts of Alexandra, at the tail end of the Metro.

So that was her grand plan, to run away like a four-year-old? First she'd run away from Russ's apartment; now she was running away from Judith's house.

As the blonde student opened the bathroom door in the Low Library basement, an older woman was trying to enter. The newcomer had short, wavy grey hair; a darker grey blazer; black slacks; and a red-and-white striped blouse. A faculty member? A middle-manager in the administrative offices? In her forties or early fifties, probably; around Judith's age. Old enough to have been a student at Columbia, in the days when Jerry Isaacs was not leading mass protests.

"Are you all right?" the woman asked, nodding slightly toward the sink, where water was cascading onto Miranda's hand and over the porcelain side, onto the pile of soggy paper towels on the floor by Miranda's boots.

Quickly, Miranda shut off the faucet. "Just a minor accident. Sorry."

With another nod, the woman turned toward the stalls.

"Have you ever—?" Oh for heaven's sake, what was she thinking of asking this total stranger: *Have you ever heard of Jerry Isaacs?* "Have you ever cut yourself really deep on a piece of glass?" Miranda held out her thumb.

"Damn. Is it bleeding?" The woman moved a few quick steps closer, her loafers padding softly on the floor. "I might have a Band-Aid." She began sweeping things around inside her large grey pocketbook until she retrieved a thick wallet. "What kind of glass was it?"

From a picture frame and a photo of my supposed father who wasn't a hero after all.

"Do you think the glass was dirty?" the woman continued. Triumphantly, she slid out a worn-looking, extra-wide Band-Aid from inside her wallet.

Miranda took the Band-Aid but kept it in her fist instead of opening it. The woman was directly across from her. She had brown eyes, some kind of sweet-light perfume, and a gold wedding band. The top two buttons of her blouse were unfastened, and there was a small blue ink spot like a *bindi* just to the left of the third button. If she was the age she appeared, she'd no doubt gone through her own share of pain by now—divorced and remarried, perhaps; laid off from more than one job; argued so badly with her grown daughter that she saw her grandchildren only at Thanksgiving and Christmas dinners; bailed her son out of jail.

"Have you ever," Miranda asked, "learned that someone really close to you had done something awful and never told you?"

The woman pushed her wallet inside her bag.

"I'm sorry," Miranda quickly added. "I'm being way too nosy. Forget that I asked."

The woman rested her lower back and her elbows against the edge of the nearest sink. "Well, no one over the age of two is ever one hundred percent honest with anyone else, no matter how close they are."

"Sure, but there are big lies versus little lies."

"Actually, I think the big ones are easier to get away with."

"Really? Why?"

"How many do you tell over a lifetime? Scores of little white lies, but the whoppers? Probably no more than one or two. And they're so big and outrageous that nobody would ever dream you'd be capable of something like that, so there's no suspicion, no confrontation. It's those scores of little lies that you can't keep track of, week after week, that erode your relationships." Reaching inside her bag again, the woman immediately drew out something small enough to hide inside her palm and popped it in her mouth. "But what do I know? My ex was a compulsive gambler and kept it secret from me for two years."

"Wow."

Someone in heavy shoes was moving briskly, with strong thuds, on the marble floor outside the bathroom.

"What did you do when you found out about the gambling?" Miranda asked. "How did you find out?"

"Typical ways. First, a couple of checks I wrote from our bank account bounced. He claimed he'd just forgotten to deposit his paycheck, and of course I believed him. Then he started having to go to a lot of 'business conferences' in places like Vegas and Atlantic City, every other week. And there were all these supposed expenses he needed money for; car repairs and dental bills and I can't even remember what else. Finally, after his third major 'dental work,' I confronted him, and he did the whole mea culpa. Apologies. Promises. He lasted three months in Gamblers Anonymous. But I was two steps ahead of him by then; I'd already canceled the credit cards and gotten a new one in my name only. So when he fell off the wagon, which of course he did, and he called me from the casino in Atlantic City, livid that he couldn't use the old credit card? I changed the locks on the house."

"So you gave him one chance."

"Sure."

Any minute, another person might enter the ladies' room, and their conversation would halt. The grey-haired woman probably had to be back to work or class soon. Miranda couldn't hide there forever. "Do you know what time this building closes?" she asked.

"I'm not positive. Five o'clock, I would guess." The woman hiked the strap of her bag higher on her shoulder. "Good luck to you with the big secret in your life. And your thumb." She disappeared inside the second stall as a deep chime abruptly sounded somewhere outside.

Miranda pasted the Band-Aid firmly on her skin. *Secrets*, she should have told the woman; *plural. Could you wish me luck with all of my secrets?*

Down the tiered staircase from Low Library, commanding the plaza again. Where was the curb where Jerry and Judith had sat and talked about his plans to help the grape workers and campaign for Bobby Kennedy?

"Come to our march show on Sunday?"

"What?"

A kid was—oh shit—a boy with long brown hair was shoving a white piece of paper at her.

"We're having an art show on Sunday at Dodge Hall. The Visual Arts Department students and faculty."

Oh. Oh. Okay. "Thank you." She took the paper. The kid moved on to someone else.

Was his arm tired from holding out flyers, like Judith's and Jerry's arms had been?

We're going to try to keep the sit-in going all night again in President Kirk's office, so we need supporters here on the plaza. Can you come? Jerry had said to Judith.

Onto the pathway made of red bricks set in a diagonal pattern, next to a row of well-spaced trees, to a fence of tall iron spikes with gold-shining crowns on top and, beyond that, to a street curb where a boy with hair like the Beatles once shared a can of Coke with a high school senior. Then that senior took the subway southward, transferred to the express, transferred again to the IND line, and went home to Brooklyn.

Dammit.

Miranda swirled around.

Clutching her sling tight against her chest, she ran back, past the fence, down the brick pathway, onto the plaza, to the stone bench. On the ground next to the bench, a silver frame and a torn, black-and-white photo lay in a pile of shattered glass. She pulled a section of *The Washington Post* out of her shoulder bag, wrapped the newspaper around the frame and the photo of some asshole who might or might not be her father, and shoved the whole damn mess into her bag.

AS SOON AS SHE EMERGED FROM THE SUBWAY at Church Avenue, there was a parade of two-story and three-story red-brick and beige-brick buildings, lined up nonstop one after another, along both sides of the street and in both directions, with small shops on the ground floor and apartments above. The buildings, the fire escapes, and even some of the faded red, green, and blue awnings were probably the same ones that nineteen-year-old Judith had passed, thirty-three years ago, trudging home from City College, trying to figure out what to tell her parents about the thing growing inside her.

However, the shops that were housed inside those buildings had changed over the thirty-three years. Where were the places Judith had loved? Lamston's 5 and 10. Ebinger's Bakery. Dubin's Bakery.

Now it was T-Mobile. Pharmacy. Fish store. Halal grocery. Chinese takeout. Jewelry repair. Laundromat. Payday lender. Hair salon. Electronics. Another jewelry repair.

Just like everything else, it was not the world that Judith had always told Miranda about.

They had lived in a tall brick apartment building on one of the side streets that branched off of Church Avenue and its lines of stores, Judith and her three brothers and Grandma Bessie and Grandpa Seymour and later Miranda, too, for the first five years of her life. It could have been the very street where Miranda was walking, a canyon of huge apartment towers, each one four or six stories tall and half a block long, dark red brick and beige brick and brown brick and patterns of different colored bricks, some with carvings above the windows and some with parapets at the roof, some with stone arches and some with Greek-style columns and one with a coat of arms sculpted at the entrance; almost any of those could have been Grandma and Grandpa's apartment. That part of Judith's story, at least, was true, because Miranda had seen some of it herself when she lived there. The building where Grandma and Grandpa lived had a wide staircase with a wooden banister leading up from the entrance foyer, and the hallway floor was made of beige, yellow, and green terrazzo. Grandpa Seymour claimed that he'd once cut out a long piece of the floor to make a seesaw for Judith, and the super had to cover up the missing section, which was why there was a stretch of carpet from the front door to the bottom of the staircase.

And at the next corner, and the next, and the next, were more canyoned streets with more towering dark apartment buildings, an endless jagged skyline of bricks, in every direction. Six-story dull-red brick. Six-story beige-and-brown checkerboard. Four-story red-and-dark-red diamond pattern. Air-conditioner units in the windows. Brick arches above the windows. Fire escapes. Plaster columns. Gold-trimmed columns. White-trimmed columns. Columns topped by lion's heads. Flowers carved above the front door. Names carved: Belle Court. Argyle. Beverly Manor. Court Royale.

Yes, Judith had been a terrified nineteen-year-old, pregnant with no good options, when she walked through these canyons of dark buildings crammed with windows peering at her. The easiest choice, or certainly the most conventional one, would have been to tell Jerry so that he would marry her. And the Jerry of her story might even have done so, because he wasn't—at least, in the story that Judith told, that was supposed to be the truth—a bad person. If Judith's parents and the rest of her world had quickly figured out the real reason Judith and Jerry were so abruptly getting married, and Baby Miranda was born too suspiciously early, no one would have confronted Judith about it, back in those days. She could have barreled through with her lie.

Yet she hadn't. That nineteen-year-old Judith hadn't taken the easy route. She'd had the courage to see that the fantasy of marriage with Jerry wouldn't work and to raise a baby on her own, even in the face of all the social disapproval of that era. She'd given Miranda a family and a home and love, or at least she thought she had.

But she hadn't given Miranda—or Jerry—the truth.

From the minute Miranda was born, she was raised in a crib of lies much much bigger and much much worse than a little cover story about what month her parents had supposedly been married. Even her very name was a lie—Isaacs, as phony as the wedding ring Judith had bought for herself. Lies with each diaper; lies with each spoonful of mashed banana. Mommy and Daddy, at the head of the revolution. Mommy and Daddy, getting married in a park wearing jeans and a peace necklace. Handsome young Daddy, dramatically dead in a car accident. Judith insisting that Miranda join her to light a *yahrzeit* candle for Jerry every March on the day that he hadn't, in fact, died.

The sky was a dreary grey-white. It was too cold to keep walking, and Miranda's feet were aching in her boots.

Maybe Jerry would have been a good father. Just like Grandpa Seymour with little-girl Judith, he would have brought little Miranda to protest marches perched on his shoulders or hand in hand as she skipped alongside him, carrying her miniature protest sign. Pink; she would have painted her protest sign pink. Carefully printing on it, maybe, "War is Bad." And oh, Jerry would have taken her on his motorcycle—thrilling Miranda, terrifying Judith. He would have gotten her a kid-size helmet, and she would have wrapped her pudgy arms around his waist—no, more likely he would have seated her in front of him, where he could grasp her and see her, when she was too young to be trusted to keep holding him.

Or maybe he would've been a jerk. Maybe Judith was right and he would've been dashing off to useless protest rallies across the country every other month, singing her to sleep with "We Shall Overcome" but forgetting to pick her up at day care when he'd promised. He might not have been around to bring her home from the police station after she was caught shoplifting, as Bill had been. He might not have stayed up with her as Judith had when she ripped up the third and fourth and fifth drafts of her history essays in high school, until she finally was satisfied with the tenth draft. If Miranda wasn't going to fantasize about Jerry the revolutionary leader anymore, then she also shouldn't fantasize about Jerry the perfect father.

But she would never know what kind of father Jerry might have been, because Judith had cheated her and Jerry both out of that knowledge.

He hadn't died, thirty-two years ago. He might even be alive now. For thirty-two years, she could've had a father.

Dammit, she needed to sit down. Her thumb was starting to bleed through the Columbia-bathroom woman's Band-Aid. Where was Church Avenue, with its subway station and laundromat and Chinese restaurant that might have chairs to sit on? Was it one more block away? Two blocks? Three? No, the next corner was full of still more huge buildings, a looming dark lifeless canyon and it looked exactly like the last street, and the three streets before that. Red brick. Brown brick. Fire escapes. Plaster columns. Parapets.

Nineteen-year-old Judith, walking through these streets, no doubt thought she was protecting Miranda with her fairy tales. But once she hid the first secret and invented the first tale, everything spiraled wider and wider, lies curling into other lies, secrets into more secrets. Once Judith had created a father that Miranda didn't have to be embarrassed about, why not make him someone to be proud of, as well? If he was going to be a leader of the sit-in at Columbia, why not also at the demonstration in Chicago? Then, if that was Miranda's story, it had to be the story Judith told to Ted and Lily, too, because they could hardly have a different version from their big sister.

And it wasn't only Judith; shit, the whole family must have consented to participate in the charade. Even Grandpa Seymour had lied to Miranda, every Saturday when he bought her ice cream and took her on walks. Grandpa and Grandma, and her uncles and aunts, all of them, bathing her in lie after lie after lie.

People keep secrets for all kinds of reasons, Judith had said. *To avoid hurting other people. To protect their jobs. Sometimes I think people just get so used to their public version of the truth, if they've been doing it for a long time, that they forget the secret they've been hiding.*

Did the Laceys and the Lauterbachs and the Andersons hide secrets from each other, through all their long years of being married? They must have! None of them were saints. Yet their marriages endured.

No one over the age of two is ever one hundred percent honest with anyone else, no matter how close they are, the woman in the bathroom at Columbia had said. *It's those scores of little lies that you can't even keep track of, week after week, that erode your relationships.*

Miranda must have walked a couple of miles already, in and around these brick canyons of Judith's childhood neighborhood. Her arm sank heavily in the sling pinioned across her chest, and her collarbone ached dully, and her feet ached sharply, and her thumb throbbed; this was really stretching the orthopedist's "it's okay to walk" advice beyond the limit, this and the stupid anti-war protest three days ago. Using her right arm to support the left and the sling eased the pressure a little, but it was such an awkward way to walk, like an old lady hugging herself against the cold air. Like a mother hugging an infant to her chest.

Okay, so maybe nineteen-year-old Judith had truly felt that she was stuck, and lying to her newborn daughter was the best of a set of lousy choices. *To avoid hurting other people.* It would be impossible to explain to a two-year-old that Mommy didn't want to be tied down to an irresponsible Daddy who wouldn't love Miranda enough to stay home and be her Daddy… But why couldn't Judith have told the real story once Miranda was an adult—at eighteen, twenty, twenty-one—instead of waiting nearly thirty-three years? Why couldn't she have trusted Miranda?

Why couldn't Miranda have trusted Russ and their commitment to each other enough to admit to the kidnapping? And the drunk driving arrest.

Why couldn't Ronit have trusted Miranda enough to tell her about Tali any time in the past six years?

Why couldn't Russ have trusted that the Miranda he'd known for two years—the Miranda he'd proposed to on the third-floor balcony of the main building at Ellis Island—was the real one and be wiling to aborb an occasional lapse? Even a felony lapse.

And now he would trust her even less. Now, if she told him the truth about her parents, he would know she came from a family of liars, instead of the family of radical leaders he'd admired.

So she wouldn't tell him? On their next date, they'd discuss the Academy Awards and the new Afghan restaurant?

This had to stop. Or begin. If Judith was really going to be her mother, and Russ was really going to be her husband, there had to be more honesty.

Why didn't you tell me the truth about Jerry?
Did you ever regret not telling Jerry about me?
Do you really think of me as a liar?
What else should I know?
Why didn't you trust me?
Russ, I was arrested for drunk driving eleven days ago.
I'm sorry.

She needed to get back to Washington, to have those conversations.

Which meant, she needed to find Church Street and the subway to take her to Penn Station, to catch the Amtrak to Washington, which meant she needed to get out of this labyrinth of brick canyons.

Another street. A six-story dark brick building. Six-story beige brick. Carlyle. Beverly Arms. Albemarle Arms. White pillars. Stone columns. Lion's head. Metal archway. Parapet. Tower. Fire escapes. Air conditioners. Her boots pounded on the empty sidewalk.

Something sharp hit her hip. Every step.

Her thumb hurt.

Her arm pulled down the sling.

The grey sky was melting darker.

She had to walk faster.

Dark brick. Beige brick. Parapet. White pillars. Brick columns. Archway. Fire escape. Where where where the hell was Church Street with the T-Mobile and the pharmacy and the laundromat and the subway station?

It was her shoulder bag with the stupid picture frame that was hitting her hip.

She needed breath. She needed the subway. She needed Penn Station, she needed a new Band-Aid, she needed to run, no she wasn't supposed to run; she needed to stop running. She didn't need a hotel. She needed to go home.

CHAPTER TWENTY-FIVE

WHEN MIRANDA SLOWLY WALKED INTO THE semi-dark living room at almost midnight, Judith was wearing a long, faded, yellow sweater over a pair of yoga pants and holding a glass of water. She was sitting in Bill's armchair.

"Are you angry with me?" Judith asked.

The only other place to sit in the room was the couch, and it was too far away from Judith, so Miranda went into the kitchen to fetch a chair. She planted it opposite the armchair. "Is the story true?"

"The story?"

"The one you told me yesterday. About how you and Jerry Isaacs met. And how he never actually led any big protests and never got arrested at the Democratic convention in Chicago and never met Cesar Chavez picketing grapes. And never died in a car accident when I was a baby."

"Yes."

"All of it?"

Judith whistled out a soft breath. "Yes."

Except for their voices, the house was utterly silent. There was no music from Lily upstairs, no footsteps; even the cold radiators were asleep. Through the living room's uncurtained bay window, faint shafts of light from the streetlamps pinpointed the white lampshade next to Judith, the pale yellow of her sweater, the beige cushions on the couch.

"I'm angry," Miranda finally replied. "And I'm hurt. And I don't know what I'm feeling. You were a scared, pregnant teenager, and you did what you thought would be the best thing for me and you. I get that. Besides which—" Miranda pulled off the rubber band holding back her hair. "Considering how many secrets I've been keeping, I suppose I'd be a hypocrite to criticize you for the same thing, wouldn't I?" She reached out, and Judith gave her the glass of water. She took a long sip. "But," she added. Rising out of her seat, she stretched her right arm to place the glass on the marble-topped table where Bill's Italian-English dictionary no longer waited. "As secrets go, yours was a whale. It's a lot more serious than me not telling my fiancé I was once arrested for kidnapping, and that one itself was pretty bad. Think about it: I've spent my whole life believing that my father was dead. And believing that when he was alive, he and you were a pair of brave, pioneering, dedicated leaders who had a major role in the history of the Sixties, who carved out a legacy that I should carry on."

It was too dark to see Judith's face in detail. She could have been about to cry or to argue, or simply anticipating.

"Some of it's true." Judith breathed heavily.

"Not that much, from what you told me."

"I'm the same person you've always known. And you're the same person. We haven't changed."

"Don't play dumb. You know what I'm saying. I feel like I've been living my whole life in a bowl of pea soup. Or living someone else's life. Everything I've always assumed is wiped out. When I was little, and I felt anxious or scared or didn't want to do something, I used to think about you and Jerry facing right up against the muzzles of police rifles in Chicago or walking arm in arm with farmworkers marching toward the grape fields, to give myself courage. It's true. One time in fourth grade, we all had to do science projects and talk about them in front of the class. I was terrified, because I knew mine was actually sloppy, and I was sure the teacher would tear me apart. I'd supposedly planted tomato seeds in various different ways, to see if, you know, watering three times a day or once a day or adding fertilizer or whatever, if any variations would make a difference. A typical elementary school science project. But I'd gotten careless, and I hadn't kept track of what I'd done to each plant. So I was going to pretend to cough and sneeze; then you'd think I was sick and let me stay home. But, I swear, when I looked at you, I tried to picture you pretending you were too sick to march with my daddy against the Vietnam War. And I knew you would never do that."

A single car skidded outside, then picked up speed. For that instant, the headlights sent a bright flash through the bay window, before the street and the room went deep-grey again.

"I'm sorry," Judith said softly.

There was maybe two feet's worth of distance between their chairs. Judith had one leg crossed over the other; she was wearing dirty white sneakers. The sling around Miranda's arm was probably filthy by now, too, and little shards of glass were no doubt still clinging to her wool slacks. Every bone and muscle in her body just wanted to fall onto a bed, even if it was Ted's narrow, bunk-hard mattress.

But the imaginary Judith and Jerry Isaacs wouldn't abandon a protest rally just because they were tired, would they?

"I can understand why you made up that fairy tale when I was a kid," Miranda continued. "It would be too confusing for a little girl to hear that her mommy didn't want to marry her daddy. But why didn't you ever tell me the truth after I was an adult? You've had ten years, eleven years, at least."

"You're right." Judith stopped. The silence became heavier, like thick snow slowly falling. "It just happened, Miranda," she began again. "I didn't... I never made a conscious plan about if or when I'd tell you; I only coped moment by moment. I had to make a lot of decisions on the spot. How to explain to Grandma and Grandpa. Whether to reenroll at City College. All those things. After a while, after my life became a bit more settled, I more or less assumed I'd tell you the truth eventually, but... Oh, I didn't want to upset you while you were in high school and needed to get good grades to apply to college. And then once you were at Georgetown, I still didn't want to upset you, because your courses there were so tough. And then you had your new job at the Center, so of course it was important for you to make a good first impression, and I wouldn't want to distract you. As time went on, and the image of your father became more baked in, it just got harder and harder to dig out of the story I'd put us into. Does that make sense?"

"I don't... No! No, it doesn't. In all those years? You think I'm so fragile? You didn't trust me?"

"It wasn't a case of trust. I—" Again, Judith stopped. "I meant to protect you. Because I love you. But I suppose," she said quietly, "that I was just protecting myself."

Miranda wrapped her hair band around a couple of fingers.

"It's late," Judith added. "We've both got work tomorrow. We should go to bed."

"You didn't have to wait up for me."

"Not only because of you, actually."

Miranda stretched forward again, to flick on the lamp next to Judith, and a cone of weak light expanded into the room, fuzzily exposing the right side of Judith's face and her right shoulder. "Why else?"

From underneath her chair, Judith pulled out a thick sheaf of stapled, legal-size papers. "I got a letter from Bill's lawyer. He's filing for divorce." She held the packet in the air above her lap, like a tray.

Shit.

"So it's not just a midlife fling?" Miranda asked.

"Apparently not."

"Are you okay?"

In the new, pale lamplight, there was a tiny upward tilt on Judith's mouth. "Deep down inside? I'm not surprised. Yes, I've been acting as if Bill was merely having a midlife crisis. Give him space. See what happens. See if he gets over it and wants me to take him back, and then do I want him back? All that social worker BS. But I knew. Bill isn't a quick-fling kind of person." Unhooking her knees, Judith spread the packet of papers on her lap and began pressing them flat. "But now I've learned my lesson, thanks to you. I'm not pretending anymore. Who did I think I was protecting this time? I told Lily and Ted today that their dad and I are getting divorced. I didn't tell them about the girlfriend, because I think Bill should have to look them in the face about that, but I made it goddam clear to him that if he doesn't do it soon, then I will."

Bill and Judith were finished. Kaput. No more marriage. No more Italian-English dictionary. They would never nag each other about taking their blood pressure medications when they turned sixty-five, or take turns filling prescriptions because Medicare didn't cover the cost. Even after twenty-two years, and two teenage kids, a marriage could end, just like that, within a few months.

Miranda scraped her chair closer. "Why did you marry Bill?"

"Okay, Miranda, I know you never liked him."

"No, no, that's not what I mean. I'm not trying to take a cheap shot. I'm honestly wondering—Well, how can a person be sure that another person is Mister Right?"

"Why did I think Bill was right for me and Jerry wasn't?"

"Something like that."

"How can you be sure whether Russ is right for you?"

"No! Well, yes, that's part of it. And shit, I'm sure Russ is wondering the same thing. Isn't it natural, when you're about to get married, to have last-minute doubts?"

"You can't compare one marriage with another, or one husband with another. You know that. There isn't a formula. Bill isn't Russ. Or Jerry." Judith was still pressing the pages on her lap with her palms. "Bill was caring and good and reliable and intelligent, and he liked you too, which you probably don't believe. And he was what I needed at that time. He was someone I could count on; someone I could just sit with. All of that was important, Miranda."

"He was the opposite of Jerry Isaacs. Reliable."

"Of course. I'm not an idiot, I knew that was partly why I was marrying him."

Caring and good and reliable and intelligent. Someone a wife could count on. Taking care of each other, like the Andersons and the Laceys from the bus to Canada. Trust, Russ would insist. Of course there had to be love and good sex. And picking up his own dirty T-shirts. Except for the sex and the T-shirts, a lot of that was the basis of friendship, too. What about shared hobbies, like running or visiting Ellis Island together? Being willing to kidnap a daughter?

"Did you ever try to find him again? To tell him about me?" Miranda asked.

Maybe it was the wrong night to ask that question, when it was getting late, as Judith had said, and they were both tired, and Judith was already feeling so shaken by Bill's lawyer's letter on top of her long confession to Miranda yesterday; or maybe it would always be the wrong question to ask.

Judith was staring at the pages on her lap, even though they were lying face-down, so that she couldn't actually read anything. "I suppose you've Googled him."

"Tons of times."

"You found that professor in North Carolina?"

"Yeah. You too?"

Judith grimaced. As she wrapped her arms around herself, the batch of papers tumbled off her lap and onto the carpet and her sneakers. "Of course

I wondered. Where he was; what he was doing. But there wasn't anything like Google until much later, so I didn't have many ways to search. I looked up his mother once, a few years ago." She made a short noise, somewhere between "huh" and a laugh. "She was still in Des Moines. But I got cold feet and never contacted her. Honestly, I don't know what I would have said if I'd called either one of them. Shit." When Judith bent over to start collecting the papers from the floor, her hands were like an old woman's, slow and shaking.

"You never heard from him again?"

"Not after that winter that I was pregnant with you."

"He could still be alive."

"Yes."

It had to be way past midnight. Beyond the lamp's weak cone of light, the living room and the world outside the window were heavy grey, greyer than Judith's hair; at least there weren't any hints of sunrise yet. Judith sat a little forward in her chair—formerly Bill's chair—with her hands tightly holding onto the short, messy stack of papers, as if she was ready to jump up. Ready, for instance, to hug Miranda, if Miranda walked over to her.

Miranda stood. "It's late, like you said. And I have a couple of emails to write."

"What? At this hour?"

"They're important, too." She lifted her own chair, to return it to the kitchen.

"The real history isn't so terrible," Judith said.

Miranda lowered the chair.

"We truly did try to make the world better. Especially Jerry."

"I guess so."

"You've built the life that Jerry and I didn't. Working on the drug-insurance bill for the elderly. Taking Lily to the anti-war protest. Those aren't lies. Those don't belong to someone else's life."

For some stupid reason, Miranda's mouth wanted to smile. "Okay, Mom. Do you want to go to the next protest march with Lily and me?"

DEAR RONIT,

Thank you for coming to see me at the coffee bar.

I am so so sorry about Tali; I can't even imagine how awful it is for you, and how much you must miss her.

I'm sorry I didn't say all that when we talked.

If you're still in the U.S., I would like to see you again, to be a friend in any way I can. And if you're back in Israel by now, I hope that being with your family, in the country you love, is helping you. I also hope that we can stay in touch, with emails and phone calls.

I'd still like to climb Masada with your dad.

I'll be thinking of you.

Your friend,
Miranda

RUSS: I SHOULD HAVE TOLD YOU THIS ALREADY: I was arrested for drunk driving eleven days ago. —M

CHAPTER TWENTY-SIX

A CLUSTER OF TEENAGERS HAD UNFOLDED SOME beach chairs on the empty marble floor next to Lincoln's statue, a few yards from the top of the staircase where Russ and Miranda stood. Sitting in the chairs, they were imitating Lincoln's pose, arms on the armrests, one leg slightly bent, the other foot protruding in front, while a burly boy in a puffy green jacket snapped their photos.

"My brother claims that he and some friends once tried to climb up to touch Lincoln's shoes." With the remains of the oversized hot pretzel he was chewing, Russ pointed toward the statue's sheer, ten-foot-high pedestal and the chain surrounding it. "I don't know how they thought they could do it."

"With a ladder," Miranda mumbled.

"There probably wasn't so much security around all the monuments, when we were kids." Russ proffered the pretzel toward Miranda. She shook her head.

"Do you want to begin?" she asked.

He froze the pretzel in the air, then lowered his arm and shoved the pretzel into his coat pocket. After another glance toward Lincoln, where the teenagers had started folding their chairs back up, he nodded in the direction of Miranda's sling. "How's your collarbone?"

Okay, she could match his tone. Careful. Factual. Like trying to walk on a balance beam. "It doesn't really hurt, unless I have a sudden jolt. I should be able to start physical therapy next week."

"That sounds pretty good."

"But I won't be able to go running for maybe four months."

"Four months? That's tough."

"I can take long walks."

"I guess that's better than nothing."

"Yeah."

The teenagers, laughing, were carrying their chairs down the marble stairs past Russ and Miranda, who stood motionless like two more of the columns guarding Lincoln on his platform. Russ was too far away for Miranda to touch the smooth wool of his coat sleeve.

"You have an attorney handling the DUI?" Russ continued, watching the teenagers.

"Of course."

"Who is it?"

"His name? Victor Knaplund."

"I don't know him. How'd you find him?"

"From Brenda." They could go on like this for minutes after minutes after minutes, maybe even half an hour, dancing with trivial questions. When was her next X-ray? When was her next court date? Was she still taking Motrin? Did she think it worked better than Advil? What was the name of the other car owner's lawyer?

"You probably think," she said, and then she stupidly had to clear her throat, thereby proclaiming to Russ that she was nervous, "that I'm some sort of reckless Calamity Jane. Kidnapping. Drunk driving."

Russ didn't rush in to deny what she'd said.

So she was going to have to proceed. "It hasn't been easy for me to tell you all my sordid history—well, obviously it hasn't, since I never said a word about Tali and the kidnapping until you learned about it from the FBI vetting. And I truly am sorry that I wasn't honest with you about that, and because of it, you might lose your job. I wish I could redo it all, I really do. Or if there was something I could do now to help you with your work situation; if you want me to talk to your boss, or anybody. And the drunk driving—I can't explain why I was such an idiot. I know I can't handle more than half a glass of wine. So I have a lot to account for, I realize that. But nobody likes to confess embarrassing things about themselves, even to the people closest to them. It's tempting just to keep quiet, isn't it?"

Russ still didn't respond. Not even a nod.

"Or make up a story."

His hands were thrust deep into the pockets of grey coat—the front pockets, not like Jerry Isaacs, who'd walked with his hands shoved into the rear pockets of his jeans. He sucked in his pale bottom lip as he scraped one foot closer to the other.

With the teenagers gone, the air around them was totally quiet, too late and dark and cold for any tourists. It was almost the same spot where little-girl Miranda used to pose, gazing at the long expanse of tiered stairs and grass and trees and the Reflecting Pool that stretched out in front of her and pretending to be Martin Luther King Jr. declaiming his "I Have a Dream Speech," just the way Grandpa Seymour had recited it to her. Just the way her father hadn't actually spoken to the crowds from the steps at Columbia.

She waited, staring at the greying pool and trees, counting farther than Tali could ever count in Hebrew. "Don't you have any reaction to what I said?" she finally demanded.

"I'm glad you weren't injured more seriously."

"That's it? I just poured my heart out, and all you've got is a cliché you could say to any stranger?"

"What do you want? You're the one who's been complaining that we've had this conversation already, numerous times, where you confess and I criticize. What's the point of repeating the pattern? There's probably nothing I can say about the DUI that you haven't already thought or that Victor Knaplund hasn't already told you. You could have killed someone, or yourself. You could have caused significant damage. The courts take DUI very, very seriously. I'm sure you'll never do it again. Do you really want me to pile on?"

"So clichés are better? Clichés and trivia? You're—" she was going too far "—becoming a cold stone, just like your father."

"Don't throw empty insults at me."

"I don't know. How empty is it? What did you ask your father to do for you when you dropped out of Yale?"

Russ didn't twitch.

Then he swirled around. "Let's go." He began striding down the cascading marble stairs.

THEY MOVED SILENTLY AND QUICKLY ON THEIR old running route, on the sidewalk that curved around the Memorial, to the rear of the building, across the grassy traffic circle, past the two towering bronze sculptures, and onto the pedestrian walkway of Arlington Memorial Bridge. If this were one of the dozens of weekends they'd run together, Russ's sneakers would be hitting heavily on the concrete, his sweaty neck smelling of talcum, his arm brushing against her to point out a kid with crazy blue hair, or the newest protest installation, or the boats on the Potomac.

Now, on the bridge, Russ inched his right hand along the top of the marble-columned guardwall. On the Virginia side of the Potomac, lights sparkled haphazardly throughout the windows of a cluster of tall, modern office buildings. Cars whooshed past them in both directions along all of the bridge's six lanes, the nearest ones just a step down from where they walked.

"All the stories I've told you about myself—going to Yale, volunteering on the investigations against G.E. and the PCBs, getting on the Law Journal, working my ass off—all that's true. It is. Up to a point." Russ halted only for a moment before he resumed walking, going more rapidly and gripping the wall more tightly. "I did everything I was supposed to. The first year. Then, in my second year, it all changed. For one thing, the Law Journal took up a lot of time, as much as a full-time job, though that wasn't just me; that's the case for everyone who does it. And the career pressure gets worse your second year. But mainly, I was increasingly absorbed in the G.E. project. It was more intense than I've probably made it sound, interviewing the families about their thyroid and liver problems, writing press releases, drafting memos for the lawyers. In other words—" From his pocket, he pulled the half-eaten pretzel and held it out again to Miranda. Again, she shook her head. He put it back. "I was skipping classes constantly. I was weeks behind in my reading, and my fall-term evaluations sucked."

Miranda didn't have enough breath in her lungs to walk as fast as he was going. She had to walk faster. But she had to hold onto her sling so it didn't jiggle her collarbone.

"Even that crap wasn't the real issue, though. The thing is, I started asking myself: Why am I here? Why am I in law school? What am I accomplishing here, working a hundred hours a week, that actually helps anyone in the real world? Yeah, I can cite case law up to the moon and back, so what? If Brown and Kendall are both walking their dogs, and the dogs start to fight, and Kendall takes a stick and starts beating the dogs to separate them, and Brown is standing behind him, and Kendall accidentally pokes Brown in the eye with the stick—The work I'd been doing on the G.E. case was helping more real people than any moot court memos I wrote at Yale, and I didn't need a law degree to do it. So, midway through second year, I dropped out.

"Which is not all that unusual, okay? People burn out, they need a break, they have family emergencies, they get sick, all that crap. Yale actually has a process for that kind of thing; I suppose most law schools do. You go to the dean to request a leave. But not me. I just quit. Burned my bridges. I went and worked almost full-time—unpaid, still—on the PCB case. And I also worked as a bagger at the Grand Union, to make some money. For almost two years."

So those were the two years when Russ was supposedly doing an internship on the G.E. case as part of a special program at Yale.

A lone, small motorboat cut a line through the dark Potomac water as it sped southward, trailing flecks of bright foam.

Russ kept walking fast with his face aimed toward the river, not at Miranda or even at the pavement ahead, letting out one breath, then another, then another. "You want the whole truth? Okay. Well, guess what? After about twenty months of that regime, writing PR memos on the G.E. case and bagging the goddam groceries, I realized I was wrong about the usefulness of law school, a hundred and eighty degrees completely fucking wrong. The civic and environmental groups had started filing legal briefs against G.E., which requires lawyers. And I saw what the government lawyers could accomplish, the E.P.A. mainly, and the Justice Department. The E.P.A. forced G.E. to sign consent decrees to contain and clean up its pollution, and Justice was the backstop with the authority to issue fines if G.E. didn't comply. And what was I doing? Writing press releases? Writing up notes for the real lawyers to use? I'd been a complete asshole, and my original plan had been correct, and I needed that JD.

"And then I was in trouble. Because I'd dropped out of Yale without arranging a leave in advance with the dean; I'd violated procedures. Also, it was coming on two years that I'd been out of school, which was another problem under Yale's policy. And now I wanted to return, and it wasn't at all guaranteed that I could.

"So I—I went to my father. I pretended to myself that he wasn't my actual father, that he was just a professor I was asking for a reference." Pausing a second time, Russ leaned forward against the wall and rested his elbows on the top. "I asked him," he said to the dark water, "if he knew the dean or another high muckety-muck at Yale Law School, and if he'd put in a good word for me."

We told him the last time, if he'd decided to drop out of Yale and devote himself to his—his other interests—Well that was his responsibility, and just what did he expect—

Abigail had basically told the truth.

An airplane, approaching low for a landing at Reagan National, roared in the sky.

"And he said yes," Russ added.

Yes?

All the fights between them, all those years, about Enron, about unions, about Grandpa Seymour, about the Steinmann department stores, about Russ's previous job clerking for one of the most liberal appellate court judges, about Russ's eagerness to investigate corporate crimes in the U.S. Attorney's office; all of their supposedly passionate arguments about basic principles and life choices. Russ walking out during their engagement dinner because his father was defending Enron. Russ lying when the U.S. Attorney asked if he was related to Henry Steinmann.

Abigail had also said: *The biggest pleasure for everyone will be seeing Russell and you standing under the* chuppah. She hadn't said: *everyone else.*

"As soon as he said yes," Russ was saying, "I was so disgusted with myself that I couldn't even look at my own fingers when I brushed my teeth."

In the dark water downstream, the George Mason bridge was just a thin black strand. Russ was still leaning against the guardwall. It was getting too cold to just stand, without moving; Miranda fastened the top button of her coat.

"I told him no thanks, and I went in to see the dean myself. I had no real argument in my defense. I talked about what I'd learned from the PCB project and what I'd learned in my first year at Yale, why I wanted to be a lawyer, and my LSAT scores, and Law Journal, and my top-grade evaluations the first year before they slipped, any ammunition I could muster. And maybe it was my earnestness, or maybe the dean likes clean rivers, I don't know, but he agreed to readmit me. The following September, I was back at Yale. And I hauled ass. And I graduated. And after that, okay, it's pretty much what you already know."

They were more than halfway across the bridge. The tail lights and headlights of the cars spanning the lanes alongside them were two continuous streams of slightly sparkling color, red toward Virginia and yellow-white toward the District. No other pedestrians, though, were shivering on the concrete walkway along with them. Miranda began moving again; Russ caught up.

"Your father said yes," Miranda echoed.

"Yes." Russ let out a long breath. "What I found out later is that all the crap with Yale was happening right around the time my father's newest book was being rejected by every publisher he tried, including the one who'd published his first three. And it was the second book this had happened with. He actually hadn't published a book in something like ten years—long before you took his seminar, in fact. For a tenured professor at Georgetown to be turned down like that? It must have been mortifying."

Another airplane zoomed in loud toward the airport.

"I think that's why he said yes. His world was crumbling, and he wanted to hang on to whatever was left, no matter how shredded. Including his family."

Miranda shook her head. "You're overcomplicating it. He said yes because they're your parents, and they love you. Just like I said yes to Ronit."

Maybe Russ was looking at her; Miranda kept staring straight ahead. Looking at him would be a step too much.

"You forgave Ronit for dragging you into the kidnapping," he half-asked, half-said, "because you loved her."

"I guess… Or I understood why she did it, anyway."

Their legs were moving out of sync, because Russ's stride was longer than hers. His right foot went forward, then a few counts later her left, then his right. She would have to move faster, or else add a few skipping steps now and then, but skipping was probably as bad for her collarbone as everything else.

This time, Russ's long exhale didn't sound as deep. "I'm sorry if I've been, um, cold. And judgmental. You have to admit it's a hell of a load you've thrown at me this past month. How can I even keep track of the emotions you accuse me of hiding? As soon as I start getting used to Miranda the kidnapper, it's Miranda with the broken collarbone, and then it's Miranda the drunk driver, and I really want Miranda the health-care crusader who runs faster than I do and hates asparagus."

There might have been a hint of a smile in his voice. Maybe, in another sentence or two, she would look at him. "Don't forget Russ Steinmann the prosecutor for the People versus Miranda Isaacs," she said meanwhile. "That's a new Russ for me to take in."

"And Russ Steinmann the hypocrite, who asks his father for a favor."

"That one's so minor by comparison. It disappears in a puff. It's not a hundred-pound lead weight like abetting a felony kidnapping and then keeping it a secret and jeopardizing your job."

A shot of wet, frigid wind slapped them. They had, maybe, five more minutes before they would arrive at the end of the bridge and would need to make a decision. Find a restaurant and eat a delayed dinner together? Take the Metro separately to their separate beds?

"Right," Russ said. "About my job."

Of course. That was the Miranda he wouldn't smile about.

"I quit last Friday," he added.

The rush-hour flood of autos had suddenly slowed, their horns honking in a shrill symphony, bright red brake lights jerking to life, probably protesting a traffic jam or an accident up ahead.

"What?" she tried to ask.

He continued calmly, whether she'd managed to verbalize her question or not. "I've been doing a lot of thinking these last few weeks, while I've been sitting around my office being the ghost who wasn't there. The corpse in the middle of the floor. What was I waiting for? Even if I was ultimately cleared in the security investigation, which is doubtful, Lou would find a dozen excuses not to make my job permanent. So I decided to get out on my own terms. Which meant, before I quit cold, I needed to consider where I might go." His voice had actually started to lilt up a little from its calm tone. "And I've been seriously looking at the other side."

"WHAT?"

The cars were honking and flashing their lights frantically as if they were as startled as Miranda was. She grabbed Russ's sleeve, jerking him to a halt in front of an old-fashioned lamp post that hit him with its beam. "You're going to go work for a corporate law firm you hate and defend those business criminals?" No. This was even worse than Miranda Isaacs the kidnapper.

"Wha—No! What do you think I am?" he almost shouted, shaking loose. "I meant the different other side."

"How many other sides are there?"

"All this time, I've been focused like an arrow on the government's role in law enforcement. The U.S. Attorney's office; the appellate division where I clerked." Making a fist, he lightly punched a marble column. "But that's not the only way to fight corporate malfeasance. You remember my friend Greg from Yale? We got together for dinner a couple weeks ago —By the way, you should try the place we went. It specializes in exotic burgers. Ostrich. Elk—"

"Never mind burgers! What about your other-side idea?"

"I'm getting to that. Greg works for the Public Interest Defense Council; have I told you about it? It's a nonprofit that represents consumer interests, and among the things they do is litigation. Suing corporations that sell unsafe products or violate workers' rights, for instance. Also suing governmental agencies like the FDA or the FTC or state AGs, if they're not enforcing consumer protection laws. You see?"

Standing on the bridge, car lights flashing on him, then off, then on, like spotlights sweeping back and forth across a stage, it was the old excited Russ once again, the Russ of last fall when he'd told her about being assigned to the big Veterans Affairs bribery case. Grinning. Glowing. Charging ahead. The Russ she loved.

"Greg couldn't offer me a job outright; his Council doesn't have any openings. But the point is, there are all sorts of ways of doing the kind of work I've wanted to do, Miranda! In fact, Greg recommended me to a fellow he knows at an environmental NGO. Whether I get hired there or somewhere else, I can represent the people who are directly being hurt—the moms who buy the cribs that break, the folks who drink the poisoned water, the families whose yards are polluted by PCBs. Maybe the threat of my lawsuits will spur some companies to change, and other times my lawsuits will get the attention of the government agencies. I'll still be fighting the same good fights your parents fought." And, finally, he broke out into a full, genuine smile.

Oh no.

"Actually," she began.

"THAT'S A MIND-FUCK," HE SAID. "Your dad might still be alive."

"Alive, and no hero."

They sat inches apart on a marble bench on the Virginia side of the bridge, along the road leading to Arlington National Cemetery. She hugged her sling; he drummed his thighs.

"More of a hero than most people," Russ insisted. "He tried to help at Columbia and on Bobby Kennedy's campaign and with the grape pickers. He inspired you to go work for Mort and the Center, to change the world."

"No. My mother's fairy tale about him is what inspired me."

"Okay, but maybe he's still been working on inspiring causes all these years. Maybe he helped organize that anti-war rally last weekend."

"Maybe he's doing PR for Exxon."

"Maybe he's been researching solar energy."

"Maybe he lobbies for the NRA."

"Why do you want to make him into an asshole?"

"Why do you want to make him a hero?"

"Because I'd rather think of your father as a hero than an asshole."

An evening jogger abruptly sped past them, heading toward the bridge, a yellow reflector vest over his dark Spandex shirt. He was moving twice as fast as Miranda or Russ had ever run that same route.

"Do you want to find him?" Russ added.

Miranda leaned carefully against the marble wall behind the bench, tilting her head back.

Hi… Dad.

I'm the daughter you didn't know you had.

Do you remember Judith, the high school girl from the sit-in at Columbia in 1968?

Her parents bailed you out of jail.

Rich man. Poor man. Beggar man. Thief. Jerry Isaacs could be doing PR for Exxon, or he could have discovered a cure for cancer. He could be a drug addict, or he could finally be speaking on the stage at anti-war rallies. He could even be one of the people on the bus up to Canada to fill their prescriptions, his hair grey and cut short, bifocals covering his chocolate eyes. If she didn't look for him, she could invent any story she wanted. But that would only be a story, not the truth.

"You could ask him all the questions you've been wondering about since you were little."

"If I could find him. I've Googled him a zillion times, and I never came up with anything except for some professor in North Carolina who's obviously not him. Mom doesn't know where he is, either."

"How about California? The last anyone knew, he was helping the grape pickers there, and he kept going back. People up in—what city did he say? Oakland? They might remember him."

"That seems like a long shot. Thirty-three years ago."

"Maybe he re-enrolled in college. You could check the alumni records at Cooper Union."

"Or every other university in the United States."

"It's a start."

"What if he doesn't want to meet me? He might have another whole family."

"True. But the man your mother described sounds like he'd be pretty welcoming."

"He wouldn't be the man we thought he was."

"He'd be your father."

It was pointless, imagining any type of dramatic father-daughter reunion. She'd Googled and Googled and there was no—

Except that she'd been looking for the wrong Jerome Isaacs. She'd searched for obituaries from 1971 for Jerome Isaacs, big-time anti-war activist. But what if there was a Jerry Isaacs still alive in Oakland, California, who'd stuck around long after the grape boycott ended, driving a city bus, doing odd jobs? A Jerry who never got his name in the newspaper.

Or Malka Isaacs, in Iowa; a name Miranda hadn't even known about until two days ago. Her grandmother. She would be in her late seventies or early eighties by now. Sure, she might still be alive. Miranda's mother had found a Malka Isaacs in Des Moines via Google only a few years ago. Even if she was no longer living in Des Moines, it wasn't a very common name, and she could probably be found, wherever she was. Wouldn't she know how to reach her son?

"Do you want to go to California to look for him?" Russ asked, and he slowly reached out to her shoulders. "On our honeymoon?"

She put her good hand against his cheek. No stubble; he'd shaved before he met with her.

"I do love you, you know."

"I love you, too. But will you clean up your crumbs and your dirty T-shirts from now on?"

"Will you let me take your wine glass away after you've drunk half of it?"

"I guess that's a fair deal. If the honeymoon includes Iowa."

Russ would never sit at a table with Jerry Isaacs, awestruck, his mouth open slightly, breathing a little fast, asking for details on how Jerry planned his big protest marches and if he'd expected to be arrested at the Democratic Convention in Chicago and whether he was nervous speaking in front of crowds. Still, they might sit at a table together somewhere, someday—in a coffee shop? in a suburban Iowa split-level house? in an aging-hippie commune in Mendocino?—and if Jerry was still as talkative and warm and friendly as he'd been at nineteen, they could have a good conversation about all kinds of things. Camping at Big Sur. The Academy Awards. The possibility of war in Iraq, and whether the protests last weekend would have any impact on Bush and Cheney. Miranda.

What would the Jerry of 1970 have thought about his future daughter helping to kidnap her friend's daughter?

You were too tough on her, he would tell Russ. After all, she was his daughter, and he would defend her, like any good parent.

He and Miranda could compare notes on their respective overnights in jail.

Her father had had dreams, even if he might never have achieved much. And her mother had invented the story of Jerry Isaacs the martyred radical protest leader because she wanted Miranda to have dreams of her own. That wasn't, as her mother had said, such a terrible history. Finding the actual Jerry Isaacs might not be such a big dream, but it was something to start with. There would be more.

ACKNOWLEDGMENTS

In the end, I think every novelist is alone with her work; only she can decide which words, which plot development, which character traits, are right.

But if she's like me, the novelist couldn't have reached that point without assistance from dozens of other people. Here are some of those who helped make *I Meant to Tell You* possible:

Jean Berman, Sharon Goldzweig, Nancy Haber, Howard Herman, Kate Spota, and Gary Sunden spent hours explaining all sorts of legal processes, career paths, and the grind of law school.

Freddie Brooks, Gail Fier, Edith Kirsch, Yehudit Moch, Jan Orzeck, Marianne Ringl, Liz Salen, and Ron Schweiger brought the world of 1960s Flatbush (in Brooklyn) and City College to life.

Similarly, Deborah Bernick, Judith and Irving Lieberman, Jean Rosenthal, and Ellen Simon described what it's like to live in Washington DC—including the best neighborhoods for finding an edgy bar and the most popular ethnic food.

Breaking my toe in 2021 gave me some direct insight into what one of my characters will endure; in addition, Sophie Gamer, Adele Holmes, Ben Kligler, and Jenna Scholnick took time to walk me through other medical procedures.

David Pelzer and Dave Dozier—who both volunteered with Cesar Chavez and the United Farm Workers during the grape boycott of the 1960s—provided an invaluable inside look into the foot-soldiering of that movement.

I'm glad none of you are reading the earliest drafts of this novel. (It actually began as a four-generation saga, told in reverse chronological order—and who knows, maybe someday I'll retrieve the two abandoned generations for a prequel, with the true stories of Jacob, Sarah, Seymour, and Bessie.) Huge thanks to the editors, workshop teachers, and fellow writers who helped me turn that sprawling four-generation mess into a readable book, including Julia Ballerini, Charlie Drees, Jason Effman, Elizabeth Ehrlich, Emily Elkind, Diana Forbes, Eric Goodman, Nick Gorski, Judy Graeff, Masha Hamilton, Scott Alexander Hess, Dakota Klaes, Laura Martin, Patricia McGovern, Sandra Newman, Kathy Pestotnik, Sean Prentiss, Bruce Rose, Michele Rubin, Julia Schiavone, Sophia Seidner, Scott Smith, Anna Tran, Jessie Vanamee, Kate Wheeler, Joyce Yaeger, and Ray Ziemer. Added thanks to Karen Curley for her eagle-eyed proofreading.

Then there are the bits of odd-lot information that a writer suddenly realizes she needs. What model of car would a newly minted MBA drive in the mid-1990s? What are the most common mistakes that a native Hebrew speaker would make in learning English? Thanks to Robert Calem, Anita Gilodo, Moran Lantner, and Lila Rieman for an assortment of obscure knowledge.

Thanks and incalculable thanks to Kimberly Verhines, the director of Stephen F. Austin State University Press, for wanting to publish this book, and Meredith Janning for all her work in making it a reality.

And finally, to my family: To Pete, Joe, and Sophie, thank you forever for your faith in me—and for putting up with me.

Photo: Jolene Siana/@jolenesiana 2017

FRAN HAWTHORNE has been writing novels since she was four years old, although she was sidetracked for several decades by journalism. During that award-winning career, she wrote eight nonfiction books, mainly about consumer activism, the drug industry, and the financial world. For instance, *Ethical Chic* (Beacon Press) was named one of the best business books of 2012 by *Library Journal*, and *Pension Dumping* (Bloomberg Press) was a *Foreword* magazine 2008 Book of the Year. She's also been an editor or regular contributor for *The New York Times*, *Business Week*, *Fortune*, and many other publications. But Fran never abandoned her true love: with the publication of her debut novel, *The Heirs*, in 2018 and now *I Meant to Tell You*, Fran is firmly committed to fiction. She also writes book reviews for the *New York Journal of Books*.